"Let me help you."

Still bearing the gruesome wounds of his death, he appeared to be etched into the very air with the acid of his anger, dark and crisp at the edges, so tightly focused it hurt to look too closely.

"This isn't good for you, Gordon. It isn't right. Your death was tragic, but it's up to the police to find the man who did it. Your job now is to make peace with—"

He cut her off with a sudden roar and circled her in a series of blurs and jerks, ending up close to her face. *"He's mine!"*

Suddenly she was pressed from all sides—the impossible weight of anger, squeezing her, crushing her chest and bowing her neck and making her heart struggle to beat at all. She couldn't cry out or call for help and she couldn't do anything more than soundlessly mouth his name as she crumpled to the ground. "Gordon . . . Gordon, *no*—"

GHOST WHISPERER™

Based on the hit TV series created by John Gray

REVENGE

DORANNA DURGIN

POCKET STAR

New York   London   Toronto   Sydney

Pocket Star Books
A Division of Simon & Schuster, Inc.
1230 Avenue of the Americas
New York, NY 10020

This book is a work of fiction. Names, characters, places, and incidents either are products of the author's imagination or are used fictitiously. Any resemblance to actual events or locales or persons, living or dead, is entirely coincidental.

First Pocket Star Books paperback edition October 2008

POCKET STAR BOOKS and colophon are registered trademarks of Simon & Schuster, Inc.

For information about special discounts for bulk purchases, please contact Simon & Schuster Special Sales at 1-800-456-6798 or business@simonandschuster.com.

Cover design by Alan Dingman

Manufactured in the United States of America

10 9 8 7 6 5 4 3 2 1

ISBN-13: 978-1-4165-5094-5
ISBN-10:   1-4165-5094-1

*Dedicated to my family—my mom, Mona;
my dad, Chuck; my sister, Nancy; and Tom—
who truly understand*

REVENGE

PROLOGUE

GORDON REESE LEFT the Whetstone Bar, and left his old way of life behind.

The chilly spring night closed in around him—spring peepers singing from the road ditch as though they were out in the country and not along this cracked sidewalk on the edge of town where only a block farther down, the sidewalk itself petered out to packed dirt and weedy grass choked by the exhaust of cars headed for Grandview.

Gordon knew how they felt. That's how he'd been—choked by his past, his small-town memories clinging to him and refusing to let go.

But no longer. He'd come to the bar; he'd said his good-byes. And now he felt free to move on to his new life.

He breathed deeply of the freedom . . . found it tasted of new-mown grass and the deep cool dew of night. He rotated his shoulders inside his leather jacket and strode confidently into the night. Away from the bar, past the phone booth that hadn't worked for nearly a year, past the old bait shack to the wide gravel lot before the garage on the corner that served as unofficial overflow parking for the Whetstone. None of it was lit, of course—not even the gas station after hours.

There, just past the bait shack, he caught the scent of beer and fresh cigarette smoke layered over old. Gravel crunched; movement flashed in the corner of his eye.

He turned just fast enough to see a blur of movement slashing toward him . . . but not fast enough to duck.

Gordon Reese left the Whetstone Bar, and left his life behind.

He comes to himself in fury, in resentment and blame. Familiar fingers of temper wrap around his awareness; they feel like a homecoming. They feel safe. They feel like something he knows how to do.

And, thinking of his last moments of life, of those fleeting impressions of sound and vision, he knows on whom he will spend that temper—for as long as it takes to exact revenge for what he's lost.

1

DELIA BANKS CROUCHED by the front display window of SAME AS IT NEVER WAS antiques, not the least bit dressed for cleaning. Flowing blouse, dark slacks, multiple bracelets jangling, and long dark hair tossed out of the way over her shoulder, she tackled the small handprints and smeary mystery marks with Windex. "I don't get it," she said. "These weren't on the glass when we closed last night. And they're on the *inside*."

"Energetic mice?" Melinda Gordon suggested, admittedly without giving it much thought. She sat behind the marble-topped sales counter at the back of the store, scrolling through the online listings for local estate sales on her beloved laptop. *Ooh, nice.* "This looks good—JWC is having an estate sale not far from here a week from now." She reached for her pen and a pad of SAME AS IT NEVER WAS stationery to note the particulars in an absently neat hand. The counter otherwise held the business phone, the register, and an appropriately antique keepsake box where Melinda stashed notes and paper clips and other clutter bits. Beyond that, the counter gleamed as clear as she could keep it, with gift wrapping papers, small bags, and ribbons on the shelves beneath. Every possible personal touch . . . and it made her customers' eyes light up when they saw the care with which their purchases were handled.

"Not mice," Delia said, still at work. "So definitely not mice. Mice always leave . . ."

Melinda looked up, perfectly willing to play fill-in-the-blank. "Poop?"

"I was going to say *signs*." Delia flipped the rag over to buff the window one last time and pushed herself to her feet. "Oof. I swear, this used to be easier." She gave Melinda a wry glance, tugging her blouse into place over her generously shapely form. "You just wait, Miss Young-and-Beautiful."

"I'm supposed to buy that?" Melinda looked up from the laptop screen, giving Delia—forty-something, mother to teenaged Ned, as fit as stair-climbing could make her—a skeptical look writ large.

"Yes," Delia told her. "And if you say *You're only as old as you feel* or anything like it, I'll . . ." And there she trailed off, because Delia was too gentle at heart to come up with anything truly wicked.

But sensing a note of true frustration in Delia's voice, Melinda held up her hands in surrender. "Okay, okay," she said. "You win. You're old. Happy now?"

Delia appeared to give this some thought. "Strangely," she said, "not so much." And went to return the cleaning supplies to the back room, a long narrow space crammed with furniture making its way to the sales floor, following restorations and cleanup downstairs. The cramped space was defined mostly by a desk, with just enough room for Melinda to engage in a hastily clandestine encounter with an unexpected visitor of the spiritual sort.

Once, before her store partner Andrea had been killed in the crash of Flight 395, Melinda hadn't gone to such extremes—hadn't rushed to hide such encounters. But as Delia spent more time in the store, Melinda had grown used to concealing her gifts once again. Too many personal betrayals had taught her well, and she knew Delia wasn't even close to coming to terms with her recently acquired knowledge that her employer and friend spent a great deal of time talking to earthbound spirits.

A very versatile place, that back room. Not to mention that it was the only route to the bathroom.

Melinda tucked her long, dark hair behind her ear and returned her attention to the laptop, found she'd reached the end of the estate sales—never a

long list, not unless she went all the way into the
city, or sometimes west to Albany—and clicked
on the link that would take her back to the local
paper. That, too, was usually short and sweet . . .
headlines at a glance, done for the day, and no trees
killed for it.

She glanced around the store as the page loaded,
satisfied that all was ready for the day—the clothing sorted by size if nothing else, off in a niche to
the side; the furniture and wood floor gleaming;
the whimsical bathtub with its glass ornaments
full to overflowing but no more; and the shelves
of heavenly soaps and lotions neatly arranged and
dusted. Hmm. This could be a lotion-sniffing day,
at that. Outside, Grandview was settling into its
day, the morning pedestrian rush hour through the
town square tapering off to a trickle. The line at
Village Java just might be getting short enough to
handle . . .

"Hey," she called back to Delia. "You up for
some coffee?"

"Coffee might help me *get* up," Delia responded,
with a faintness that suggested she was probably
washing her hands in the little bathroom.

*swingbatterbatterswing a kaleidoscope of sound
and motion and bursting colors and a sudden explosion of darkness and the astringent smell of ants*

The counter swooped in her vision; Melinda
gasped, catching herself just before she toppled

from the stool and into the hard countertop. "Well," she murmured, straightening. *Ants?* "That was so very special." She ran a hand over the smooth, deep green velvet of her corsetlike vest and tugged the overlong sleeves of a lace-edged poet's blouse back into place. "Now I *really* need that coffee." Melinda scanned the store again—this time with narrowed eyes, looking for any sign of spiritual influence.

But no flickering lamps; no lotions gone askew. Except . . . the seasonal section nearest the door— vintage spring clothing and a darling wicker baby carriage beside a turn-of-the-century croquet set— looked subtly disturbed. She focused in on it but realized quickly enough that Delia had moved the carriage in order to clean the glass.

So. Nothing.

But a spirit so fragmented . . . so confused that it was able to communicate only in short jumbled pieces . . .

Melinda could definitely count on a return engagement or two, until whoever it was sorted themselves out well enough to communicate more clearly. She took a deep breath, made the mental note to stay off ladders and other tricky high places until this particular spirit had crossed over, and returned to the online news.

Because, after all, this was her life: ghosts on board.

The headline startled her out of serenity mode. *Local Man Murdered in Bayview.* Whoa.

"Did you hear about this?" she called back to Delia, lowering her voice as Delia appeared in the doorway, still smoothing lavender lotion over her hands, her eyebrows raised in unspoken question. Melinda gestured at the laptop monitor. "The murder?"

"On the radio this morning." Delia moved in to look over Melinda's shoulder, where the screen displayed a photo beside the headlines. "Oh, and he looks so young, too."

"Just starting a new life," Melinda murmured, picking up on the story lead-in. *Gordon Reese, murdered . . .*

"That's what they said on the radio, that he'd been hanging with a rough crew—one of them died young, one went to jail, and Gordon himself had a nasty temper, ran hot all the time—but then he met his wife . . . went to school, got a degree, went into her family business. They run a B&B on the edge of town, and they have that great honey over in the market—you know, the creamed honeys, and the honey with the comb—"

"Oh! Right—the Honey Bs stuff! I've seen it. I never dared to get any. Put that stuff on Jim's french toast and my head might just explode."

"I guess they just had a baby," Delia said, and her voice held all the wistfulness of a mother who knew her son's father would never see him grow up.

"That's so sad." But when Melinda turned back to her laptop, a flurry of activity outside the store caught her eye. Early spring morning, grass so very green, flowers so very thick and bright along the sidewalks, the war memorial standing tall in the middle of it all. Only a few stragglers from the morning traffic flow, now, and the first of the day's shoppers, and—

The murdered man's ghost.

Gordon Reese. A clear and strong angry ghost etched with unnaturally acidic sharpness—not vague, not hazy, not uncertain. A ghost with purpose and plenty of energy.

She thought at first that he was looking for her—looking and hadn't quite found her. But that didn't fit, because he wasn't *looking* at all. In fact, his entire being focused on the man before him—a man who walked, oblivious, through the square, coffee in one hand, briefcase in the other, and distraction on his face.

Or maybe not so oblivious, for as the ghost kept pace—not walking, but flickering from spot to spot so quickly his movement was nothing but a blur—the man stumbled slightly, barely keeping hold of his coffee. He steadied himself, giving the sidewalk a bemused look as though he might find a gaping crack there, just as the angry spirit halted his dizzying harassment and leaned into the man so their faces nearly touched, bellowing something without sound, but with a force that made the air around them ripple with vehemence.

Spirits, Melinda had found, had a very poor understanding of personal space. Either that or they just didn't care, but to the same effect. *In your face* turned quite literal at times.

And then the ghost was gone. Worn out . . . distracted . . . or so beside himself that he couldn't hold his presence here.

"Melinda?" Delia said, acting as though it wasn't the first time, or the second.

"Hmm?" Melinda straightened, bouncing back into cover-your-tracks mode as she pushed the laptop lid down, ready to clear the counter and make way for the day. And then she hesitated, seeing the look on Delia's face and realizing her friend had seen too much in recent weeks to fall for cheerful misdirection any longer. So she said, "Trust me. You don't want to know."

"Maybe not, then," Delia said, acting a little sorry that she hadn't just played along with the cheerful misdirection. "But how about that coffee?"

"Sounds great." Melinda tucked the laptop beneath the counter. She had found a spirit struggling with confusion and a spirit struggling with anger, but neither of them was ready to cross over and neither was ready to come to her for help, so . . . yeah. Coffee sounded just about right, for the beginning of what might turn out to be a long day.

It feels good, the anger. It feels strong. And with it, with the toll he exacts from the man who, tire iron in hand, left him for dead, he feels something else, too—a flutter of energy, siphoned from this man he's vowed to haunt. Each time the man stumbles, not knowing why, each time he feels the punch of anger in his gut, not knowing why . . . the raw exhilaration from that flickering fear goes down like hot whiskey, leaving a hunger for more.

And he knew just how to get it.

And a long day it was—made that way by fruitless waiting for a recurrence of either of Melinda's visitors. Endless expectation, no results.

"Maybe tomorrow," Melinda murmured, for now just happy to be home, the place where she'd once been safe from visitors but lately seemed to experience intrusions on a regular basis. She headed for the closet, reaching for the leather buttons of her vest . . . and her fingers stopped, hovering, before they got there.

Huh. Pale gold dog hair . . . slightly crinkly, clinging to the green velvet of her vest. She moved into the light of the bedroom bay window, plucking the hair away. Strange. She didn't recall brush-

ing up against any dogs during the day—not even
Delia's big, happy golden retriever Bob.

"Mel?" Jim's voice filtered up the stairs of the
house, an old structure under ongoing renova-
tion—if no longer one that regularly blew circuits,
lost the capacity to heat itself, or shed unexpected
bits and pieces during rough weather.

Usually.

"Just getting undressed," she called back to him,
and knew immediately that she'd left herself wide
open for—

"Ah," he said, and a smile touched his words
even from the distant kitchen. "My favorite."

"Do I smell burning hamburger?" Melinda
grinned as she unfastened the small leather buttons of the vest, quickly inspecting it for more dog
hair as she hung it in the old freestanding ward-
robe and just as quickly shrugged out of her poet's
shirt and snug black jeans. She traded them for a
comfortable long-sleeved tee and low-slung yoga
pants, revealing just a little gap of bare skin that
would drive Jim mildly insane. And since the fur-
nace was working just fine to keep the house warm
on a cold spring night, she padded downstairs in
bare feet, pulling her hair up into a sloppy ponytail
along the way.

"It's taco salad," Jim said as she entered the
kitchen. He stirred a frypan of perfectly unburnt
ground beef, already simmering with taco sea-

soning, chili beans, and French-style dressing; it smelled heavenly. "A hint of burn just adds a special essence."

"Hmm," she said, most skeptically. She went straight to the cabinet to pull down dishes, making it only as far as the cooking island before she set them down and circled back behind Jim to snake her arms around his waist. Unlike her, he hadn't yet changed from his work clothes, but he'd untucked and unbuttoned his paramedic uniform shirt, and he had a distinctly adorable end-of-the-day rumple to him. Melinda rested her cheek against his back and felt the play of muscle as he turned the heat down and reached for the frypan cover; one of his hands covered both of hers and gave them a squeeze.

"One of those days?" he asked.

His voice rumbled against her ear; she smiled. "Not really. A good day, actually. Flowers blooming, grass growing, trees budding—it might just be spring."

"Uh-huh." He took a step sideways and turned as he leaned against the counter; her cheek ended up against his chest, warm from the reflected heat of the stove. He drew her in closer, kissing the top of her head. "Do I sound convinced?"

"I've got a reminder ghost, that's all."

"I get the feeling that's not the same as a tying-a-string-around-your-finger reminder."

"Does anyone even do that anymore?" She lifted her face to look at him, pondering the line of his jaw and the proximity of same. Hmm, tempting. "No . . . more like life-is-short-sometimes, appreciate-what-you-have."

"Want to talk about it?"

Melinda shrugged, a restless gesture. "He's not really even mine, yet. I just saw him. And read about him. You must have heard—the man who was killed over in Bayview?"

He stilled against her, an instant of not-breathing and then a deeper breath to follow. "Yeah," he said. "The guys were talking about it today. The crew from Bayview was pretty upset over it. I guess they'd patched him up a time or two after bar fights. They were pulling for him when he started this new-life thing."

"It doesn't seem fair," she mused, tightening her hold on him—giving back some of what he'd just given her. "But what was he even doing out there? At the bar again?"

"Saying good-bye, is the way I hear it." Jim stroked her back, an absent gesture; she knew if she looked, she'd find his gaze far away. Thinking about what he'd heard, how he'd heard it. Why he'd heard it.

She'd have to read that article more carefully. "He's angry, and I can't blame him. First I thought he might be looking for me, but I'm not so sure. He was pretty focused on this man in the square . . . really taking him on. Once he gets a little more experience, he could make a real impact."

"You'll get through to him before then," Jim said, so full of matter-of-fact confidence that she stretched up to kiss him except

swingbatterbatterswing lichen crumbles and melts into swirling soup erupts into lava lamp Day-Glo stench

"I gotcha," Jim said, and he did, holding her upright when she would have flailed for balance, then holding her an extra moment while she caught her breath. "Was that him?"

"No." But her voice came out a little shaky, and she hated that. She took a deep breath and stepped away, just to prove to herself that she could—but couldn't stop her arms from coming up to warm her stomach and chest where she no longer touched him. "That's my other ghost from the day."

"Busy day," he noted.

"He—I *think* it's a he—is pretty much the opposite of Gordon Reese. Has no idea what's going on, who he is . . . He's not new, but he hasn't been aware of himself until now. He's got a lot of catching up to do before he can cross over." *If he can even do it.* Sometimes, it was too late. Sometimes, those confused spirits never did gain the strength and understanding they needed.

"Hey," he said. "Maybe you should take it easy

tonight. Muster your mojo, or whatever it is that you do when you watch one of those sappy movies of yours." He shook his head. "I don't know how many times I've said it—I just can't understand how you deal with this stuff."

"Are you kidding?" She smiled at him, genuine and suddenly full of energy. "*I'm* the lucky one. I get these reminders . . . I never get to take anything for granted. That means I don't have to worry about waking up fifty years from now and realizing I wasted my time with you."

He raised his eyebrows, taking in all the implications of that. "I guess that makes me the lucky one, too."

Except suddenly, she smelled something, and this time it wasn't Day-Glo stench. She wrinkled her nose. "Except I think dinner is burning. Seriously."

"Hmm. Just as well." He reached to turn off the burner. "Eat light. I have some exercise planned."

He follows the man home. Finds it stings when the man's wife greets him singsong from the kitchen. Finds the warmth in her eyes a physical blow—one he quickly assuages by circling around the man so quickly he feels the power build, feels the fear trickle in, and the man stumbles. *Craig,* she calls him, and urges him to sit, quickly checking his forehead, his flushed cheeks.

But Craig doesn't have a fever. Craig only has Gordon Reese, the man he killed, the man he walked away from.

The man he *thought* he walked away from.

The woman pulls a letter from the mail for Craig's attention, and her expression has turned hopeful. Gordon suddenly realizes that they're discussing children, discussing adoption, discussing *family*.

Gordon has family. Gordon turned his life inside out and upside down and remade himself, and in return he has family—his incredible Carol, his little baby girl.

But they no longer have him.

And there, hovering around Craig, drinking in the energy derived of uncertainty and fear, Gordon decides that Craig's family will lose him, too.

Jim opened his eyes to a midnight darkness that wasn't quite complete. Not with the bed beside him still warm but empty and the bathroom light on down the hall. "Mel?" he called, sleepy but waking up fast. That light only came on when there was trouble—something more than a quick bathroom break.

Ghost trouble, mainly.

"It's fine," she called. "Go to sleep."

But her voice held a puzzlement that made him

sit up, and he turned on the light beside the bed. "Too late," he said. "What's up?"

She must have seen the light; she came back into the bedroom, though not with any speed. She, too, looked sleepy. Adorably sleepy, with her wavy dark hair mussed and her eyes half-mast. And ooh yeah, she'd put on that red satin robe. His favorite. If you didn't count the black satin, and the flowing white satin, or the—

All right. So they were all his favorites. And the red satin seemed to be what had her attention; she held a section of it between her hands and never looked away from it even as he pulled her down to sit beside him. She said, "Did we get a dog while I wasn't looking? Or have I just been spending so much time with Bob the wonder dog that I'm bringing his hair home with me?"

Jim looked at the section of robe in question. Red. Shiny. Touch-me satin. "Not seeing it."

"What?" She looked away from the robe for the first time to double-check his expression, truly startled. "Oh, no. Don't tell me we have *two* of them!"

He got it then. A ghost dog. *Another* ghost dog. "You're kidding. Another Homer?"

"Except Homer is all the fun and none of the hair. So far, this dog is nothing *but* hair!" She wasn't kidding; her voice rose in frustration.

He did his best to hide his smile. He really did. She gave him an incredulous look; he held up both hands in a mea culpa and shook his head. "Everything you deal with . . . and it's the Cheshire ghost dog that—"

He didn't get to finish. She dropped the robe; her hands were everywhere—poking here, tickling there. "Don't make me hurt you, Jim Clancy!"

Aha. She'd started it; that made her fair game. He grabbed her up, pulling her close even as he flipped her over. She squealed, of course, but couldn't keep it up, not when she was laughing so hard. In the next moment he was comfortably on his side again, arms clasped around her, covers only a modest tangle around them. A deep breath, a satisfied smile, and he closed his eyes.

"The light," she said, but when he twisted to turn it off, she made no attempt to escape, only snuggled deeper as he drew the covers up around both of them. Her voice fell to a murmur. "You did that on purpose."

"Maybe," he said, which was as close as he'd get to a confession—not that it mattered. The heavy pattern of her breathing told him she was well on her way to sleep. Good. With a bevy of ghosts making the scene—one an angry ghost at that—she'd need the rest. She'd push herself with this one . . . he knew the signs well enough. And she wouldn't let up on herself until she'd done every-thing she could—which wouldn't include asking for help.

He'd learned to work around that, though, as much as anyone could. In such small ways as this.

He smiled again, breathed the scent of her, and followed her into sleep.

2

Don't watch, Delia. Melinda walked out into the square, ostensibly on her way to a Village Java run—because there had to be at least one of those each morning—and ruing the loss of the previous day's clear sky and bright sun. The clouds hung overhead in a featureless mass, obscuring the fact that a sky even existed; the air had enough of a bite so Melinda crossed her arms over her fitted coat—a vintage sidesaddle habit jacket, snug in the bodice, square flaring tails to midthigh, rescued from a barn trunk with the skirt long gone—holding in the warmth as she could. *Don't watch, Delia, because if things go well, I'm about to play tag with a ghost.*

And she knew what that looked like. No matter how she reminded herself to keep the conversation discreet, the spirits were as *real* and present to her as anyone she met on the street. Soon enough she'd be gesturing, making expressive faces, turning circles in the middle of the sidewalk . . .

Especially with this one. With the anger he carried, and the energy he burned . . .

But she thought he'd be learning better, and faster. He was going to spend a lot of downtime in recharge mode if he didn't control himself.

But she saw nothing—not the ghost, and not the man he'd been harassing. So maybe it was all about the coffee after all. She checked her watch—she'd planned her trip for the time the man had hustled through the square the day before, but then again . . . he'd looked in a hurry. Late, perhaps—meaning if he was on time today, she'd have missed him already. She'd try earlier tomorrow.

She did a slow three-sixty—saw Delia watching, puzzled, from the store, pretended she didn't—and shrugged. *Brrr.* She'd need that coffee if she was ever to get warm, that's for sure. According to Weather Underground online, tomorrow should be nicer . . . easier to linger. She and Jim could meet for lunch if he wasn't out on a call. She turned on her heel to head for Village Java and

oozing filaments and fine fluorescent bug wings melting into stark oozing gravel and whamwham-wham! *the blows rocked her*

and Melinda found herself on the ground, or nearly so—folded over herself, hands braced on the sidewalk, and knees about to touch down.

"Here, are you all right?" A man's voice, startled and concerned; his hand steadied her arm.

"I'm fine," she said, putting the casual lightness into her tone that came as second nature after so much practice. "I must have tripped." Figures—go looking for one earthbound spirit, find the other. She pushed her hair out of her face, took a quick, clandestine look around just in case the spirit had indeed manifested in some fashion, and then, as she was accepting a hand up, finally looked at her good Samaritan. "Oh!" she said. "Hello!"

He did a tiny double take, responding to her recognition. "Have we met? I'm so sorry, I don't remember." He looked less hassled than the day before; no doubt his ghost had taken some time to recharge after the display Melinda had seen. Today he was neat in a casual light jacket and dress slacks, his briefcase on the sidewalk beside him, his close-trimmed extended goatee and neatly cut hair asserting his professional status.

She allowed him to help her to her feet. "I guess I've seen you in the square," she said. "I own the antique store." She gestured at it. "Big windows. Not so many customers first thing in the morning. Faces tend to become familiar."

"My wife loves antiquing," he said, his gaze settling on the store. Melinda took the opportunity to check again. Still no signs of spirits—not her mystery vertigo spirit or the angry murder victim—

and she was ready when the man turned back to her. "I keep meaning to tell her about your little place. We live in Bayview," he added, "or I'm sure she would have found it on her own."

"Oh!" Melinda's all-purpose exclamation of pleasant discovery perfectly suited the moment. "I hope she stops by. We have some new things coming in before the weekend—perfect timing. I don't have any cards with me, but I'd be glad to drop one off at your office—?"

She did have the cards, of course. But if she just handed one over, she'd know nothing more than before he'd picked her up off the sidewalk.

"Craig Lusak," he said, apparently deciding introductions were in order. "I've got the little law office tucked away just out of the square proper."

"Melinda Gordon." She shook his hand, found it confident and warm, and wondered again what connection this man had with the angry spirit. She had just enough time to ponder whether their encounter from the day before had been a mistake of some kind when black anger brushed the edges of her awareness.

The blur of movement gave her far too little warning for the contorted rictus of fury that suddenly appeared within inches of her face, snarling her away. She couldn't help the little shriek of surprise, the quick jump back—and by then the spirit had circled his target three times, leaving

Craig Lusak confused and disoriented and trying to hide it.

She knew how to play that game. "Sorry," she said, offering an apologetic shrug. "Something flew into my eye." That was close enough to the truth—and she wasn't ready to mention the spirit, not until she had a better understanding of the connection between them.

He made a visible effort to smile at her—even as Gordon Reese dashed between them again, right up to her face *again*. He bellowed silently at her, so close she couldn't even attempt to see the words on his lips; the sound came lagged and distorted, like ripples on water. *"Mine-ine-ine!"* Mine.

Well, just because it didn't make sense now didn't mean it wouldn't later.

"I wonder," she said abruptly, when Lusak seemed on the verge of polite flight from this awkward social dance, "since you're a lawyer, do you know anything about the man who was killed the other day? Gordon Reese, from Bayview?"

Round and round Reese went, as though he were a spider spinning a web of anger—and then he was gone. Not drained, but gone. Learning already, Melinda guessed, not to push it to the limit. Lusak pulled himself together, shook off the lingering effect of the ethereal attack, and cleared his throat. "I'm not that kind of lawyer, I'm afraid. I work as a children's advocate and I mediate custody arrangements. Why do you ask? Were you a friend?"

"In a manner of speaking." This time, she had the warning—the black anger, brushing up against her awareness—but she still jerked in surprise when Gordon rushed her. This time he added a little push, making her stumble back a step.

"Mine-ine-ine!" he bellowed—still silent, as though the shout itself was so loud it was beyond hearing.

Melinda batted at her fictional bug. "Darn, that thing's persistent!" And so was Gordon Reese. If he'd only slow down . . . if he'd talk to her, instead of shoving her around . . .

He clearly realized she could see him. He clearly didn't want anything to do with her. Whatever he was doing in this square, he hadn't come here looking for her, as so many did. No, he'd come for Craig Lusak. But this time he didn't go flickering around; he stood between them, scowling so strongly that his face remained distorted—not to mention that the side of his head was gruesomely smashed and bloody, gray matter exposed.

He'd died, suddenly and violently; he'd left a family behind. And yet . . . he'd been drawn to Craig Lusak?

Lusak, Melinda thought, deserved a little search-engine time. Because he'd never said he *didn't* know anything about Gordon; his response to her had been as vague as her own when she was obscuring her interaction with a spirit. She wasn't quite ready to let him off the hook, either. "If you do hear anything . . . ? My husband is a paramedic, and you know how it is—they're all pretty tight. The Bayview crew is pretty shook up. I think everyone's really hoping this killer will be caught."

"It must be very hard on them," Lusak said. "Small town, everyone knows everyone."

"Well, almost everyone, or we would have met earlier." Melinda smiled at him, knowing when to back off. If Lusak had any connection to Gordon Reese, he was very cool about it, and pushing wouldn't do anything to change that. It might even drive the hidden things deeper.

And as Lusak smiled and nodded and gave the square a surreptitiously wary look—no doubt feeling the waves of glaring energy pouring off Reese even if faintly and even if he had no idea what he perceived—Melinda wished him a good day. She'd planted the seeds; she'd be able to go back to him after she'd learned a little more about him.

But for now . . . as she smiled and moved aside so Lusak could pick up his briefcase and pass, she stepped in front of Gordon and said in a low voice, "I want to talk to you."

"Excuse me?" Lusak said, half turning.

"Melinda!" And that was Delia, calling from fifty feet away as she closed in at a fast pace—an authoritative pace. "I saw you fall—is everything okay?" But she was looking at Lusak as she spoke, and Melinda knew her concern was truly triggered by this strange man who'd lingered over her after the fall. A friend's protectiveness, at just the wrong moment.

"I'm serious," Melinda said under her breath to Gordon, who scowled at her with deep, unabated resentment and then flickered around her at fast-forward speed as if just to show that he could. Melinda didn't even try to follow his movement. "We need to talk."

"Leave him," Gordon snarled, his voice a deckle-edged rasp against her ears. *"He's mine now."*

Delia's assertive stride faltered as she reached them; looking from one to the other, she tried to sort out the nonverbal cues—not much chance of that, with Lusak baffled by Gordon's energy and Melinda's behavior, and Melinda caught in conversation between two worlds. Delia said, "Melinda?"

"This is Craig Lusak," Melinda offered, stepping boldly into the confusion. "He has an office just outside the square. I'd say I threw myself at his feet, but we're both happily married."

"More than happily, from what I see of you and Jim," Delia said, a little more pointedly than necessary as she glanced to Lusak.

"Craig's wife might come antiquing here sometime," Melinda said, desperation edging her

voice—for Gordon wouldn't stay here long. Not as
fixated as he was, not as set to *maximum ghostly
rage* as he remained. "Did you mention her name,
Craig?"

"Jeannie," Lusak said, looking bemused.

Melinda really couldn't blame him. Between
whirlwind Gordon and whirlwind Delia—and perhaps a little of whirlwind Melinda—he deserved a
little bemusement. "We'll keep an eye out for her,"
she promised, and gave Delia a meaningful eye.

Delia's response came just a beat too late to look
genuine, but her smile was convincing enough.
"Yes, of course. Did Melinda mention we're getting
some things in before the weekend?"

Ah, teamwork. It gave Melinda the moment to
turn to Gordon, to mouth at him *I mean it* even
though such pronouncements generally meant very
little to those who had passed but were still here,
tangled in their issues and their obsessions. Gordon, she felt safe enough to conclude, was one of
those tangled in obsession. In sudden inspiration,
as Delia chatted with Lusak, Melinda stepped right
up to the spirit, reversing their roles, and said in a
low voice, "You'd better talk to me. Because I'm *not*
leaving him and I'm *not* going away, and I'm going
to be in your face every step of the way—"

Gordon roared in no-longer-human rage, his
features distorting, running down his face in inky
trails. He quite suddenly expanded into several

times his normal size, collapsed into himself, and speed-jerked directly through Lusak, disappearing on the other side. Melinda briefly held her breath, letting it out in a sigh. Inspiration, maybe. Mistake . . .

Maybe.

Lusak had stiffened and now held a hand to his stomach, looking as though he had just experienced a most distasteful belch. "Excuse me, ladies," he said. "Breakfast may not be agreeing with me." His expression made it clear there'd be no lingering, not this time.

"Oh, I'm sorry," Melinda said. "I hope you feel better."

Lusak hastened away, and Delia barely waited until he was out of earshot. "What was that all about?" she asked, and at least she kept her voice low. "Aside from being totally strange. You know it was totally strange, right?"

And there was Gordon, back again—still aggressive, still seething. Still stuck in bleeding and oozing mode. The paper hadn't said exactly how he'd died, but the term *blunt force trauma* flashed through Melinda's thoughts. Gordon leered close. "He's *mine*."

"Oh yeah," Melinda said to Delia. "Definitely on the strange side. In fact, you might well say it still is."

Delia finally understood. "What? Again?" She backed a few steps.

"Same song, different verse." And to Gordon, "That's not the way it works."

"I, um . . . I left the store open," Delia said. "See you there?"

"With coffee," Melinda assured her, as if she wasn't looking straight at Mr. Gruesome. She headed for the familiar purple and green Village Java storefront, but as she passed Gordon she murmured, "Come with me," and at the first opportunity she left the sidewalk and sat on one of the slatted benches to cross one leg over the other and contemplate the towering war memorial. An instant later Gordon, too, towered over her.

She glanced up at him. "Look, I get it. You're mad. You're *really* mad. But I'm here to help."

"Stay away from that one. He's mine."

She gave him a thoughtful examination. Aside from the gruesome factor, he didn't look much like the man described in the newspaper. The family man just graduated from school, the new business manager for the B&B and honey farm. He wore scuffed steel-toed boots and worn, rugged jeans, a flannel shirt over a T-shirt and a tough-guy leather jacket over that. Unlike the first time she'd seen him, he was now unshaven, and his hair had needed a cut a subjective month earlier.

He wasn't the man who'd died. He was the man he'd given up—the person he'd left behind. "You're different," she observed, wondering if he'd noticed . . . if he'd made a choice, or slid into it in his distress, perhaps unwittingly.

"This works for me," he growled, and his words rumbled and distorted as though he'd spoken them inside an empty metal drum.

"And the other didn't?"

"I'm dead, aren't I?" Gordon snarled closer, his body briefly expanding with his rage, then settling back under control. *"I'm dead, and my killer lives. That won't last long."*

"Gordon," Melinda started, but hesitated; she folded her hands on her knees as if this outward sign of composure could keep her settled on the inside. She'd dealt with angry spirits before, but Gordon . . . Gordon contained the fury of a man betrayed by more than just any one person. By *life*. She could understand that, and a year ago—two years ago— she could have waited him out, acted as a calm anchor for him, guided him to an emotional place where he was ready to see the light, to walk into it.

But things were different now. Now Gordon's anger manifested clearly on his chosen target. Now, once he figured it out, he could do more than make Lusak miserable. He could kill him, just as Ely Fisher had nearly killed Judge Merrick. Ely had been an older ghost—an experienced one. But Gordon's rage . . . it was fresh and harsh and deep, and it drew on a lifetime of rogue behavior. *He could do it*. What she'd been through in this past year told her that; the fear tightening down her throat told her that.

So she didn't argue with him. She had his attention; that was enough for now. Instead she asked quietly, "Why Lusak?"

Gordon flickered behind her, to the side of her, directly in front of her; Melinda closed her eyes and could still see him with her inner eye, a wash of red over all. He repeated, *"My killer lives!"*

She had the sense he'd stilled; she opened her eyes to find him right there, etched again in unnatural crystal clarity. When he spoke, his voice was controlled and quiet and perfectly normal . . . and it still left a chill in her bones. *"He's mine,"* Gordon said. *"Don't talk to me about any damned light. Don't talk to me about love and peace. My love cries her heart out. My peace bled out on the filthy gravel with my brains. Revenge is my peace, now."*

And he was gone.

"Whoa," she murmured to herself. And she spent another moment looking at the war memorial, and then she took a deep breath, stood, smoothed down the dense black wool of the sidesaddle habit jacket, and headed for Village Java.

"Thank goodness," Delia said, accepting her coffee with eager hands. "Somehow I just really need this right now." She took a sip, savored it with her eyes closed, and set it aside to return to the task at

hand—stickering gift bags with custom SAME AS
IT NEVER WAS ovals. She opened her mouth, hesitated there, and gave the faintest shake of her head
as she pressed her lips together.

Well. She was *trying*.

Melinda went into the back and grabbed the
window-cleaning supplies, and when she re-
emerged, Delia said, "The look on Craig Lusak's
face . . ." And she took a deep breath. "Could he
see it, too? Whatever you were seeing?"

"Hmm?" She hadn't expected that particular
question. Points to Delia for approaching her co-
nundrum creatively. "No, not that I could tell. But
Gordon is definitely having an effect on him." She
moved the wicker carriage in order to reach the
front display window. Yup, she'd been right when
she'd spotted that smudge upon returning to the
shop. More fingerprints, a smear or two, one entire
palm print. Now, what was who up to?

"Gordon?" Delia said, and her voice went up a
notch, heading for sharp. "As in Gordon Reese? As
in the man we were reading about yesterday morning? You think you're seeing Gordon Reese?"

Long practice made her voice matter-of-fact and
allowed her to ignore the implication that she only
thought she saw the man. "Yes. And he's very unhappy. Craig Lusak is in trouble, if I can't convince
Gordon to . . . well, to take a breath and think
about things."

"Take a breath," Delia repeated. "Okay, that's a good one." More coffee. A few more bags stickered. "Craig Lusak—he's the man you were watching in the square yesterday morning."

"I was watching Gordon," Melinda said, reaching to eradicate one final stray fingerprint on the glass. "But Gordon's attached himself to Craig, so I guess I was watching them both."

Delia said nothing. She stickered. She sipped coffee. She quite visibly said nothing, and as Melinda stood, shifted the carriage back into place, and returned the cleaning supplies to the back room, the saying-nothing vibes hovered so obviously that she thought she might well start seeing those, too. And finally Delia slapped her hand down on the stack of finished bags and said, "Okay. Let's say you saw . . . *something*. Whatever." She frowned. "Why Craig? Why not be with someone he loved? I mean, did he even *know* Craig Lusak?"

"Not according to Craig." Melinda nursed her own coffee, a reassuring two-handed hold, and absently plucked away a long, crisp dog hair from her sleeve. "The thing is, Gordon seems to think Craig is the one who killed him."

Whatever Delia had expected, it hadn't been that. Maybe she'd been looking for something sentimental, something more *Touched by an Angel*. A couple of years ago, she'd have had better odds. Not so much, lately. Delia made several attempts to find words, and then sat straighter, tucked her hair behind her ear—the rebellious ear, the one with multiple piercings all the way up the back curve—and said quietly, "Then what are you going to do?"

Melinda shrugged. "Try to calm him. Try to get him to cross over. Whatever that takes."

"But if Craig . . ." Delia stopped, rolled her eyes. "I can't even make myself say it. He seemed so nice! But if . . . , then shouldn't you—"

Melinda shook her head, and sharply. "I help earthbound spirits, Delia—I offer closure to those left behind. But I don't *interfere* with the affairs of the living. Not beyond delivering the odd message or two, and believe me, some of those are *really* odd."

"But you could call in a tip . . ."

Steep learning curve, especially for those who didn't really want to know. She knew that look in Delia's eye—knew her friend was straddling the line where part of her played along and part of her still wanted nothing to do with it, nor truly believed any of it. When all was said and done, Delia could still easily fall back to that place. And Melinda . . .

Melinda tread carefully. She cared too much to have this go wrong. "Gordon's been through a lot," she said. "His death was sudden and violent, and he may not yet truly understand what happened.

He could be confused about what he saw." But she remembered the look on Gordon's face and knew that he wasn't confused at all. He *knew*. It didn't mean he was right, but it meant he was dangerous.

It meant she couldn't just wait for him to sort things out. Not for his sake; not for Lusak's sake.

She gathered her thoughts back to the conversation and shook her head. "The point is, I can't call in a tip with the little I know."

"Then what are you going to do?"

Melinda eyed her laptop, tucked away behind the counter. "I need to know more, that's what."

More about Gordon Reese. And more about the man he believed had killed him.

He lives it again.

Gordon Reese leaves the Whetstone Bar, and leaves his old way of life behind.

The chilly spring night closes in around him—spring peepers singing from the road ditch as though they are out in the country and not along this cracked sidewalk on the edge of town where only a block farther down, the sidewalk itself peters out to packed dirt and weedy grass choked by the exhaust of cars headed for Grandview . . .

Let's go get Whet! A familiar voice, a friend's voice. Any friend's voice. And Carol's face, golden brown hair short and wispy around her ears and the base of her neck, her eyes big and blue and worried. *No more,* those eyes said. *No more,* Gordon's own voice agreed.

No more, he told them all. *Here's to good times. Here's to you all. Here's to the future.*

And fresh night air and lurching movement and a tremendous blow, a tearing separation of body and soul, a blurry swirl of stars and the shift of gravel and the thump of something—some*one*— falling to the ground.

A man hurries away. *Neat clothes, light jacket, short, crisply styled hair, trimmed extended goatee.* And the world sucks away into black and red and grief, into new hope turned to anger, into potentials screaming away into nothing, and then nothing left but revenge . . .

Jim might have been on the couch with his sock-covered feet sticking off the other end, and he might have had his eyes closed, and he might have been bone-tired after working an end-of-shift car accident with an entrapped driver and child, but when Melinda opened the door and rustled in with the accompaniment of crinkling plastic bags and closed it with her little shut-door-with-foot maneuver, he definitely wasn't asleep. And when she made a little *oops* noise and suddenly got a whole lot quieter, he couldn't help but smile. "Already awake," he said. "Not necessarily conscious, though."

"Perfect!"

That got one eye cracked open, though all he could see was the back of the couch and her shoulders as she passed by—dark hair flowing down her back, that tailored vintage whatever-it-was following the narrow lines of her waist to flare over her hips. Not that he could see that much, but he'd seen it that morning and it had made its usual impression. "What," he said, the one eye still open, "about me not being conscious is *perfect*?"

"No, perfect that this is the night I brought home takeout." Unfazed, she headed for the kitchen, where more rustling announced the swift unpacking of the bags. "Not to mention the gooey."

That was almost worth sitting up. "You brought home the gooey?"

"Well, it's *a* gooey. Only proper examination and testing will determine whether it assumes the title of *the* gooey. I found it in the market. There's honey, nuts, cinnamon—"

"Sugar crash," he said, feeling too heavy on the couch to get up. "Right here and now. Just from listening."

"Well, then, here." She reappeared in the living room and set a plate on the coffee table, already heaped with cashew chicken, then paused long enough to unbutton the coat and reveal the snug soft turtleneck beneath. "My penance for being late. We had a sudden rush at the store—a field trip bus from a retirement community. Delia had to get home for Ned, so it took me a little longer than I expected to wrap things up." With the coat hung up, she briefly disappeared into the kitchen again, returning with her own plate and a batch of napkins. Another trip and she had sparkling flavored water and he had a beer, and she stood in front of the couch to give his legs a meaningful look.

"What?" he said, as if in surprise. "Am I in your way?"

She gave him one of *those looks*—a sideways glint from almond eyes—and set about carefully moving his legs on her own, swiveling them around so he had little choice but to sit and contemplate the meal. "There you go," she said, and patted his knee.

Oh, no. She thought she'd give him a little pat on the knee, did she? He snatched her right off her feet and into his lap, while she gave the requisite shriek and struggle and subsided with an unconvincing, "God, you're a beast."

"Uh-huh," he said, deeply moved . . . not so much. "So I hear you were picking up a new guy this morning."

"You did, did you? Checking up on me?"

"I wish I could say guilty as charged, but it was Tim." He righted her, and she slid off his lap to sit beside him, already reaching for a cashew from his plate. Clearly impressed by his prowess, oh yes. "He was Delia-watching. Probably best if you don't mention that to her."

"She's still a little gun-shy," Melinda agreed. "As for Craig Lusak, actually, I think he picked *me* up. Right up off the sidewalk. Was that the most embarrassing thing, or what?"

He gave her a sharp look. "I thought Tim was kidding when he said you fell for someone else."

"Nope," she said, cheerfully enough. She snagged the chopsticks and scooped herself an expert mouthful of sweet and sour chicken before heading off to the kitchen again, this time to return with her laptop; she'd apparently dumped her case in there with the food. "So here's the thing," she said, so casually that she took him completely off guard. "Gordon Reese thinks Craig Lusak is his killer."

Killer. Suddenly the conversation took on a whole new layer. "That's why you were out there," he realized. "Talking to Gordon."

"Actually, I was getting coffee. But you know how it is. All things come to the Grandview square." She hunted for the AC adapter plug that generally hung around the coffee table and plugged the laptop in, lifting the lid. As the machine booted up, she picked out a chunk of chicken covered with sauce, timed its drips, and made the dash to her mouth. Almost got there, too—just a little sauce on her chin. She made a face at it, swiped it off with a finger, and licked the finger clean. "Ah, here we go. I want to see what I can find out about our Mr. Lusak." She shook her head and added, "Honestly, he doesn't seem like the type."

Something in the pit of Jim's stomach went cold. He put down his laden chopsticks and asked quietly, "And what would you do if he was?"

"What I'm doing now," she said, quite firmly. She didn't pin him with another sideways look, for which he had to give her points; they'd had this conversation before. "Seeing what I can find." But within a few moments—enough time for him to force down a goodly portion of food even if he wasn't quite tasting it—frustration crossed her features. "Well, it doesn't seem as though that's going to be a whole lot. Not this way."

"Not on the Internet radar?"

"Not so much." She'd ignored her own food, and now she turned to it, sitting back to balance the plate on her knees. "He's listed with the Grandview Chamber of Commerce, but that just gives me his business address. I could have walked down the street to find that. Otherwise, if he has any presence on the Web, he's covered his tracks pretty well."

"No MySpace page for Craig Lusak of Grandview? What's he do, anyway?" It was too early to relax. Not finding anything now just meant she'd have to dig deeper in more conventional ways. More personal ways.

More vulnerable ways.

"He's a lawyer. A children's advocate." But she answered absently, her eyes narrowed slightly in thought; the expression emphasized the sweep of her lashes, the high angle of her cheekbones.

"Look, Mel," he said, and put his own food down to move a little closer. "I know you have to do this. But if there's the slightest chance . . ." He stopped, rubbing a finger at the bridge of his nose where the day's fatigue seemed to have set in. "It was a brutal murder, Mel."

"You've heard about it," she told him. "I've *seen* it."

Silence sat between them for a long moment, then each of them took a breath to speak again at exactly the same time, stopping short as they realized it. Melinda laughed—a sound he loved well, light and taking delight in the silly moments of life as few people bothered to do. She said, "You first."

"I was just thinking. The point is to cross this guy over, right? Maybe the place to start is with his family. See if there's something he needs that'll do the trick. Give the police some time to get close to the killer, whoever he is."

She thought about it another moment. "Okay," she said. "I can do that." But as he reacted with relief, she tipped her head in warning, holding up a finger to stop him from going any further with it. *"But,"* she added, "I'm not passing up any opportunities to learn more about Craig Lusak. Not if they come my way."

And that, he knew, was about as good as he was going to get. "Just . . ." he started, and hesitated on words he seemed to say far too often.

She knew them, too. "I will," she said. "Now, do you want to try the gooey?"

"The gooey sounds perfect." He planted a kiss on her temple and released her; she gathered up her plate, finishing a last few bites on the way into the kitchen while he took a deep breath, followed by a deep slug of beer. Then gave the beer a second look, thinking . . . Probably not the best thing to mix with something that claimed honey, nuts, and cinnamon as its big taste factors. Coffee, maybe. Decaf, so he could tackle that sticky window in the laundry room and make an early night of it.

From within the kitchen, Melinda made a faint noise; crockery hit the floor and smashed. Silverware bounced. Jim shot up out of the couch, fatigue obliterated by alarm, and made it to the kitchen in a few plunging strides.

Melinda lay on the floor by the stove island, curled into a tight ball with her arms over her head—protective, but not protective enough, not to judge by her tight shaking, by her cries of fear. "Mel!" Right down beside her he went, amid the smeared food and broken plate, but when he touched her, she shrieked, batting at him.

Backing off—not an option. He drew her in anyway, pulling her into his lap, expert fingers checking her head for lumps and bumps even as he tucked long tangled hair away from her face. Nothing there . . . totally a ghost thing. God, he wished they would lighten up. Lately she'd had none of the easy ones. None of the simple ones.

He kissed the top of her head and wrapped his arms around her and waited, and after what seemed like an hour or two but in truth added up only to minutes, she quite suddenly quit trembling and took a deep watery breath and turned to him.

"Hey," he said. "Welcome back."

"That," she said in return, somewhat muffled by his shirt, "was really, really unpleasant. I seriously can't figure out what's going on with this one."

"Yeah, well you know what I say to *this* ghost?" Jim raised his head and lifted his voice. "You! Get your act together! You want some help, then quit messing with the one person who can help you!" Then, in his normal tone of voice, "What do you think? Maybe he'll listen?"

She was silent for a moment. Then she said, "Well, who knows. Maybe you'll reach him, on some sort of he-man level. I'm pretty sure it's a guy, after all."

"He-man?" He hadn't stopped stroking her hair,

but mainly that was because he loved stroking her hair. "I don't know whether to be impressed with myself or offended."

"Your choice?" she suggested, and sat up on her own, brushing off her turtleneck—spending, in fact, an inordinate amount of time picking at the fabric over her hip, which looked perfectly spotless to him.

"Don't tell me," he said. "Dog hair?"

"Dog hair," she confirmed. And then, looking at the mess of the plate and the food, another sort of horror crossed her face. "Oh! Don't tell me I'd already made it to the counter! Don't tell me I dropped the gooey here somewhere!"

Jim leaned back against the stove island, resting his forearm across one upraised knee. "Never fear," he said. "The gooey is safe."

"Well, then." She climbed to her feet, resolute and not entirely convincing. "That's all that matters."

But the little wrinkle of worry between her brows didn't go away.

3

MELINDA HESITATED AT the office door of Professor Rick Payne, finding it closed but for a crack of light, and pondered whether this made the door officially open or officially closed. Since she was—quite deliberately—within the semester's posted office hours, she settled on a firm knock and pushed the door open without actually entering.

Well, maybe a foot across the threshold. Because otherwise, as she knew from experience, she was likely to wait some time before she actually caught his attention.

Indeed, he was crouched before his desk, peering into the side of an empty jar with a notepad perched over the top of it, and he didn't so much as look her way. He rotated the jar, cocking his head; he squinted slightly.

Maybe not so empty after all.

Just when she thought she'd have to do some

obvious and borderline obnoxious throat-clearing, Payne said, "Did you know that a cricket's tympanic organs can vibrate up to twenty thousand cycles per second? That's well beyond the sensitivity of human ears, somewhat like a certain dearly departed recently encountered. And of course the temperature can be determined by counting the number of times a cricket chirps in fifteen seconds and adding forty to the number."

"I didn't know that," Melinda said, and she was pretty sure her tone also indicated that she didn't care.

"Cricket breeding and fighting was once a popular pastime in China. In fact, crickets are partially to blame for the decline of the Southern Song dynasty; the last premier, Jia Sidao, supposedly neglected important affairs of state to watch his fighting crickets. Not unlike certain modern-day politicians with their little personal distractions."

"Uh-huh," she said, as flatly as possible. She looked at her watch—at both the watches she currently wore, each a sweet little vintage dial, loose on her wrist because she could never seem to get them to fit snugly anyway.

"And while in general they'll eat just about anything—plants being preferred, but get them stuck inside and they'll snack on clothes and papers, too—we sometimes turn the tables by frying them up. In fact, in the early nineties the New York

Entomological Society celebrated its hundredth anniversary with a banquet that included gourmet roasted crickets, cricket and vegetable tempura, and a dessert of chocolate cricket torte."

"And how was it?" Melinda asked dryly.

That, finally, got his attention. He looked up from the jar and said, "What? Oh, no, not me. I prefer a little more creepy with my crawly. But I've had other—"

"No." She stepped into the office, cutting him off as firmly as she dared. "Really. Don't need to know. But I could use some information on—"

"Typical," he said. "Here to use and abuse me." He swiped the jar off the desk, made it to the window in two brisk steps, and jimmied open the screen to upend the jar outside. "He'll be someone else's snack, now. I keep telling them that screen needs to be fixed, by the way."

Melinda didn't tear at her hair—consciously stopped herself from that—but tucked it behind her ear and smiled prettily in a way that very well got his attention. She said, "Look, I had to take a taxi to get here and I really need to get back to the store as soon as possible—"

"Oh ho," he said, and sat on the edge of his desk, never minding that he shoved a stack of papers aside with his hip to do it. "What of the inimitable red Saturn?"

"The Saturn is fine. But I won't be driving it

until I can figure out what I've been seeing, and just at this moment that doesn't seem likely." She hadn't been able to argue with Jim; if she'd been driving when the mystery spirit tried to connect with her the previous evening, she'd have run off the road—or worse, taken someone else with her. Generally, the spirits who reached out to her were careful. They might distract her at a stoplight, or they might even mess with the vehicle in some way that took her right to the edge of danger and didn't do her nerves or her blood pressure any good at all, but they hadn't yet crossed that line.

This time, she couldn't take the chance. Until this spirit was communicating better—or at least less intrusively—she was grounded.

And really, really out of sorts about it.

"Oh? Tell me more. All the gruesome details. Especially any parts about crickets."

Melinda crossed her arms, realized it made her look childishly peeved, and deliberately relaxed them at her sides again. "It's hard to describe," she said. "It's not just seeing, it's smelling and tasting and feeling. The only thing that's the same each time is the *batterbatter* chant. And there are generally ants."

"Whoa. It seems you've stumped even my prodigiously profligate genius. The *batterbatter* chant?"

She gave him a disbelieving look. "You've never played baseball? *Swing, batter batter . . . ?*"

He looked startled, then disappointed. "Oh. *That batterbatter* chant. More mundane than I'd hoped."

"Trust me, there's nothing mundane about this one. The colors have smells, the ants *taste . . .*"

Payne laughed shortly. "Sounds more like an acid trip."

"Well, it's not. It's got to mean something, and unless I figure it out, I'm grounded. And the thing is, I've got things to do. *Important* things." She thought of Craig Lusak—possibly a killer, possibly wrongly targeted for revenge by a furious spirit who could, once he got his act together, very well succeed.

"Like what?"

"Oh my God, you are so *nosy.*" Her hands went to her hips in spite of herself. "I would slap your hand if it was anywhere near!"

"If it was anywhere near, you'd have reason," he said, never at a loss for words, or for the little smirky smile that so rarely expanded into a genuine expression. "Ants. In dreams, they signify a dissatisfaction with your daily life. Maybe you feel neglected or insignificant. Petty annoyances abound. And you need to learn cooperation. You see? This would be a perfect opportunity to practice—"

"If it's a dream, it's not *my* dream," she pointed out.

"Well, then." The half smile again. "Ants also

symbolize hard work, diligence, and industry, not to mention social conformity and mass action. Also not to mention they eat dead things."

"They eat *dead things*?" Melinda repeated.

"Sure." He shrugged. "Since we're talking about the dearly departed and all, who knows? Could be relevant."

"Well, I can see this was a great use of my time." It wasn't really fair, and she knew it. What had she really given him to go on? "Nothing that connects ants and . . . well, baseball?"

"Not unless you're talking team mascot."

She sighed. "Great." And fumbled in her purse for her phone.

"What, that's it? Those are my only clues? Ants and baseball?"

"Melting bug wings. Day-Glo stench." She checked the *calls placed* menu, looking for the taxi number.

"Okay, now we're just back to my original supposition. Acid trip. Not that I'd know anything about that, but the Paumarí—they hail from Amazonian Brazil—have this great snuff called *ebene;* it's made from the inner bark of trees from the *Virola* genus—actually, of the nutmeg family . . ." He'd finally caught on to her exasperated expression; his words trailed off. "Not the subject at hand, however. Put that phone away. I'll drive you back into town."

"And you'll think about what I've seen? Let me know if anything else comes to mind?"

"Would I be a gentleman if I didn't?" But at that he stopped as he slid off the edge of the desk, and he and Melinda exchanged a long look—he somewhat deer-in-the-headlights, she very much and-do-you-really-want-to-go-there? He gave a short, decisive shake of his head. "Never mind. We'll leave that one."

"Probably for the best," she agreed. "But I appreciate the ride anyway."

"Melinda." Delia looked up from the counter in surprise, where she fussed with the arrangement of several jewelry pieces on velvet—all art nouveau and art deco, all arrived only that morning. Delia herself had an extra bit of sparkle today, in a lilac top with shirring in all the right places and dangly earrings made of glass beads with a metallic glint, and yes, definitely a hint more makeup than usual. "I didn't see the taxi pull up."

"I got a ride with a friend. Lunch date with Tim today, by any chance?"

Delia pulled a face. "Am I obvious?"

"I think it's perfect," Melinda declared, pulling off her coat—still the sidesaddle habit against the chill, but today was brighter and had inspired a lightweight blouse with overlong cuffs, plenty of the delicate detailing and fine touches that she loved. "Let me stash my things, and I'll be out to help. What you're doing there is a great start."

But when she came back out, Delia was no longer alone; the jewelry board had been tucked away behind the counter, and Delia spoke to a woman who looked to be in her midthirties. "We did get in some new things, but I'm afraid we haven't gone over them yet."

"I knew I might be jumping the gun," the woman said. Average height, average weight, she was neatly dressed in what Melinda thought of as outdoorsy semiformal, her dark blond hair elegantly cut. "I just had the chance to come in, and after what happened in the square the other day . . ."

Delia turned to Melinda. "This is Jeannie Lusak. We met her husband in the square."

As if Melinda wasn't excruciatingly aware of that name right now. "Oh!" she said. "Hello! I'm so glad you could make it in."

"Craig wanted me to apologize for his abrupt departure the other day. He . . . hasn't been feeling well. Some odd virus. But he was a little worried about you," she added, looking at Melinda. "I hope you're okay?"

Melinda made a dismissive gesture. "Probably just . . . well, some odd virus." She grinned. "I'm fine. But you know, since you came all the way in here, we could let you look at some of the things we've pulled out so far. They aren't priced, but if there's anything you're interested in, I'll make a note to get back to you about them."

Jeannie's face opened up into delight. "Could I? That would be so fun—like a treasure hunt."

"Sure. Of course, there are things we haven't cleaned up yet—and a thing or two I suspect we'll weed out as not quite our style—so you're going to see it all in its unglory, so to speak."

"Even better," Jeannie said. "Almost as good as going antique hunting myself. I just haven't had time for that since Craig moved his office out here. The lease terms are so much better, but with our . . . well, it always seems like I'm running somewhere." She stopped short, seemed to consider her words, and said, "Gosh, I'm sorry. That was a whine-fest."

"Not at all," Melinda said, as Delia pulled out the very jewelry board she'd been working on and Melinda brought up the box that held the rest of the pieces. In the back she had a little vanity table, a washstand, and a collection of ladies' toiletry items, all from the turn of the century and early 1900s, but they'd start here. "It can be hard enough even when you work down the street from one another! My husband Jim is a paramedic, and on the days we meet for lunch out in the square, that's wonderful, but when he starts covering extra shifts, it seems like nothing quite fits together anymore."

Delia said, "You know, I'm still working some

real estate along with my time here—I don't even fit together with myself sometimes! Add Ned into the equation . . ."

Jeannie laughed. "You're both very kind." She poked at a ring still in the box. "Ooh, look at this one. Do you suppose it'll clean up well?"

It was a mess, dirty and dull, but Melinda laughed. "Wow, you *do* have an eye. That's probably the best piece of the batch. It's art nouveau, from the late eighteen hundreds, and that's a ruby under the dirt—plus those two brilliant-cut diamonds on the sides, and rose-cut diamonds on the winglike sections. Ten of them, if I counted right. I'm pretty sure it's platinum over gold, but I'll have to check on that. I can definitely get you a quote on it, if you're interested."

"I love these old things," Jeannie mused. "Somehow they carry the time along with them, until they're more than just *things*, if you know what I mean." She stopped, looked at them, and laughed. "Of course you know!"

"Yes," Melinda said. "I've always felt that way. This store is my way of preserving not just things, but someone's memories."

"I'm learning to see things that way," Delia said. "When I first came in here, I just thought of it as a decorator's dream!"

"Those lamps!" Melinda said, and laughed, remembering a particular frantic Realtor in need of replacement lamps for a showing.

"Those lamps," Delia agreed. "Look where it got me!"

Jeannie turned the ring on her finger, gone pensive. "Is that why you asked Craig about Gordon Reese?" she said, quite suddenly. "Your husband, I mean. Was he called to the scene that night?"

Melinda had as much as told Lusak not, but apparently Lusak hadn't shared that much. It made her wonder how much he *did* share with his wife . . . and how much he kept secret from her. Because if Gordon was right, if Lusak *had* killed him . . . when it came down to it, Melinda might well betray this woman's trust.

And still.

So she pretended not to see Delia's sudden questioning glance and said, "He wasn't, but he heard about it. I guess it was pretty bad. And what with Gordon's new life, his new family, it just all seems particularly wrenching."

Jeannie shuddered. "I can't stand the thought that Craig was in that part of town that night."

In the back corner of the store, something dark flickered into movement. *You stay out of this,* Melinda thought fiercely at Gordon Reese.

Not that he could hear her. Or that he'd heed her if he could.

And Delia was already saying, with some surprise, "He was there?"

"Not *there*," Jeannie said, and she stopped playing with the ring to give Delia a look that was part horror, part surprise. "That end of town. He was coming home. The car got a flat, and he was hoping the garage on the corner could patch it up so he wouldn't have to drive on the little spare tire. It's a rough area . . . he even took his tire iron with him." She laughed, but it wasn't convincing—more as though it hid a remembered shudder. "He thought it would look casual enough, since he was dealing with the tire. The station was closed, of course. But he went right by that bar—the Whetstone. And I guess it happened somewhere around there."

Gordon appeared suddenly behind her, looming over her, bowed as though in a great wind, blood and matter from his battered head running down the side of his face. *"Right there!"* he bellowed and disappeared again, not without popping a lightbulb or two on the way.

As one, the women recoiled, and then looked at one another sheepishly, embarrassed at how easily they'd jumped. As if they could have been anything but edgy, with the energy Gordon had so suddenly splashed around the place. Nothing to do but laugh it off, of course. "Must be a power surge," Melinda said. "These old buildings . . ."

"Right," Delia said, less convincingly. "A power surge."

"How about if I put that aside for you?" Melinda said to Jeannie, holding her hand out for the ring. "I'll see how it cleans up and follow through on the information they sent on the piece, see if I can verify it. Then I can quote you a price. No pressure. If you don't want it, it'll look marvelous as the centerpiece to our display out here."

And inside her own thoughts, she kept hearing the words *tire iron* and seeing Gordon's injuries and thinking *blunt force trauma* and seeing Delia's shocked face at her revelation about Gordon's intent with Craig Lusak, hearing her response: *Then what are you going to do?*

Good question.

But Melinda still didn't know nearly enough. And she still needed to get Gordon crossed over, to ease his mind somehow. To keep him from taking things into his own hands—or from slipping further into the Dark Side.

Subtly, Delia nudged her foot; Melinda blinked and found Jeannie holding the ring out. "Right," she said, taking it and offering a smile in return. "Just let me put this in the back with a note."

She left Delia and Jeannie speculating about the woman who'd owned the jewelry—what her house must have been like, her life, her times—and headed for the back, silently admonishing herself.

The intention was to make a good impression on Jeannie in the hope she'd come back to the store. In the hope of more casual contact. She should probably suggest a lunch date—and actually, she could use a good, educated gaze roaming Bayview. A small commission, perhaps . . .

swingbatterbatter . . .

It came as a whisper, volume increasing with each word but still so faint she might not have paid any attention at all without knowing where it would lead. But this time, she knew—and this time, she stopped short and said, "*No.* If you want to talk to me, you figure out how to do it properly."

"Oh, I'm sorry!" Jeannie sounded startled, not far behind her. "I knew I shouldn't have come back here—"

Melinda whirled to find her there in the doorway, embarrassed. "Jeannie! No, no—" She reached for the cell phone sitting on her desk, second nature after so many years of covering her unusual conversations. "Incoming call—someone I don't want to talk to. I was just . . . soliloquizing."

"Now that's a word you don't hear every day." No doubt that little wrinkle on Jeannie's brow was the little voice in her head noting that she hadn't heard a ringtone, but like most people, she didn't push it. "I just wondered if I needed to put down a deposit to hold that ring. I really would like a first chance at it."

"No, it's no problem, really. It wouldn't be out on display yet in any event—not until I have a chance to clean it. And actually, I was thinking . . ." She took a breath, shoved every trace of the *batterbatter* chant out of her mind, and said, "I was thinking, it's obvious you have a good eye, and I could really use a spotter in the Bayview area. Would you be interested? I'd pay a small commission on anything you found for us that sold."

"Really?" Jeannie said, confusion giving way to delight and then to doubt. "But you only just met me."

"Oh, but Craig and I are practically neighbors." Melinda smiled at her. "Really, it's a no-brainer. I won't acquire anything I don't think will sell, and I don't pay commission on anything that *doesn't* sell. But I have a feeling it'll work out."

Jeannie smiled. "I see what you mean. And thank you. With things working out the way they are . . . well, I'd love to be a spotter. You just have to promise to let me know if I drive you nuts by going overboard."

"It's a deal." Melinda held out her hand in an exaggerated wheeler-dealer fashion; her smile faltered only slightly as Gordon flickered into place behind Jeannie, wrath entrenched on his features. He'd grown even scruffier—reverted, she realized, to the man he'd been before he'd ever met his wife, ever considered finding another way to live. But he didn't act out on Jeannie; he lurked there, glaring at Melinda, and with resolute practice, she pretended not to see him at all—at least, not as she ushered Jeannie back into the store and said her good-byes, adding with regret that she supposed she needed to respond to that phone call after all.

But once she turned around, she marched straight back into the long, narrow storage area, and she knew what she'd find. *Who* she'd find. "Let me help you," she said, preempting whatever he'd prepared himself to shout at her. She knew he wasn't ready—just looking at him told her as much. Reverted to the persona of nearly two years earlier, yet still bearing the gruesome wounds of his death, he appeared to be etched into the very air with the acid of his anger, dark and crisp at the edges, so tightly focused it hurt to look too closely—almost as if she'd just barely crossed her eyes in the process. "This isn't good for you, Gordon. It isn't right. Your death was tragic, but it's up to the police to find the man who did it. Your job now is to make peace with—"

He cut her off with a sudden roar of silence and he circled her in a series of blurs and jerks, ending up in her face. *"Leave it alone!"*

She did her best not to react to his visual antics—not to flinch away when he appeared so suddenly before her. She bit her lip and took a breath and persevered. "—make peace with your situation. Say good-bye to your wife. I can do that for you, if it'll help—"

"Leave it to me!"

"God, do you not *have* an indoor voice?" Melinda closed her eyes, seeking inspiration. Not to mention patience. Hard to talk to a broken record, but sometimes all it took was finding that one crack, that one tiny entry point . . . the words to break through the defense mechanisms.

Because when it came right down to it, this was about Gordon Reese being unable to face the pain of what he'd lost—the disappointment of the happily-ever-after within his reach that had been so cruelly destroyed. So much easier to blow himself into this tremendous fury than to see or feel those things, and until he could, there'd be no crossing into the Light.

Melinda caught the faint desperation in her own thoughts, found herself both startled and dismayed. Patience used to be enough to help earthbound spirits—patience and understanding. Spirits wouldn't come to her if they didn't want help on some level; she had only to find the best way to give it.

But things were different now. Spirits like Gordon could do real harm in the living world, and he was so very vulnerable to the now-active Dark Side—just exactly the wounded, powerful, and angry soul ripe for recruitment. So now Melinda didn't have the time for patience. She had to find a way to get through; she had to push. But when she opened her eyes—finally, resigned to that need—she found herself alone. "Gordon," she said anyway, suspecting that he didn't trust her enough to leave her completely, "this isn't your fight. You have an obligation to your family. They need the peace of knowing *you're* at peace, and that's not ever going to happen if you go hunting the man who killed—"

"He's mine!" There he was, right in front of her, etched in anger, and Melinda cried out her startlement—and then he disappeared in a blur, but she instinctively knew he hadn't gone, that he'd come *toward* her and enveloped her, and quite suddenly pressure closed in on her from all sides—the impossible weight of anger, squeezing her in, crushing her chest and bowing her neck and making her heart struggle to beat at all. She couldn't cry out and she couldn't call for help and she couldn't do anything more than soundlessly mouth his name as she crumpled to the ground in slow-motion resistance. "Gordon . . . Gordon, *no*—"

"What?" Delia's voice behind her, surprised and then frightened. "Melinda, what on earth—? Are you all right?"

Faintly, Melinda felt Delia's hands on her shoulders, heard the jangle of bracelets by her ears. She fought to breathe, to speak—the pressure seemed to crush down even harder; Melinda's vision went gray and then dark—and then quite suddenly she was free and gasping for breath, half sitting and half lying on the floor with Delia's hands supporting her. "Gordon!" she cried, both a plea and a remonstration.

He appeared before her—crouching, his forearms resting on his knees, scuffed steel-toed boots and work-worn jeans and leather jacket. She thought she smelled beer and smoke and sweat. For the first time he spoke in normal tones—but low and confident and threatening. *"You getting the picture?"* he said. *"So will the one who killed me, by the time I'm done with him. If I have to take care of you first, so be it. Stay out of my way, bitch."*

Melinda gasped, as much from affront as from the physical assault. And Gordon disappeared, leaving Delia's voice alone in her ears. "Talk to me, Melinda! Dammit, I'm calling nine-one-one—"

"No!" Melinda shifted from her hip to her knees and paused there to take a deep breath. Her heart still pounded in her chest, but it was slowing, and if her stomach felt slightly sick, it was from implications and not from the imminent danger of fainting. "I'm fine. It was just . . . a conversation that got out of hand."

"Some conversation," Delia said, her voice as dry as it could be considering her lingering concern.

Melinda tucked her hair behind her ear, gave her friend a wry look. "You have no idea," she said. "He's really holding on to his anger."

Delia's expression suddenly shuttered. She realized she'd been drawn into discussing the ramifications of identifying a killer with the testimony of a dead man, and now she felt threatened and maybe even embarrassed by it. Full retreat mode. She stood, holding out a hand. "You okay? Ready to get off that truly nasty floor?"

Typical storeroom floor, concrete and dust bunnies and fine grit from who knows what. Melinda grimaced and took the proffered hand and knew it was time to drop any mention of Gordon. With Delia, she couldn't afford to push. Couldn't afford to lose.

Unfortunately, with Gordon, she couldn't afford to *not* push—because now even more, she couldn't let him slip away into his dark anger. Not so far that he couldn't come back.

Not so far that the living would pay the price.

4

MELINDA'S FOOT PRESSED down on the nonexistent brake an instant before Jim did the same—over there on the driver's side of her Saturn, where she should have been. Where Jim sat instead, newly home from an early Saturday morning shift with nothing more than breakfast and a shower between him and the night of work. He slanted her an amused glance, as if he'd sensed her copiloting. "Might as well relax and enjoy the it's-spring factor," he suggested. "Like, for instance, I'm enjoying that dress."

Melinda smoothed the skirt, palest of lilac colors with lace inset and ribbon details. Not, she suspected, what Jim referred to. She had a strong suspicion that he'd been taken by the low sweetheart neckline, the delicately tied shoulder straps, and the snug empire waist made more shapely by the perfectly placed lacing at the sides. "This is my it's-spring dress," she told him. "Problem is, it has a lot of ties and laces, and I'm not sure I'll be able to get out of it without help."

His hands tightened noticeably on the steering wheel. After a moment he said, "Just how long do you think we'll be at this home visit?"

Melinda laughed. "As long as it takes, my grandmother would say. But seriously, probably not too long. They won't be ready to hear about Gordon, and Gordon definitely isn't ready to talk to them. So this is just preliminary stuff. As in, I need to know more about Gordon before I can reach him." She sobered. "And I definitely need to reach him before he goes too far with Craig Lusak. Right now he's just gathering strength, figuring out how to handle himself. And getting his kicks out of torturing Lusak."

Jim, too, sobered. "About that, Mel . . ."

Melinda sighed, but kept her tone light. "You're going to say this no matter what I do, aren't you?"

"I wouldn't be a good husband if I didn't," he said. "Or a good friend, or . . . well, someone who loves you."

"Oh," she said. "When you put it that way . . ."

He smiled slightly, not taking his eyes from the tree-lined road. Spring buds had swelled into bright green early leaves; the roadside grasses and early greens poked up from remnants of last year's growth. It was a bit too early for butterflies and

Bambi, but birds fluttered in the shadows of the undergrowth, digging up grubs and fussing at each other.

Melinda suspected Jim saw little of those delights and that when his hands tightened on the wheel again, this time his inspiration had nothing to do with spring. He said, "You know that Lusak was in the area. You even know he was carrying a tire iron, which could easily have inflicted the injuries you've described. And Gordon still thinks he's the killer. If now isn't time to call the police, then when is?"

"I'm not sure," Melinda admitted. She ran her thumb over a bit of ribbon detail on her dress. "I only know it doesn't feel right yet."

"It doesn't feel anywhere near right to know this guy is working down the street from your shop, either."

"*And* from the station," she reminded him. "In fact, you're between him and me."

He was silent another moment, but she didn't think he'd given up, and she was right. He gave her another glance, turned onto the road that would take them on a looping route around to the other side of Grandview, and said, "You know I've got friends on the force. I can drop a word; I can even say it's something I heard on the street."

Melinda laughed. "Does Grandview even *have* a 'street'?"

His jaw tightened. "This isn't funny, Melinda. We're talking about a murderer. And if you know something about Gordon's death—and by extension, if *I* know something—then we've got an obligation to do something about it. To report it."

"No," Melinda agreed, "it's *not* funny. But Craig Lusak had a flat tire and he went looking for help. I'm not sure it's fair to turn his life upside down just because he happened to have that flat tire in the same area that Gordon was killed."

"If he didn't do it, then he'll be cleared. It doesn't have to be a big deal."

Melinda felt her mouth tighten. "That doesn't mean it won't be. You know as well as I do that the police make mistakes . . . it seems these days more than ever, there's a rush to judgment. He's a children's advocate, Jim—can you imagine what it would do to his practice if the police fixated on him thanks to a tip from me, and he turns out to be innocent? He's going to pay the price anyway, and you know it." And then she stepped on the nonexistent brake again as they came to a stop sign.

He shook his head, amused. "You can't stand it, can you? Sharing your spiffy red SUV."

"Maybe not for much longer," she said, glad enough to drop the conversation about Lusak.

"Oh?" He hesitated there at the stop sign—no one waiting behind them, no one waiting on them to turn. "You're getting a handle on your other visitor?"

"Yes and no." She shifted in the seat, progressed to a wiggle, and barely stopped herself from going for the nonexistent accelerator. "You're doing that on purpose!"

"Maybe you should just sit on my lap," he suggested, finally moving forward and turning toward the B&B. "You know, do all the actual driving unless there's a problem, and then I can take over."

"Ha, ha," she said. "I think I'm figuring out how to get out of this dress on my own after all."

He said firmly, "I didn't hear that." And then, as they approached a driveway sign for the Honey Bs, he added, "Seriously, what makes you think it's safe now?"

"I'm learning to shut him out," Melinda said, simply enough so she knew she'd get a reaction, and she did—the jerk of his attention off the road for an instant, the surprise on his face. She knew why, too. She'd never before deliberately shut anyone out. Even as they drove her to extremes or to tears or ended important relationships in her life, she'd made room for earthbound spirits to reach out to her. But this time . . . "I don't think he understands that he's not communicating in any meaningful way, or even that he's endangering me. The only way I can think to get through to him is to make it clear what he's doing isn't acceptable."

"Whoa," Jim said, still surprised; the guilt swamped her.

"If he'd shown any signs of changing what he was doing, of trying something new—"

"No, I get it." He pulled into the tiny gravel parking area of the Honey Bs, beside an old cream-colored GMC and directly outside the small building that housed the honey shop; before he cut the engine, he turned to her. "I get it, I'm just . . . well, that must have been hard. Really hard. All this time, the extremes you've gone to to stay available to these people . . . Shutting someone out must go against everything you are."

Gratitude flushed through her body, hovering in her throat and prickling her upper arms into gooseflesh. "I take it back," she said. "I have absolutely no idea how to get out of this dress without help."

He grinned. "As it happens, I think I know where to start."

She'd been frightened by Gordon at first. Frightened, trying not to show it. A diminutive woman, so nicely rounded, golden brown hair cut spicy-short and eyes as big and eloquently expressive as eyes could be. Eyes that suddenly made him think differently about eyes in general. They left him mystified. They left him staring. And so those eyes had narrowed at him, and her hands had tightened on the handle of the grocery cart, and he'd only just barely escaped with his toes and his knees intact, breaking out of his trance to remove himself from the rear end of her car, where he waited while his buddies bought beer.

He'd tried to sneer at her, to show her he hadn't been affected at all. But the sneer hadn't come, and somehow he'd found himself helping to load her groceries in the trunk.

She hadn't wanted that, either. She didn't like him. She didn't want him anywhere around.

Too bad she'd been wearing that cute top, the one with the short girly sleeves and the scooped neck and the embroidered logo for the Honey Bs— that damned cheerful bee tangled up in two uppercase Bs.

Dead now, hunting peace or hunting revenge or hunting he didn't know what, Gordon sees it unfold, over and over, whether he wants to or not. His sudden interest in bees, the look on her face when he first walks into the store. The wariness giving way to enthusiasm as she discusses the minutiae of the business. Slowly, so slowly, gaining her trust, even as they realize they have certain things from their past in common, intersecting circles of friends and more. Keeping her very existence a secret from the Whetstone Bar crew until right before they married.

Those eyes . . .

That smile . . .

The soft girly belly gone big with pregnancy, then shrunken again, but lightly silvered with stretch marks.

Holding the baby . . .

The baby . . .

And the tears.

Those eyes gone red and face blotchy and golden brown hair just shoved behind her ears even when it was barely long enough to manage and *those eyes and tears and the baby and*—

And those grieving eyes deserved to be avenged.

Jim held the door for Melinda at the quaintly signed Honey Shack, a small outbuilding with hours neatly posted on a whiteboard and a little bell to ring for help—but entering the store triggered a loud buzz in the background, and Melinda was betting they wouldn't be alone long. The door behind the counter led to the back half of the building, and although she got glimpses of processing equipment, she also saw a door to another room, one filled with colorful toys and the flicker of reflected television light.

"I take it you didn't call ahead," Jim said.

Melinda trailed her fingers over a row of creamed cinnamon honey, plucking a jar from the shelf. "Too formal," she said. "I'm betting we end up with someone in the family, and that's—"

She hesitated as a figure approached from the back room, a young woman with a small baby—dressed in pink, with a little pink headband on her barely hair—in a sling sack at her chest. The woman's huge dark eyes dominated a face marked by grief. Melinda cast Jim a quick smile. "That's more than good enough."

The woman sat behind a long, low counter, its wooden top scarred by years of service, and picked up a stack of labels for sorting. "Hi," she said. "If you have any questions, let me know."

Smiling, Melinda slid a business card across the counter, watched the surprise of it register on the woman's face. Carol Reese, she would bet— Gordon's wife. "I probably should have called ahead, but this was a great excuse to come out and get some of your honey, so I took a chance. I wondered if you might be interested in having a small outlet for your honey in town." And then, when the woman didn't quite seem to know what to say, Melinda did what often worked—kept right on talking, giving her time to get her bearings. "I know, I know, the market already carries some of your goods, but I thought it might be nice to have an outlet that isn't so dependent on the weather. Not that we could carry a huge sampling, but we could keep the stock fresh that way—"

Jim, bless him, wandered the short aisles, pondering the honey offerings and leaving her to do her thing. The woman glanced his way and said, "But doesn't this say you have an antiques store?"

"I do," Melinda agreed, cheerful enough. "But we do have a small selection of what I like to think of as luxuries that evoke the feel of the past. Handmade soaps, scented lotions, bath salts . . . We even have some beeswax candles. I think your honey— with those charming homemade labels and the family business behind it—would fit right in." She put down the glass jar of creamed honey. "I know you'll need to discuss it. But meanwhile I'll treat myself to one of these."

"That's a favorite," the woman said. She glanced at Jim. "Did you see we have a habañero blend? It's surprisingly good—just enough habañero to widen your eyes after you swallow. It's over on that wall there." She nodded, her hands busy at the minimalist register, and Melinda didn't even have to look to know Jim had swallowed that bait. The door buzzer sounded again, and an older couple entered with the look of those out on a Saturday drive who've Discovered Something. On their heels came a man who did not seem to be sharing their good day; he frowned at the shelves of delectables and poked at a shelf of jars, without any of the reverence Melinda felt at these homegrown and beautifully presented offerings. The woman greeted them as she'd greeted Jim and Melinda, and turned back to the register.

"There's something else," Melinda said, lowering her voice slightly now that they were no longer alone. "You're Carol Reese, aren't you?"

She expected the suddenly wary look, the retreat, and Carol Reese said, "Why do you ask?"

"I have a friend," Melinda said, although she stretched the truth with that one. Gordon Reese almost certainly didn't consider her a friend. More like an interfering annoyance. "He's going through a hard time; you might say he's at a turning point. I thought if I could learn a little more about your husband, I might be able to help my friend. You know, show him he has options."

"I don't know what good that would do," Carol said, her bitterness surfacing even as one hand instinctively covered the baby. "Gordon's *options* didn't do him much good."

"You don't think so?" Melinda asked, letting her surprise show. She looked at the honey shack, obvious about it; she reached a hand toward the baby, letting it fall short but obvious about that, too. "It seems to me he had plenty of good in his life."

"And yet the old life caught up to him." Carol stabbed at the register *enter* key. "That's seven fifty. Unless you want some of the habañero?"

Melinda glanced at Jim, found him hefting a jar. "It looks as though we do. So you think someone from his past confronted him outside the bar?"

Carol ran a hand through her hair, looking to

be at her wit's end, and at the end of her emotional
stamina to boot. Tears glittered in her eyes; her nose
reddened slightly. She glanced at the other customers and lowered her voice. "He went back to the
bar to meet them, to say good-bye. But those guys,
they weren't the type to do what was done to Gordon. Losers and boozers, but not up to anything
more than a bar fight here and there, you know?"
She looked at Melinda's delicate summer dress, the
ribbons and layers of eyelet lace, and she looked at
Jim—he might be tired after his swapped-out shift,
but he was clean and shaven and Melinda had very
good reason to know that he smelled good. He
looked good, too, that dark thick hair over strong,
handsome features and a body he kept fit by working out between calls at the station. And Carol said
bitterly, "Then again, maybe you *don't* know."

"You might be surprised," Melinda said, but
quietly enough so Carol wouldn't feel she had anything to prove.

Carol took a deep breath, swiped at her eyes
one after the other, and steadied the sleeping baby
with one hand as she added the habañero honey
mix to the tab. "You know, I don't think I'm the
right person to talk to. Not right now. You should
try his friend Howie. He's from the old gang, but
he always seemed to understand what Gordon was
doing. Was *trying* to do. He knows things from the
past that Gordon tried to hide from me."

"As much about the before as the after?" Melinda suggested.

"That's one way to put it." She'd regained some of her composure; her hands were deft in handling the money, quick in bagging the honey. "Just don't expect him to put on company manners for you. He hasn't got any of those."

"Ah," Melinda said, making a mental checkmark. "Well, if it helps my friend, I'm sure it'll be worth it."

Carol gave her a resentful look, something mixed of bitterness and envy. "Aren't you lucky, to still believe in happy endings." She scribbled a name and address on the back of scrap paper and dropped it into the bag.

"Yes," Melinda said, quite firmly. She glanced at Jim, who had drifted for the door—not impatient, just anticipating. "In fact, I do. But my version of a happy ending just might surprise you." She scooped up the bag with the honey, cradling it in the crook of her arm. "I'll come back, if that's all right, to see what the rest of the family thinks about putting some stock in my store."

"Sure," Carol said, a verbal shrug. She looked again at the business card, one hand lightly caressing the back of the baby's head as she stirred slightly, and as Melinda turned away, Carol tucked the card in the front of the register where it would be seen.

Melinda hadn't learned much, but it was a first step. And she had a reason to come back . . . and another trail to follow.

With Gordon's temper and strength rising, she wouldn't waste any time following it.

"Maybe I should drive," Melinda suggested as they approached the Saturn and Jim headed for the driver's side. Spring seemed to have infected her, putting a lilt in her walk, and she gave Jim a sideways look—a beguiling look.

"Hey," he said, "that's why I'm *here*."

"You're here because it's a way to spend a beautiful spring day together." But when he just looked at her, his hand closed firmly around the keys, she sighed, swinging the bitty little thing they called a purse these days. "Well, and because of a certain seriously confused spirit. But really, I'm—" She stopped; breezy confidence made way for startled hesitation and then determination. *"No,"* she said. "That's not the way to talk to me. But I'm listening. Try something else."

As odd as he found it, those times she looked directly at nothing or reacted specifically to nothing, Jim found this odder yet—watching the fierce concentration in her eyes as this time, she didn't look at anything at all, not even him. He swiftly came to her side, one hand reaching out and then hesitating, not touching her in the end. Not interfering, just . . . being there. Just in case. And with extreme strength of will, not even removing the very breakable honey from the crook of her arm as she insisted, "I want to help you. Please. Try something else. See if you can come through to me— yes! I can see—" But her shoulders, attentive and leaning forward just the slightest bit, relaxed in disappointment; she sighed.

Jim let his hand fall. "Gone?"

"Gone," she confirmed. "But I still think—I *hope*—this is the thing to do. If my grandmother were here—" She stopped herself, took a breath, and shook her head, a clear admonishment of self. "You'd think after all this time . . ."

"Nope." He drew her close, wrapped his arms around her, rested his cheek against her hair. "Some people are just like that—you never stop missing them. Doesn't make you needy, makes her remarkable."

"Oh," she said, and he could feel her stillness as she absorbed the thought. "You're a good man, Jim Clancy."

"That I am," he agreed, releasing her to toss the keys and grab them out of the air. "But I'm still driving."

"Nuts!" But she took that defeat in good grace and without argument; it was clear enough that this particular spirit still had a lot to learn. She reached into the honey bag, rustled around until she came up with the scrap paper, and presented it to him with a flourish. "There you are, then," she told him. "Bayview, if I'm not mistaken. And I'm thinking it's a good thing I packed that picnic lunch. Think you can find a park between here and there?"

"All part of the service," he said, and plucked the paper from her. A single glance at the address made him most grateful to be along for this excursion, picnic lunch with lovely wife in damned fine spring dress notwithstanding.

Even a small town like Bayview had its bad neighborhoods.

5

MELINDA GORDON.
She made Carol cry. *Nosy, nosy, nosy.* She
isn't part of this. She's distracting and interfering
and problematic. She should stay *out* of this.

He'll convince her.

"Okay, yes." Melinda looked down the street, eyeing the aging homes and ragged yards and dilapi-
dated chain-link fence. And to think they'd bought
their *own* place as a fixer-upper. "I'm glad you're
here. Not that I wouldn't have done this anyway."

"I know," Jim said. "That's what scares me."

"It'll be fine," she said, releasing the seat belt.
"You'll see." But before she got out of the SUV,
she reached around to the back where she'd stowed
the dark lilac bolero vest that turned this dress into
something more demure—a dress of layers, rather
than a flirty summer thing. It'd be fine, but she

wasn't asking for trouble, either. "What do you think about waiting here? I have the feeling he'll be more talkative that way."

He gave her a steady look, as if measuring her determination. "Outside the Saturn," he said. "Looking obvious."

"I can live with that." She picked up her purse, decided that it, too, was too flirty, and tucked it away beside her seat. "He might not even be home," she said as she opened the door, but the small truck in the driveway suggested otherwise, and Jim didn't respond. He, too, exited the SUV; he came around to lean back on the front fender, arms crossed. Definitely in protective possessive mode. And while Melinda didn't appreciate being hovered over in general, there were times . . .

This was one of them.

She cleared her throat, sent him a breezy smile, and walked the cracked sidewalk to the front door. She'd only just lifted her hand to knock when it jerked open.

Howie, last name unknown, stood in front of her, wiping his hands on a rag. He wore old jeans and an old T-shirt covered with gray dust; his hair was buzzed short in the kind of cut that said *because this way I don't have to mess with it* and his cheeks held weekender stubble. She guessed him to be the same age as Gordon Reese—perhaps five years older than Melinda herself—but some wear and tear showed at the skin around his eyes and mouth. "Not buying anything," he grunted at her.

"That's good, because I'm not selling anything." She held out her hand. "My name is Melinda Gordon, and I'm hoping you can spare a few moments to talk. Carol Reese sent me your way."

He looked at her hand, then at his own, and shook his head. "No offense," he said. "I'm building a barbecue." His gaze lifted, focusing out to the street—to where Jim waited. His eyes narrowed slightly, but then he seemed to shrug inside. *Yeah, yeah,* his eyes said when he looked back at her. *I get it. You've got a chaperone.* His voice had flattened slightly when he spoke again. "So Carol sent you?"

"You sound surprised." More like skeptical and disbelieving, but confrontation wasn't the way to go with this man.

"She's not my biggest fan." Howie flicked another glance out at Jim and leaned against the door frame. He wasn't going to ask her in, and she was fine with that. She didn't think she had anything to fear from this man—most people lived up to the faith you put in them—but Jim wouldn't feel nearly as relaxed about seeing that door close behind her.

"I think in this case, she hoped you could help."

He snorted. "I doubt she's right. And this really

isn't a good time." He gave his dirty hands a meaningful glance.

"It's just that I have this friend," Melinda said, talking a little more quickly. If he thought she'd discourage that easily, he'd misread *fun spring outfit* for *lack of fortitude*. "He's going through a hard time right now. What Gordon did with his life is amazing, and I thought if I could learn more, understand more . . ."

He gave her equally mixed puzzlement and scorn. "Gordon is *dead*. That's what he did with his life. That's what all his changes got him."

"Do you really believe that?" She asked it quietly, unexpectedly; it took him back.

He made a rough, indecipherable gesture and didn't look at her. Behind her, a large vehicle drove down the narrow street, moving slowly; a quick glance showed her a cream-colored SUV. It pulled in somewhere down the street, the rough engine making a tough transition from idle to stop.

"What happened to him—that was chance. Bad luck. Completely and totally unfair. But what he *did*—that was inspiring."

"Made his life not like mine, you mean?"

Wow. Major chip on that shoulder; lots of smoldering resentment. Melinda couldn't help but wonder what Carol had expected her to get from this conversation. "If you want to take it that way, I suppose. But that's not what this is about."

"Leave it alone." Gordon's voice, a raspy whisper, flinched across her nerves. It came from all around, but the flicker of movement—a ripple in the air— came from the driveway, distorting the truck and flowing outward in fading rings of darkness. *Rings of anger.*

Howie flinched, obviously perceiving the splashed emotion. He drew himself upright with a resolute expression and asked, "What do you want, then?"

Progress! "To understand Gordon better. What made him decide it was time for a change?"

He snorted again. "Not Carol, like everyone thought." He thought twice about that, shook his head, and added, "Well, yeah, but she didn't *make* him change. It was more like he saw something in her, and he went for it." His expression softened as he spoke; something of envy touched his features. But just that fast, he shook it off. "Gordon had a tough start. No big special sob story, so don't go looking for one. His father worked too hard and drank too much, his mother died too young. It happens."

"To you?"

He scowled. "I thought this wasn't about me."

She winced. "You're right. I'm sorry. Please . . . so Gordon didn't finish high school?" That much had been in the paper.

"We went looking for work together." Howie

shrugged. "We found it. And we found the Whetstone. It suited us. It still suits me, if you want to know." He shook his head. "But Carol, she had this whole different way of looking at life. She has family. She has this vision of what she thinks life can be. She has a way of carrying it with her. Gordon saw that."

Melinda thought it sounded as though Howie had seen it, too.

He gave her a sudden strange look, as if realizing he'd said too much and he didn't even know her at that. She had the feeling he was about to end the conversation—and she didn't have enough, she didn't have nearly enough. Without understanding Gordon, she'd never reach past his anger—or get him to reach past his anger, either. "With all of that," she said, a little too quickly, "what was he doing back at the Whetstone?"

Howie gave her a dark look. "Some people say he was going out behind Carol's back. How's that for inspiration?"

She shook her head. "I don't think you believe that."

"You're damned pushy," he scowled. "Too damned sure of yourself. Maybe you don't really want to know what happened at that bar."

What? She hadn't expected that one. "What do you mean?"

Gordon blew past. *"Damned pushy."* His voice

was loud—close, and yet still from all around. Melinda took a step back, glancing around—unwilling to be caught by surprise if he came back at her.

"What?" Howie said, gone wary—a reaction that struck her as not quite right.

She didn't have a chance to respond before Gordon sent more dark ripples all around them, an instant of warning before he appeared directly in front of Melinda and growled, *"Damned pushy. Don't you learn? I'm taking care of this."*

Desperate, she blurted, "Well, you shouldn't be!"

His head pulsed; his form took on that burnt, gritty look. Before she could do so much as brace herself, he jerked forward—jerked right through her, just as he'd done to Craig Lusak. Cold wind wrapped her heart; she staggered back a step, unable to suppress a small cry of dismay. But Gordon was gone—gone, but for the warning he'd left her, clear evidence that his patience grew short, that he'd use some of his hoarded energy to make a physical impact on her.

Then again, it meant he was paying attention to her . . .

Maybe not such a bad thing after all.

She cast a quick look over her shoulder to see that Jim had straightened, definitely also paying attention . . . but that he held his ground. And then she looked back to Howie, ready to make some excuse, and found she really didn't have to. He'd paled, his ruddy complexion drained beneath that scruffy weekend unshaven look, and she got another shock on top of the chill still wrapping her bones, the surety of sudden realization.

He'd seen that.

Maybe not all of it, maybe hardly any of it. Just enough to react to it.

"Howie," she said, knowing she had no choice, not any longer. "The friend I'm talking about—it's Gordon. *That* was Gordon. He's still here, and he's mad, and I'm trying to help him find peace and cross over. Please . . . what did you mean by what you said? About not wanting to know what happened at the bar?"

But Howie pulled himself up straight and his mouth flattened; his eyes flattened, too. "You must be nuts," he said. "You're wasting my time. I've got a barbecue to build, beer to drink. You see? This life suits me perfectly. Maybe it suited Gordon, too—or maybe not, but we'll never really know, will we. What's done is done." And he closed the door in her face.

Melinda hesitated there a moment, and then she lifted her hand to the doorbell but hesitated at that, too. She had to think about this—think about her best approach, and her best reapproach.

For Howie was a key. Of that, she was certain. That he was drinking himself out of what small gifts he might have, that was also certain—just as her own mother had suppressed her gifts into migraines all her life. But what he'd meant about the bar, how to best deal with him now, and whether she might already have just enough information to help Gordon . . .

Definitely time to think about it all.

6

MELINDA APPROACHED MONDAY morning with mixed feelings; frustrated feelings. Feelings that didn't resolve one bit when she opened the front door to the sight of Rick Payne's early morning meant-to-be-a-smile, closer-to-a-smirk. She said, "Is this you-know-where-I-live thing going to be a problem?"

"Is that any way to greet a concerned friend?"

Melinda took mental inventory: after her morning shower, she'd pulled her hair back into a loose ponytail and thrown on a pair of drawstring pants and a long-sleeved tee, though she'd have opted for one that didn't expose quite so much navel had she known she was going to have company. So, safe to open the door a little wider, but she left it at that. *"Concerned* friend?" she repeated, letting her skepticism through.

"Well, then, curious friend. Do I smell bacon?"

"You smell lingering bacon molecules. Don't you have class or something?"

"Sure. But not yet." He had his professor suit on, a lightweight jacket over a button-down shirt, nice slacks; no tie. "I just got tired of waiting for the other shoe. Aren't you going to ask me in?"

"I haven't decided yet. What other shoe?"

"You know, you come to me for answers, I provide you with witty repartee and amazingly wise trivia, and then you come back after pondering same and ask better questions, entertaining me. But you didn't come back. And since you aren't driving, I thought I'd make it easy for you."

She rested the side of her face against the door's edge. "Is there even such a thing as amazingly wise trivia?"

"It would be a first, I have to admit, but do you expect anything less?"

When it came to Professor Rick Payne, she'd learned not to set expectations at all. She gave him an exaggerated shrug, knowing he'd see only half of it; the rest of her stayed hidden behind the heavy wooden door of their old house-in-progress. "Well, be that as it may, I don't have any better questions for you just now."

"You're kidding. Nothing new at all? You're still stuck on Day-Glo stench? And you really aren't going to let me in, are you?"

"What I've got," she said, "is one intensely angry

spirit trying to take his revenge on someone who may or may not be the man who just killed him and who—thanks to the changes around here—might just be capable of it, one friend of said spirit who has enough of a gift to glimpse things that confuse and frighten him straight to a beer bottle, and one really confused spirit who's been battering me with the dreams or visions we discussed. None of them wants to talk to me right now. So you know, really . . ." and she shrugged again, adding widened eyes for effect, "I got nothin'."

"Wow," Payne said. "I changed my mind. Maybe I don't want to come in. Besides, you ate all the bacon."

"Exactly."

"Another time, then," he said, but didn't move.

Melinda made a big question mark with her expression.

"Oh, come on now," he said. "That's never just it. There's some last little thing you're going to tell me, or some question will come to mind as I'm turning away . . ."

"You're not turning away," she pointed out.

"I thought I'd save us the trouble."

They looked at one another for a long moment, while Melinda marveled at his ability to hold that tiny hint of a smirky smile at the corner of his mouth.

heybatterbatter . . .

"Oh," she said, unable to help an exasperated eye roll. "Not *now*—"

"What?" Payne said, as eager as a little boy with a great big jumping frog just out of reach. "Because I don't think you're talking to me."

"Think about it," Melinda said, not to Payne at all—and not wanting this, but knowing that after yesterday's silence, after her previous efforts to re-direct this particular spirit, she couldn't shut him out now. "*Try*—"

*heybatter*BATTER STARRYSTARRYNIGHT silence frustration *hey batter?*

"Keep trying," Melinda whispered, mindful that yes, she was on the floor, her grasp on her own re-ality completely subsumed by the confused spirit and that yes, Rick Payne was babbling something at her about overdoing things to make a point and then her mind lit with fluorescent swirls and the color oozed along her skin and grew legs, and just as she thought *You've got to be here somewhere,* the legs grew bodies and suddenly she was swarm-ing with ants, fiery stinging biting *ants* and even though she thought she'd seen a glimpse of a man, shadowy and badly formed and equally swarming, suddenly all she could do was shriek and swat and swipe at herself, clearing hundreds and making way for thousands, her skin on fire and crisping with venom, invisible beneath a blanket of *antsantsants* gone.

A brief hint of dismay lingered, of frustration. And then Payne, crouched right there beside her. "Whoa, that's a serious set of pipes you've got. I'm thinking I should run, before the cops get here and arrest me as the cause of all the—"

"Shut up!" Melinda cried, much more wildly than she wanted. She came upright as far as her knees, pressed her hands to her face, took the deepest of breaths. "I mean, not *shut up*—just *not now.*"

"Okay." Surprisingly agreeable, he moved back slightly, giving her the time for another deep breath, a personal inventory from within. Because although it was no longer to be taken for granted, she was in fact perfectly whole. Not a single lingering bite; not a single remaining welt. She let her hands fall away, brushed off her arms, and used the door as support as she climbed to her feet.

Payne didn't bother to get up. He sat cross-legged against the door frame, looking up at her. "Ants, I'm guessing—based on our previous conversation and the whole shrieking, rolling, get-it-off-get-it-off body language. But you should know, there aren't any ants in this area that display that kind of swarming behavior, never mind the biting. There *was* biting, wasn't there?"

Silently, Melinda pointed out the door, a vague directional with meaning clear. The conversation was over.

"Okay, okay." He stood, brushed off his pants, and moved out onto the porch with no evident awkwardness. "But you call me when you've got your questions lined up."

She closed the door. She was perfectly aware that he stood there, his half smile in place, looking at the door for another moment—and that he headed for his car with that same smile. Not a man easily embarrassed, discouraged, or otherwise put off.

Which was just as well, because sooner or later, she'd have those questions for him.

"Hey," she said to Jim on the phone, pulling an extra long-sleeved, fine-weave shirt from the chest of drawers, and a snug cropped stretch shirt with short sleeves to layer over it. She shucked out of her pants and reached for jeans, brushing away the golden dog hair clinging to them. "I'm heading into town. Anything you want me to pick up?"

"I thought Delia had the store today." Jim's voice came overlaid with the noises of the station—background radio buzz, the rumble of a truck; she'd caught him out cleaning the rig, no doubt.

"She does, but you know me . . . I'm in restless mode." She balanced on one leg, threading her jeans with the other.

"Not getting anywhere?" He didn't specify with what; he didn't have to. And really, best not to try, not with the station active around him.

"Yes and no. Another visit from the confused one; he's really trying, but whatever happened with him, it really took him apart. I'm surprised he's been able to make even this much effort. Nothing from Gordon. I thought I might talk to Lusak."

"Be careful." Jim's voice lowered, got a little growly.

She had to admit she liked the effect. But it didn't deter her.

"Listen," she said, managing the second leg of the jeans, "I need to see if he's okay. Gordon—he's determined, and he's strong. Once he really figures out how to use the energy of the people he's attaching to, he's going to be able to do some real damage."

"Oh. *That* kind of talk."

"Not that I won't take what I can get," she warned him. "But you know, even if he's the one, I'll be right there at his office. Pretty public. And *yes,* I'll be careful."

A moment of silence—or what passed for silence, with the activity in the background—and he said, "I know. I'm sorry. It's just that lately—"

"It's not the same as it was," she finished, giving a little hop to settle the jeans around her hips.

"Are you—what're you doing?"

"As if you can't tell. I'm getting dressed. I've been pretty much unclothed the entire time we've been talking. See you for dinner, then?" She caught his growl as she cut the connection, and smiled. If nothing else, she'd definitely redirected his thoughts.

As for her own, they weren't so malleable. She tossed the phone onto the bed and finished changing, twitched the feather duvet back into place, and trotted down the stairs into the realm of the bold white-and-green vertical-striped wallpaper of their entry area and living room. The closet yielded a funky denim jacket to match her casual garb, and with the speed of long practice, she filled a leather rucksack with her sundries and pulled slouchy ankle boots onto her feet. Then she grabbed up the leftover coffee cake from breakfast and headed out to the Saturn.

Because this time, yes, she was driving. This time she felt she could put off her confused spirit if she had to—no matter how wrong it felt to shut him out that way. "Are you paying attention?" she asked him, perfectly comfortable with the possibility that he might not even be lingering anywhere nearby. "I'm going to be driving, and I can't talk to you then. But if you want to try again, I'll be at the shop soon."

Because you never knew.

But the drive into town was uneventful, and once parked, Melinda patted the steering wheel with a satisfied smile. She headed to the front entrance so as not to surprise Delia from the rear, but there on the sidewalk, she spotted her friend coming back across the square with—of course—coffee in hand. And at first Delia smiled and waved, a cheery greeting if somewhat mixed with her surprise to see Melinda at all—and then she stopped, just on the other side of the street, her jaw dropping ever so slightly and her brow rising to match.

"What?" Melinda asked, even though they weren't quite within conversational earshot, but she followed Delia's gaze and very well saw *what*. She felt her own mouth drop open briefly, and the coffee cake shifted in her grip, but she quickly closed her mouth and righted the cake and walked swiftly for the shop.

By the time she reached it, Delia had crossed the street, and they stood together to stare at the front door.

"I swear," Delia said, "I locked that door not five minutes ago. Just long enough to grab coffee!" She indicated the front door, their "Gone for Coffee, Back in Five" sign with the tall steaming mug hand-drawn at the side. "And aren't those handprints on the *inside*?"

"Looks that way," Melinda said, moving closer. "But not *this*." For there, at eye level, written in ugly slashing script with what—dry-erase marker?—was a fine bit of nastiness.

Leave it alone, bitch.

Gordon? It sounded like him; the words were

his, already used on her in anger. And he'd made no bones about it: he wanted her out of his business.

Except . . . dry-erase marker? It didn't feel right. Spirits used what they had in hand, and in Gordon's case that was more likely to be blood or gore or some physical effect upon the glass; Melinda saw none of that. And another glance at Delia confirmed perfectly that she, too, saw the ugly words.

Then again, she was able to see the smeary handprints, too, and that, over there—that was a nose print, Melinda was almost certain of it. Someone was putting a great deal of effort into leaving those handprints, that was for sure, and she suspected she'd find out what that was about sooner or later, but for now . . .

"Leave it alone, bitch?" Delia said. "That's not showing a lot of imagination."

"You don't think one of Ned's friends . . ." Melinda started, and then didn't finish, because that didn't feel right, either. Unless this was aimed at Delia?

Delia gave a decided shake of her head. "For once, peace reigns in the Banks household. Homework is being done, age-appropriate sports are being played, pizza has been doled out to homework project gatherings. Y'know, if I'd grounded him or kept him out of one of their group activities, I could almost see this—at least, from one of those kids he was hanging out with earlier this year. But he's with a pretty good bunch right now."

Melinda pulled her gaze away from the offensive lettering to catch a glimpse of wistfulness on Delia's face. "Sounds like he's growing up. Growing into himself."

Delia took a sudden deep breath. "Well, he'll always be my little boy, whether he likes it or not." And then she juggled the store keys in her hand, finding the right one, and briskly unlocked the door. "Let's get this all cleaned up. And what are you doing here, anyway? Not just bringing me whatever's in that very promising cake pan?"

"I was afraid I'd eat it all myself," Melinda said. "But no, it's just one of those days. I figured I'd do a little cleanup work in the back, walk the square . . . you know, basically make a pest of myself."

"Well!" Delia said, taking this with good humor. "All right then! Seeing as you brought food and all."

"Here." Melinda handed her the pan. "Already cut into handy serving sizes. Or so they say. I think they're skimpy, myself. Anyway, have some. I'll clean up this mess." She pulled the coffee sign off the tiny suction cup hook on the glass and tucked it away behind the window display. From the inside, the smudges looked more obvious and the writing more ominous. She gave it another moment's thought, decided again . . . no, not Gordon. Not in *marker*.

And that meant . . . who?

Feeling grim around the mouth, she went for the cleaning supplies, dumping her purse on the desk in the back and moving with quick efficiency—best to get rid of the mystery before a customer saw it. But she took the time to pull open the top desk drawer and grab the small digital camera from within. *Document it,* she decided. Because somehow, she wasn't sure this was her sort of mystery.

Though she was pretty sure she wouldn't show that picture to Jim. Not just yet.

"Good idea," Delia mumbled around a socially acceptable bite of coffee cake, as Melinda came back inside.

The nasty message was now immortalized in digital. Melinda slipped the camera into the pocket of her denim jacket and grabbed up the cleaning supplies. "And now," she said, "whatever it's about, it's gone." The job of a moment, a quick swipe of the dampened old dishtowel across the glass, and she returned to the store to work on the waist-high smudging inside.

"Do you think we'll ever know?" Delia asked, and then straightened. "Do we even *want* to know?"

"I think if it's important, we're going to find

out." The smudges were harder to remove—harder than normal handprints, as if imbued with a little spiritual energy to boot. Definitely someone out there lurking, biding their time . . . needing help and not sure how to ask for it. Though why the smudges were on the inside looking out and not on the outside looking in . . .

Well, she'd know that in time, too.

"I need to put this away." Behind her, Delia made rustling noises—paper napkin, brusque motions. "I'm meeting Tim for lunch today. Nothing more pathetic than showing up for a date with crumbs clinging to your lips."

Melinda turned just enough to give Delia an incredulous look. "Wow, hard on yourself much lately?"

"Facing facts," Delia said simply, but there was a tight edge to her voice that implied otherwise. And Melinda might have challenged her on it—*might* have, for Delia was a strong woman who often needed her own space to think these things through—but in the corner of her eye she caught a glimpse of activity . . . and from the cold wash of bitter fury that brushed across her heart, she knew what she'd find when she turned back to the door.

Gordon.

Out there in the square, set to full-speed flicker and zoom, leaving crisp-edged afterimages at each hesitation and battering himself against . . . against, yes, Craig Lusak.

"Whoa," Delia said, and hurt laced her voice. "You sure let that subject drop in a hurry."

"I—what?" Melinda turned to her, momentarily bewildered, struggling to think past Gordon's emotions even as they tightened down on her. *He's getting stronger.* For another instant she stood there staring blankly, the cleaning spray dangling from her fingers, the old towel bunched in her other hand. And then she remembered where she'd left off with that conversation. "Oh! No, that's not it. I mean, I actually wanted to tell you *baloney,* but I didn't think you'd take that very well, and then—" Wow, she wasn't doing this well at all. "I got distracted," she admitted, nodding out to the square.

Delia came around the counter, looking out the front window with a frown. "Craig Lusak?" she said, her puzzlement making it clear she didn't see what was so distracting about *that.* And then, "He doesn't look very well, does he? Carol did say he had this thing he couldn't shake."

"He's got a *thing,* all right," Melinda muttered, more grimly than she'd meant to.

Delia gave her a wary look; Melinda shrugged in return. "It's what I do," she said simply, and held out the cleaning supplies in tacit request. "Speaking of which, I'll be back in a minute."

Delia took the cleaner and towel and said, "All

righty, then," in the tone of someone who's not really happy but doesn't have a choice. Melinda offered her a quick smile—apology and gratitude both—and spun around to head out the door.

She met Lusak halfway across the square. "Hey," she said. "Are you all right? Do you need to sit down?"

His smile was short-lived and wry. "That obvious, is it?" And he let her lead him to one of the benches, easing down into the shaped wooden slats. "I feel like an old man. Or what I imagine an old man feels like, anyway. The doctors, they can't find a thing. I'm considering a freakish elimination diet."

"That's where you stop eating just about everything?"

He nodded. "And add the foods in, one by one, to see when things go wrong. Of course, if they never go right in the first place, then food sensitivities—probably not the problem after all." Again, that wry smile.

"At least you've kept your sense of humor about it."

Lusak gave a little half shrug, as if he wasn't so sure about that. And Melinda didn't blame him; Gordon was clearly having an impact.

But Gordon had apparently stomped off in a resentful fit upon her arrival, although his anger still pervaded the air. Melinda viewed this development with trepidation. Gordon, she thought, was not the sort to give up. On the other hand, if he'd figured out that her presence had a calming effect on Lusak, then he'd also realize there was little point to sticking around. He wanted to generate fear; he needed to build himself up at Lusak's expense. Build himself up, play around . . . gain the experience he needed to take care of the man he believed had killed him, once and for all.

Maybe she had a few moments after all.

"I was just coming to see you," Lusak said. "I tried a few minutes ago, but the store was closed."

A few minutes ago—when Delia was out for coffee.

When the note had been scrawled on the shop door.

"I'm sorry we missed you," she said. "But I don't suppose . . . did you see anyone? Hanging around the store?"

"A customer, you mean?" Lusak shook his head. But he'd gone distant, and Melinda wasn't sure how to take it. Lying? Or just not feeling well? He took a deep breath, made an obvious attempt to reconnect. "Actually, I wanted to say thanks for your kindness to Jeannie. She's been at loose ends lately; we're still trying to find our balance after the changes we've made, and . . . well, we're playing a waiting game with an adoption agency. It's been really hard on her. The idea of being an antiques 'spotter' really lit her up."

"Adoption!" Melinda grinned. "I had no idea!" And although part of her couldn't hide her delight at the thought of a child finding a home, she had to hide the part that wondered if theirs was really the home for any child. Because if Gordon was right about Craig Lusak . . .

Lusak looked away. "I probably shouldn't have said anything. Don't mention it to Jeannie, if you don't mind. Because—the real reason I came this way—she thinks she's found a treasure trove of a barn north of Bayview, and she hopes you'll call when it's convenient."

"Oh!" Melinda said, smiling. "Perfect! I'm at loose ends myself today—I'll call her as soon as I get back to my phone. Well, not that there aren't a million things I'm supposed to be doing, but none of them seemed quite right for the day, if you know what I mean. Or doesn't that happen to men?"

"Guild secret," Lusak said.

Melinda grinned, but wondered again—could he have done it? Killed a man in the brutal way Gordon was killed?

Under the right circumstances, anyone can do anything. She'd learned that lesson along the way—learned it early, in fact. So many of her earthbound spirits were loving family members with one simple thing left undone . . .

And so many of them weren't. Dramatic lives, dramatic deaths, lingering needs.

Lusak put a hand to his solar plexus, straightening slightly. "Talking to you has been good for me, it appears. I *do* feel better."

"Maybe you just needed to take a moment," Melinda offered. "Your job must be pretty high stress."

"It has its moments," Lusak said. He shook his head. "The things I see . . . sometimes I just . . ."

She had the feeling he was going to say something along the lines of *sometimes I just want to lose it,* but he didn't. And it was on the tip of her tongue to ask if he *had* lost it, but no—it would have been too soon, too sudden. And besides, he shook his head and stood up. "Jeannie will be glad to hear from you," he said.

Maybe not if she knew that Melinda thought her husband just might be a murderer.

7

MELINDA SAT FOR a moment after Lusak walked out of the square and down the street; she crossed one leg over the other and rested her clasped hands on her knee. "I know you're still here," she said. "You're not exactly subtle."

And there he was, bent over in front of her so his face was up to hers, his favorite intimidation tactic. She couldn't help but gasp, and yet at the same time she noticed that he'd settled into himself, no longer distorted with anger. Still mortally wounded, still actively bleeding. *"You don't know how to take a hint,"* he growled at her. *"Or maybe you don't take me seriously enough. Maybe you need a demonstration of what could happen to you."* And his hand landed on her forearm, closing around it with a dread cold that made it instantly ache to the bone.

With tremendous strength of will, she didn't

react to that touch. "Oh, I take you very seriously. But I've talked to Carol. I've talked to Howie. I know that each of them, in their own way, had tremendous belief in the changes you made in your life—belief in the person you'd always been, deep down. And I don't think that person would truly hurt me."

He snatched his hand away as if he was the one in pain. *"You* are *a fool."*

"I don't think so," she said softly.

His gaze burned, a deep black with no light to it, only cold fury. *"If you think I won't avenge myself on him—"*

"Whoa." She held up both hands—a stop-right-there gesture—and quickly remembered that she was out in public talking to thin air; she dropped them in her lap again. "That, I believe, okay? No need to prove anything to me."

His hard-edge appearance softened slightly. *"Then why waste your time?"*

Oh, never mind who was watching. They should be used to her by now anyway. She turned toward him; she caught his uncomfortable gaze and held it. "Because if you do this thing, you change your own fate—you change the essence of who you are."

He laughed, short and hard—the kind of laugh that was meant to make her squirm. *"Haven't you noticed? My* fate *is sealed. It's* happened. *Thanks to that man, it's* over.*"*

She held firm, refusing to match his raised volume. "That's not true, and you know it. You still have choices to make. It's time to cross over, to give yourself peace. You aren't going to find that here, no matter what you do."

"Says you," he snorted. He sat on the bench next to her, one arm over the back of it, legs sprawled wide. Sloppy and disrespectful. The Gordon that had been.

"Yes, I do." She shifted so she could look more directly at him. With any luck it would seem to the rest of the world as though she was taking in the huge bank of tulips bordering the sidewalk behind him. "I've been doing this for a long time, Gordon. I've seen people make hard decisions. I've seen them lose themselves. I'd hate for that to happen to you."

He snorted. *"Why? Did my story of redemption tug at your heartstrings? Buncha crap. Look where it got me."*

She narrowed her eyes at him. "That's not the way I think. Everyone deserves the chance to cross over. Everyone deserves to be at peace. Your story touched me, but you're not getting any special attention, thank you very much." Not exactly true, but that was as much for the sake of the living as for Gordon. "In fact, I'm currently in touch with two other earthbound spirits, one of whom is in worse shape than you." And the other of which, she was pretty sure, was a dog—but no reason to mention that little fact.

"*That's all very moving,*" he said with a sneer, but she was used to that, too. Like any number of those she'd helped, he was being as disagreeable as he could—just like a kid, needing her to prove she really meant what she said about helping him, even if he risked driving her off in the process.

Unless, of course, he was just plain being nasty. That had happened too.

"*All the same,*" he added, "*I'll stick with who I was. And* that *Gordon would make sure his killer paid for it.*"

"Would *that* Gordon take an innocent life so easily?"

He waved away her concerns with arrogant dismissiveness. She moved in on him, for once the one to close the distance between them. "Think about it, Gordon. Do you remember with absolute certainty what happened in those moments? Or do you just remember what happened around that time? Do you have memories, or do you have impressions?"

He gave her an incredulous look. The blood glistened on his face, a suddenly fresh flow. "*You're asking me if I remember the very moment someone bashed my brains in? The way it felt when that first blow landed? How many times he hit me before I died? Whether I lingered, or* pop, *out like a light?*"

"I'm asking you," she said steadily, "whether you remember the person who hit you. Not before, not after. As that person hit you."

"I remember enough." He sneered at her again, and this time it was an obvious cover for his inability to answer the question. "A man with a tire iron. The man I've been following. Want to see?"

"I—"

He didn't give her a choice. The world went night-dark, washed with haze around the edges. No streetlights, no window lights. There might have been a hint of neon bleeding into the sky off to the left. *The bar?* Gravel bit into the skin between her—no, *his*—shoulders. She couldn't feel his left side at all; the fingers on his left hand twitched—a purposeless, reflex movement. His mouth fell open; the noise that came out was barely human yet took all the energy she had. *He* had.

The world blurred. The stars, once pinpoints of light, fuzzed and merged with the night. And then . . .

There.

Craig Lusak. Just a glimpse. A man moving furtively. The tire iron glinted in the scant light from the bar. Gravel crunched under hard soles, pushed down into the soft spring ground.

Gordon released her; she squinted at the sudden brightness of the late morning in Grandview, barely catching herself when she would have tipped over, her left side numb and unresponsive. She flexed that hand and glared at him. "That was rude."

He shrugged, unconcerned. *"You wanted to know."*

"That's it?" she asked. "You're condemning him for *that?"*

His edges grew hard and brittle. His voice gained a faint reverberation, the anger rippling outward with his words. *"Damned right I am."*

"But he doesn't even *know* you. He has no motive—"

"Did you see the tire iron? I did. I do. Over and over and—"

"I get the picture," she said, more shortly than she might have been inclined, maybe than she should have been inclined. *Patience,* she told herself. *Understanding.* "You think it's him. So what?"

"So what?" His incredulous look might have been laughable, under other circumstances.

"Look, you want revenge, right?" She felt herself sliding toward words that would horrify Jim. "You want to mess with the guy who killed you, and you want him dead when you're done."

His eyes narrowed with suspicion. *"If you don't know the answer to that, you haven't been paying attention."*

"And how's that working for you so far?"

He didn't respond. He faded somewhat, although his crisp edges remained; his facial features wavered as he looked back at her. She took it for surprise and uncertainty, and in turn took *that* as a good sign—pursued it. "You getting satisfaction? Getting anything besides a little energy rush when Craig Lusak reacts to what you've done?"

Again, no response, but his form solidified, and his annoyance brushed at her.

"Then what do you have to lose by doing it my way for a while?"

His voice had taken on a hollow nature. *"Meaning what?"*

"Let me look into it. Let me see if I can find out for *sure* if Craig Lusak could have been your killer."

That was just *so* not a phrase one expected to say on an average day.

But it would buy time. Give him the opportunity to cool down, to back off . . . to absorb what had happened, and to make room for acceptance. Maybe even to cross over.

Gordon laughed, entirely without humor. *"Fine,"* he said. *"You do your Pollyanna do-gooder thing. Just don't expect me to buy into it. So I'll tell you what: I won't kill him. Not while you're playing detective."* He laughed again. *"But leave him alone? Not gonna happen, sweetheart."* He winked at her, a patronizing gesture. *"It's as good a deal as you're going to get."*

And of course he disappeared.

Melinda sat back on the bench, deflated. "Great," she muttered. "Jim is going to kill me."

At least, once he found out about it.

Melinda sat on the bench a short while longer, and this time she really did take in the spring flowers, the increasing number of people in the square, and the pleasure of sitting in the open air with only a light jacket on. "Right," she said to the open air. "Might as well get on with it."

An older couple were deep in discussion of the wicker carriage when Melinda entered the store. She wiggled her fingers at Delia in a quickie wave and slipped into the back room to find her phone, searching out Jeannie's number from the corner of the bulletin board. "Hey!" she said to Jeannie, and identified herself. "I know it's short notice, but Craig just mentioned your barn discovery to me, and as it happens I've got time this afternoon."

Jeannie was delighted, so after a quick call to let Jim know what she was up to, Melinda returned to the store front. The couple were gone and the carriage remained, but as she was passing through, Delia said, "Bet they'll be back. I'm going to hunt for a few final touches for that carriage display. They won't stand a chance."

"You never know, maybe I'll find something this afternoon," Melinda said, hand on the door. "I'm heading out to see what Jeannie's found."

"Is that what Craig wanted?" Delia asked it so casually that Melinda couldn't help but smile. Delia didn't want to know, but . . . she really wanted to know.

"That's why he was headed this way." Melinda shifted her weight. "I have the feeling he just missed our mystery note writer. He said he'd checked the shop a few minutes earlier and found the coffee sign, but didn't see anything on the door."

Delia wasn't slow. She looked up from her notes and said, "You don't think . . ."

Melinda shrugged. "I'm going in so many different directions right now, I don't know what to think. I'm just trying to keep track. I figure it'll all come together sooner or later."

"Y'know," Delia said, "that's what I say about Ned." She stopped, frowned slightly, and added, "It's what I *used* to say about Ned. These days . . ."

"But hey," Melinda said, picking up on that thread of melancholy again, "that's a *good* thing, right?"

"It is," Delia said, quite positively, but then had to repeat it with a little nod of her head. "It is."

Melinda narrowed her eyes most obviously. "Hmm."

"Good things," Delia admitted, "aren't always the easy things. I mean, you'd think so, but . . ."

"Change is hard," Melinda said. After all, what was Gordon facing but change? Change so profound that even after all these years, Melinda could only imagine it. And before that, change of his own making.

Too much change for one soul to accept, it seemed.

"Anyway, have fun antiquing," Delia said, returning to her notes in a most industrious manner. "Doesn't it feel strange going out with someone whose husband you think might have . . . ?"

"Like I said," Melinda responded, her tone and smile wry, "so many directions . . . just trying to keep track." She pushed the door open. "Have a good lunch with Tim."

Delia brightened at that, turning to her notes with a smile that was probably meant to be private. Melinda left her to it, heading for the Saturn. There she stopped, her hand on the keys and the door half-open, and said, "I'm going to be driving now. I would appreciate it if you could wait to talk to me until I'm *not* driving. If you don't wait, I'll have to give you a busy signal, because it's not safe."

She thought she heard a faint, passive chorus of *swing batterbatter*, and she, too, smiled a private smile as she climbed into the SUV and pulled the seat belt into place. But she didn't head for Bayview, not directly. She swung out to take the loop around Grandview, heading for the Honey Bs. It had only been a couple of days, but it'd be another week before she'd have a chance for a casual visit.

Besides, it had only taken a few days of driving restrictions to make driving the lightly traveled roads a pleasure. She turned the radio on, turned the volume up, and hummed happily along with Midnight Hour as they performed their latest.

She was still humming when she reached the Honey Bs and turned off the road into the now-familiar driveway, easing into the small gravel parking area to pull up beside the same beat-up old GMC that had been there on Saturday. "Huh," she said out loud, looking at it and then peering through the greening landscaping to locate the B&B itself, and the open stand-alone garage beside it, clearly separate from guest parking, that held a small collection of family cars. Beside that stood a little work shed, the contents of which were neatly visible through the open overhead door; she noticed a pegboard wall of tools and a bulletin board tacked full of notes and papers. She gave the big cream vehicle a backwards glance as she entered the little honey shop and, as the woman dusting the shelves turned to look at her, said, "What a co-incidence. That same SUV was there when I visited a couple of days ago."

The woman—short and chunky, with a stuffed fanny pack attached to her hip, permed steel gray hair, and tiny wrinkles fanning out from the corners of her eyes and along her lips—said, "Not so much of a coincidence when you figure Dave works here." She looked Melinda up and down—obvious, but friendly enough. "I hope you're not back because you've found a problem with the honey."

"Oh, just the opposite. In fact, I left my card. I was hoping I might carry a small stock of your honey in my shop in town. I talked to Carol about it on Saturday. You must be her mother?"

"Rebecca Donovan." The friendliness faded; the woman put her feather duster aside. "She mentioned it. Do you have any idea how much you upset her?"

Whoops. Not how she'd expected this conversation would go. "I'm so sorry to hear that. I didn't mean to."

The woman moved back around the counter, plucking Melinda's business card from the register and putting it down on the counter with the snap of a card being dealt. "What were you thinking, coming around to ask questions about Gordon?"

Careful, now. "I didn't know I'd find her here," Melinda said, moving up to the counter with what was only the truth. She shifted the bag on her shoulder to a more secure position so she could relax a little, hoping to put a more casual tone into this conversation. "But when I did, I thought she would find comfort that Gordon's life and his accomplishments could help someone."

"I suppose they could be considered inspiring, at that." Somewhat mollified, the woman didn't ease up completely; she stabbed a finger at the card as though it was a surrogate Melinda. "But asking her about the night he died? How's that supposed to help anyone? That's just nosy. Ghoulish, even. You don't know us; you have no right to anything that's not in the papers. And that," she added, glaring at nothing in particular, "is already too much."

"You didn't want his story told?" Melinda couldn't help her surprise. "Why?"

"No one's a saint," the woman snapped defensively, and then instantly seemed to wish she hadn't. She took a breath. "No one's life stands up to media scrutiny."

It was the first implication that Gordon's life changes hadn't been as profound as the news stories had suggested. Of course, the media had chosen their human-interest angle and stuck with it. But Melinda had no doubt they'd turn things around if they felt it would grab readers. No doubt this woman knew it, too. "I'm sure you're right—my own life included," Melinda said. "I think Gordon did better than most. If there's something you're worried about, I haven't seen it."

For an instant, the woman looked relieved—at Melinda's understanding, at her reassurance. And then she stiffened slightly. "You're doing it again, aren't you? Being nosy! You're just being slyer about it than you were with my daughter."

Melinda winced inside. Whatever worried this woman, it kept her defenses on full force. Maybe if she mentioned Gordon's presence . . .

But Gordon wasn't ready to talk to his family, wasn't seeking that contact. Wouldn't cooperate, and wouldn't make it anything but hurtful for Carol. The timing was definitely not right. But until it was, she wasn't likely to learn more about Gordon here.

Unless you counted what she construed from the defensiveness itself.

Out loud, she said, "I really am just trying to help."

Carol's mother crossed her arms, her expression entirely at odds with the little shop around her—the homey little touches with gingham bows and carefully hand-inked signs; the basket on the counter with a soft and lifelike plush cat sleeping within, a wee stuffed mouse curled up between its front paws; hand-drawn bees populating the rough pine walls in strategic locations. "No one asked for your help."

Not yet . . .

Maybe not ever. But it didn't matter. Melinda's role in life had been settled long ago, the day her grandmother had taken her to view the casket of a sad-faced man Melinda had also seen sitting in the church pew. She hadn't truly understood, not then. But now . . . Now, this was who she was. And she'd grown used to resistance along the way.

If not quite the high stakes inherent in Gordon's fate.

"The truth is," Melinda said, "I'm helping someone other than you. And I can see you aren't happy with that, but it's something I need to do." She shrugged; she kept her voice light and pleasant. "Of course, I did also come back to see if you were interested in stocking some honey with me."

The woman's mouth flattened. "You really do have quite a bit of nerve."

Ah, well, she hadn't thought so. Melinda turned to the shelves, scooping up several flavors of creamed honey in quick succession, deciding against the combed honey as too potentially messy. "I'll just offer tasters in the store, then; see how it works out." She'd been admiring their tasting table—mini plastic spoons, miniature tea biscuits. Add her own favorite lavender-mint-scented hand wipes off to the side, and it might serve as a neat little touch for SAME AS IT NEVER WAS.

"That's up to you," the woman said. "We're doing well enough anyway you look at it, without your *help*. So those will be full price."

"Of course," Melinda said. And thought, *You have no idea . . .*

Melinda tucked the honey away in the back seat foot well, padding it with the emergency blanket she also kept back there. For a moment after sliding in behind the wheel, she just sat there, pressing the heels of her hands to her eyes. "You're not going to make this easy, are you?" she said to the darkness of her eyelids. "None of you."

Gordon, too full of anger to look ahead at what was best for his journey or back to acknowledge the confusion of events the night he'd died. His wife and her family, too full of grief and defensiveness to give her a decent conversation about the man Gordon had been. Howie, too frightened by his faint glimpses of spirit-driven activity to do anything but sneer and pretend to be tough as he reached for a beer.

And Craig Lusak, sickened by Gordon, just trying to get on with his life—an ostensibly good man who had opportunity, means, and, with the frustration he'd built up in his life, maybe even motive.

But for now, Carol's family was a dead-end. Maybe later, when Melinda knew more . . . when she was ready to tell them just which friend she was really trying to help. But that, she knew, would be a hard, hard conversation.

Not the first. Not the last.

She took a deep breath, dropping her hands. "Howie," she said out loud, looking out into the bright green of the budding maples that spilled out from the yard to hang over this parking area. "What is it you think I don't want to know? And is it the same thing Carol's mother doesn't want me to know?"

She caught a glimpse of movement in the corner of her eye—so flighty that she at first assumed it was a shy spirit, maybe even Gordon himself. But she felt nothing unusual—none of the emotions that drifted along with such spirits, none of the physical effects—and another glimpse revealed a man, working amid a tangle of brush. Trimming, dragging branches. Hard labor.

The man straightened, turned . . . looked straight at her. Frowned.

Suddenly, Melinda had felt enough unwelcome. She started the car, shifted into gear, and pulled smoothly out onto the road, headed for Bayview and the more pleasant distraction of digging through dusty old barns in an antiquing treasure hunt.

8

Jeannie Lusak greeted her in the driveway of their modest colonial two-story in Bayview, a smile on her face and worry behind her eyes. Melinda gestured for her to climb on in, turned down the radio, and welcomed her new passenger with a smile. "So! Where are we headed for treasure hunting?"

"If we can beat the rain?" Jeannie asked, peering out the windshield at a day going from blue to silvery gray. She was dressed for it—outdoorsy informal, this time, with chinos and a three-quarter-sleeve button-up under a tidy corduroy jacket, all brown tones, playing up the gold in her hair. "It's not far. I really hope you'll think it's worth your time. It's one of those old barn collections—lots of junk from lots of attics, but I think there's some good stuff lurking around. Hopefully we'll catch them at home—it looked pretty random to me.

You know—older folks, just going about their business, halfway living the way old-timey folks used to."

"Sounds wonderful," Melinda said. "Point me in the right direction, and we'll see if we're in luck."

Jeannie sent her back to the winding state roads, as they settled in to light conversation—Melinda's plans for the store, the honey she had tucked away in the back, a few words about Gordon's family that netted a sympathetic response from Jeannie but nothing beyond—no defensiveness, no undue concern.

If Lusak had been involved in that death, Jeannie didn't have a clue. And from the concern lingering between her brows, Melinda decided Jeannie had other things to think about. "Everything okay?" she asked. "Is today really a good day for you?"

Jeannie blinked in surprise, bit her lip, and laughed—a small laugh, evidently more at herself than anything else. "You *are* perceptive," she said. "But really, today is fine. No better or worse than any other day, and I do have the time. Seems like waiting is half of what I do these days. At least now I'm *doing* something while I'm waiting."

Melinda negotiated a curve, one eye to the vehicle behind them. "Craig mentioned something about adoption," she said. "I wasn't supposed to say anything—I think he was surprised to have brought it up, you know how men are—but he did make it sound as though you've been waiting long enough to start getting anxious."

Jeannie made a sound that might have been a laugh. "That's one way to put it," she said. "We've been through our classes; we've had our social worker visits. In a strange way, I'm almost getting used to being in that mode. But this thing with Craig . . ."

"He looks like he's not feeling well," Melinda said. *Well, duh. He's being haunted to the max.*

Jeannie shook her head. "It's the strangest thing," she said. "Some days it's as though he has the flu; other days he's fine. And sometimes he starts out just fine, and then suddenly . . ." Her voice sounded strained; Melinda glanced over to find her fighting tears—her eyes already reddened, her fair complexion blotchy.

"Hey," she said, dividing her attention between Jeannie and the road. "You okay? I didn't mean to upset you."

"You?" Jeannie laughed, wiping a careful finger under her eye. "No, I should have warned you how emotional I am these days. It's just frustrating. I don't know how long he can go on like this."

He won't have to for much longer, not if I can help it. "It must be hard," Melinda said, her heart going out to that frustration.

Jeannie visibly gathered herself, sitting straighter

and adjusting the seat belt slightly at the shoulder. "A year from now, I think of us as happy and healthy, and baby's room is occupied." She wiped under the other eye and said, "How about you?"

"Oh, *us*. Yes, happy and healthy. Still practically newlywed. My husband works at the fire station, but you knew that. It's great, really—we even get to meet for lunch sometimes."

Jeannie looked wistful. "Take my word for it," she said, "don't rush those days. Enjoy every minute of them."

"We do. We are." And she hoped it was true. They certainly had more reason than most to value their time together, never taking anything for granted. Too many of those she'd helped cross over had left with messages of regret.

"Here we are," Jeannie said suddenly, as they reached a turnoff with a crooked sign languishing on the corner. ANTIQUES, it said, with an arrow, hand-painted and fading. Melinda signaled, checking the rearview to see that the other vehicle had noticed her brake lights. "This road on the left, and then it's just a few mailboxes down."

And indeed, there was another sign, equally faded and jostled by time and weather so it actually pointed off down the road. Melinda pulled into the long driveway, obscured as it was by a few trees, and emerged into an open area where no further direction awaited. As she idled there—eyeing the house, the scattering of outbuildings and old farm equipment and rusty piles of arcane plowing gear—Jeannie drew her attention to the left, where the most faded sign of all declared that particular building the Antiques Barn.

"Antiques *shed*?" Melinda suggested.

Jeannie laughed. "It's bigger than you think— it has that front shed space, but it's attached to that old barn behind it. Not that all the space is for the antiques. it's more like they overflowed back that way. If you park out in front of it and sit a moment . . . That's what I did, and someone showed up."

And indeed, with two Homerlike border collie mixes now circling the Saturn as it parked, Melinda had barely shut off the engine before a real-life version of Mrs. Claus came from the direction of the house, her permed hair curled tight to her head, her plump form compact enough to easily navigate the narrow passage between the shed and some of the old machinery, her gait rolling and un-hurried. She wore an apron, of course. It and her hands were liberally dusted with flour, and she was utterly unaware of the earthbound spirit walking along behind her—a man not much older than she was, dressed in work overalls and galoshes, looking perfectly content. She waved at them as Melinda disembarked. "Hello! Welcome to our little barn. I'll just shut the dogs up in their kennel so they won't be pestful, and you can take your time looking around. There's a little button in there that you can push if you see something you like or if you have any questions. Otherwise, feel free to leave when you've seen enough!"

"Wow," Melinda said, tucking her purse straps over her shoulder. "What a wonderful place you have here! Thank you."

"Most folks don't quite see the wonderful," the woman responded, "but through my eyes, it's all of that."

"Of course it is," Melinda said, looking past her at the older man. "It's a *home,* anyone can see that. It carries its own history."

"Well, my goodness. I suppose it does at that. My sister and I do hope the children feel the same way when we pass, but you know how children are these days. Anyway, you make yourselves at home there, and give me a buzz if you need anything. Snip, Sam!" This last to the dogs, who stopped their obsessive circling and came to orbit around the woman instead.

"Can I do anything for you?" Melinda asked as the woman turned away—but it was the man she looked at.

He smiled at her. *"No, young lady, but thank you for asking . . ."*

"For me?" the woman asked in surprise. She smiled, amused.

"I'm just waiting," he continued. *"I know I should move on—I've seen that light—but when we can go through it together is soon enough for me."*

The woman shook her head. "Why, I guess not." And then, bemused, "Young people these days—how unusual you can be. But charming, I do have to say."

Melinda smiled, the slightest of nods—to the husband, although the wife, as she turned away, took it for herself. And Melinda, glancing at Jeannie, found her also somewhat bemused. She shrugged off the moment with an airy, "Just an impulse. Let's go see what you've found, shall we?"

"Lots of tools," Jeannie said, leading the way. "They look to be in pretty good condition, and I bet if they were cleaned up, they'd bring a lot from someone who even wanted to use them. And I notice you don't carry too many truly big pieces of furniture—there's plenty of that, here—but there are some really solid smaller pieces, and I have the feeling that if some of these were cleaned up, they'd turn out to be serious gems."

The barn addition was, of course, dimly lit. They pushed the sliding door open as far as it would go, and Melinda found herself amid the most fascinating sort of clutter, a substantial gathering of age and history that cried out to be recognized as treasure by someone who knew. A secretary over there, grime gathered over blackened varnish; a cast-iron headboard over there, sweeping and fanciful enough with its whorls and curlicues to rival Melinda's own cherished bed. A wooden tool tray filled with pliers and awls and tools she didn't recognize but she thought Jim would, and *aha, perfect gift!* She'd squirrel it away in the back of the shop until the holidays . . .

She realized that Jeannie was waiting, watching her, and quite probably holding her breath, and she laughed. "It's wonderful!"

Jeannie grinned relief. "Wait'll you see this adorable little marble-topped washstand vanity table over here," she said. "You'll just have to *believe* about the marble, but I'm pretty sure that's what's under the weird decoupage treatment."

"That could be a showpiece, if we can get it cleaned off." Melinda stepped carefully between an old steamer trunk and two dining room chairs, one upended on the other. "If it could possibly be from England . . . " and then, looking at the piece, "Ooh! Yes! That's got to be walnut. And I'll bet that's original hardware, and scroll-cut supports on the gallery back, and baluster-turned legs—never mind the Christmas present I just saw, this is worth the whole trip! I don't suppose it's priced anywhere . . . ?"

"If it is, I think we'll need a flashlight to find it." Jeannie's grin had grown, and now her cheeks were flushed with excitement. "But we need to clear away some of this stuff around it anyway."

"And borrow Jim's pickup to get it over to Grandview." Melinda gave it a thoughtful look and then glanced around. "Let's see what else we can find. Might be worth renting a small van, if there's enough of it."

She felt a sudden gust of impatience, of anger; the dim light fluttered as though blocked by slowly whirling fan blades. Gordon's voice filtered through itself and back again, whispering down Melinda's neck. *"Ask her."*

Melinda pivoted away from Jeannie, ostensibly eyeing the goods around her. *"Man*ners," she said, singsong between her teeth.

Jeannie set aside a small end table, a cheap little thing. She gave the flickering light a little frown—great, that meant Gordon was manifesting to everyone right now, not just Melinda—and asked, "Did you say something?"

"Hmm? Just, oh *man,* there's a lot of stuff here."

"Do a quick triage for this first trip, and plan to come back?" Jeannie suggested.

Melinda gave a single, decisive nod. "That's a plan."

"Ask her!" Gordon appeared before her so suddenly, so close, that Melinda startled back with a squeak.

And still she caught his gaze and widened her eyes, tightening her mouth with the faintest of head shakes. She'd do this her own way.

Just that fast, he disappeared. And because she'd done the jump and squeak, she said, "Ooh! Mouse!"

"Not surprising," Jeannie laughed. "It must be a haven for them here." But she gave the open door another frown, where the faintly wavering light shone. Melinda had the impression that Gordon had put himself on fast forward again and now ran jerky laps through the barn, heedless of the furniture, turning himself into a negative strobe effect.

All righty, then. She and Gordon needed to have a talk. He wanted results, but she knew from experience that pushing it didn't always get them. Not when fragile human emotions were involved. "I think there might be a flashlight in the glove box. That would make our quick triage a lot quicker." Melinda headed for the door, strides purposeful, Jeannie's distracted acknowledgment in her ears.

But the door slammed shut, rattling in old tracks not meant for such abuse, and so close it brushed against her as she jumped back. Dust rained down with the force of its impact against the stops; Melinda reflexively covered her ears, but only for an instant. "Gordon," she said, not just

through her teeth but through now distinctly grit-
ted teeth.

"Melinda?" Jeannie said, bewildered, "Why—?"

Of course she thought Melinda had done it.
She'd been preoccupied, not looking. But for
once, Melinda didn't have a quick cover. And for
once, she didn't bother, because she had the feeling it would be a moot point in very short order.
Gordon had promised not to kill Craig Lusak, but
he hadn't promised not to dog the man. And he
distinctly hadn't promised not to dog the man's
wife, or Melinda, as she tried to learn what she
could.

Her style, it seemed, wasn't the least bit satisfac-
tory to Gordon.

"And this is better?" she muttered, knowing he
wouldn't follow the exact nature of her thoughts
but he'd know she wasn't happy.

He probably just didn't care.

Well, she didn't intend to do this here. Without
trying to explain anything, she hunted and found
the metal handle inside the door, threading her
hand through to give the kind of yank it would
take to move the abused old thing. Instead it was
her shoulder that nearly gave way as the door held
firm; she lost the air from her lungs in surprise.
"Oh, come *on*," she said, smacking the door with
the flat of her hand. "This isn't funny!"

"You didn't—?" Jeannie asked, spooked now.

She moved away from the washstand, finding a clearer spot.

"I didn't," Melinda confirmed. She tried the door again, this time prepared for its recalcitrance, and braced herself against the worn wood floor, the soles of her boots sliding. Jeannie quickly joined her, the two of them partnered in wordless effort—and tacitly admitting defeat at the same moment. They stepped back, both flexing their hands where the metal handle had bitten deep.

"I don't understand," Jeannie said, worried in the dim light, dust motes dancing high overhead in narrow slashes of light from between warped siding. "If you didn't—"

"ASK HER," Gordon thundered, suddenly there again, his very favorite ploy and *damn,* it was a good one. Melinda stumbled backward, and her last bit of patience grew abruptly thin.

"Stop it, Gordon!" she snapped. "You're not helping!"

He stood in the center of the barn addition, smug unto a borderline sneer, arms crossed and legs propped wide. *"I'm not trying to help."* But when he disappeared, Melinda felt anything but relief. She stepped away from the door, slowly, turning to look all around the barn.

"Melinda?" Jeannie said, her voice very small. "Who are you talking to?" And then, "Oh my God, *Gordon.* That's the man who was killed.

What's wrong with you? What is this all about?" But she didn't wait for any sort of an answer; she'd quite evidently had enough. "I'm beginning to think this was all a big mistake. I'm sorry. I'd like to leave now."

"That doesn't seem to be an option for either of us," Melinda said. "I'm sorry, I didn't know he'd—"

"ASK HER!" Right in front of her, his face up to hers, distorted with his impatience, dripping with his blood.

"Stop it!" She yelled right back at him, not giving an inch, knowing that Jeannie slowly backed away from her. "Do you mind? I was making a friend here—"

Too much to ask, at that. His eyes bulged, almost comically. He jumped to speed-jerk mode, circling her, drawing back to punch right through her. The breath left her body with a whoop; she doubled over, eyes tearing as she fought to draw the air back into her lungs—and fought to keep her head up, her eyes on Gordon. In the periphery of her vision, Jeannie backed away, horrified, and then ran back to the door, slamming her hands against it. "Let me out, let me out! Open this door! The buzzer, where's the buzzer—"

"No!" Melinda managed, mostly soundless. She reached out an entreating hand, took a shallow sip of air. "Don't bring her into this. Don't . . ."

Gordon spun out to the rest of the barn, speeding through the furniture, circling around them with his rage set to high and the wind rising in the energy of his passage. Dust rose; furniture tipped and splintered. Jeannie crouched by the door, arms covering her head, crying out in fear. A stray board spun through the air and smashed against the door just above her; a hapless sparrow tumbled high overhead.

"Gordon!" Melinda cried. "Gordon, that's enough! I'll ask!" No reason to be coy about it, now. If she could keep Jeannie from bolting . . .

But Gordon was caught up in his own anger, a boiling darkness that gathered in the center of the barn—roiling, tumbling darkness, engulfing the contents of the barn, casting a shadow. *Real.* Melinda straightened, horrified. She took a slow step back, and another. She'd never seen anything like it, but she didn't want to know what would happen if that anger engulfed either of them. Jeannie, drawn by Melinda's movement, caught sight of it and screamed, one of those bloodcurdling screams that should exist only in a fright flick and never in anyone's real life.

And quite suddenly there was a fourth member of the party. The man Melinda had seen behind his Mrs. Claus wife walked right through the door, his expression stern and his body language no-nonsense. "Young man!" he said. "That is quite enough." Somehow his voice, although quiet and firm, rang over the din Gordon had created.

Gordon appeared in the center of the barn addition, rocking slightly to catch his balance as though the choice hadn't been entirely his. Disheveled hair fell in his eyes; his shirt and jacket were askew. He shimmered, and Melinda knew that in his inexperience, he'd overstepped the bounds of his own resources. He'd let his anger carry him away until he was riding the wave of it, and now the old man had put a stop to that and he'd been left gasping.

"Behave yourself," the man said, just as stern, as if speaking to a naughty puppy. "This is my home. These are my guests."

Jeannie couldn't see any of it, of course; she huddled by the door, and a single sob of relief escaped as she dared to look around the settling interior. Melinda took a step toward her. "It's okay," she said. "I can explain what's happening."

"And you think that's *reassuring*?" Jeannie snapped at her.

Melinda smiled, small and sad; she couldn't help but admire that fortitude. "Maybe not," she said. "But it's all I've got." And to the old man, she said, "Thank you. He's very angry. He doesn't always play well with others."

"I can see that," the man said. "But he's on my property now, and he'll have to manage somehow."

"Who—?" Jeannie asked, staring at Melinda, and then stopped, putting her hands over her face in an obvious attempt to pull her thoughts together.

"It'll make sense in a moment," Melinda said. "I promise it will." She turned back to their host. "And you're sure there's nothing I can do for you?"

"You think she doesn't know I'm here?" The man chuckled, though his attention never left Gordon. "Or that I left something unsaid? No, it's just as I told you—I'm waiting. I don't think it'll be long now. She's not well, she just doesn't know it yet. But I can feel it."

"Just . . ." Melinda chose her words with care, thinking of what she'd seen in the past several years, what she now knew. "Be careful."

"My dear," the man said, and this time he did look at her, "why do you think I'm waiting? I don't want her to do this alone."

Melinda blinked away the sudden sting of sentimental tears, and couldn't help but smile. "That's sweet."

"I'm glad you understand." Words from a man who'd clearly seen what was out there. And with one last look at Gordon, the man stepped back, turned away. "I'll be here if you need me."

"I hope that won't be necessary." Melinda sent a stern look Gordon's way.

"I'm sure it won't be," the man said, and walked

out through the barn door just as he'd come in. Gordon said something rude and crude in his wake but remained subdued. In fact, after a sullen glance at Melinda, he disappeared.

"Must be nice," Melinda muttered.

Jeannie made a surprised noise; the door grumbled as she tugged on it, and it rolled open a foot.

"Please," Melinda said, as Jeannie braced herself to open the door the rest of the way. "Please wait. Let me explain."

Jeannie hesitated, uncertain, her hand still wrapped around the old metal handle.

"I know this is hard," Melinda said. "And I know it's crazy. I mean, really crazy. But it's still *real*."

"*Your* reality," Jeannie said. "*Your* thing. Because this definitely isn't about me. And I really don't want it to be."

"I can understand that. Trust me, I understand it better than you know." Because since she'd moved to Grandview, anything that concerned earthbound spirits had somehow become about Melinda herself. Never before had she had any indication that she was a known factor, that the ghostly grapevine kept track of who she was and what she was doing. That someone even seemed to be keeping score.

Yeah, she could definitely understand Jeannie's reaction. But . . .

"The thing is, I'm not so sure that's true. That this isn't about you." She brushed a cobweb out of her hair, dusted off her arm.

Jeannie shook her head. "That's ridiculous. I don't even know what *this* is. Besides, I've got enough going on in my life right now."

Melinda seized on that. "Exactly. And this is part of that. It's not new, it's not another thing. It's another side of something that's already happening—and maybe a way to resolve it."

Jeannie stepped away from the door, her eyes narrowing with suspicion. She didn't, in that moment, look the least bit like the friendly woman who'd first approached Melinda at the store. "What're you talking about?"

Gordon popped up right in front of Jeannie—Jeannie who couldn't see, but who recoiled from the cold anger. *"This."*

Coarse laughter, the sound of pool balls breaking, marginal lighting, the thick, heavy smell of beer . . . from the tap, from men's pores.

"The way I see it," Mikey Gomez says, smacking his beer down on the scarred bar hard enough to draw the slanting, warning gaze of the bartender-owner-bouncer, "you're saying we're not good enough for you anymore."

Gordon swallows his own beer. "You asshole, always gotta make it about you, don't you?"

More laughter, and someone slaps his back, and the

beer puts an agreeable blur on his thoughts, a blur with an aggressive edge—

He is out in the cold spring night, awkward on the ground, the stars fading into the night sky above. And there's Craig Lusak, wild around the eyes, tire jack in hand, looking over his shoulder . . . jogging away . . .

"Ask her," Gordon demanded, standing next to Jeannie but glancing over at Melinda. *"She does his laundry. She sleeps beside him. She knows, whether she wants to or not."*

But Melinda quite suddenly remembered what Howie had said. "What happened in the bar?" she asked him instead. "Howie said I wouldn't want to know. What wouldn't I want to know?"

Gordon blinked, sincerely taken by surprise. *"I don't know what he was talking about. It's not important. I wasn't killed in the bar."*

Faced with another one-sided conversation, Jeannie said, "That's it. I'm outta here."

"Gordon Reese is here," Melinda said abruptly, cornered into it. "He hasn't been able to cross over into the Light since his death; he's tortured by how things turned out for him. How he worked so very hard to turn his life around and was killed just as he succeeded."

"Well, of course that was tragic—" Jeannie seemed to respond in spite of herself, but she cut herself short and said, "Wait a minute. Gordon Reese is *here*?"

"I have a gift, Jeannie," Melinda said. As much as this part was always the same, it was also always different—different words, different reactions. "Just as Craig mediates for children, I . . . well, I work on behalf of earthbound spirits."

"Ghosts," Jeannie said flatly. "You mean ghosts."

Gordon smiled the sneery smile. *"Boo."*

"Were you really this bad?" Melinda asked him, but quickly shook her head. "No, never mind. It doesn't matter." *Or does it?* A quiet thought, but one she couldn't respond to immediately, not with Jeannie on the verge of leaving.

Of course, Melinda had the car keys. But nonetheless, once Jeannie left this barn, the opportunity for discussion would be twice as hard to create again, if it even happened. "Ghosts, yes. Earthbound spirits—those who haven't been able to cross into the Light. That happens when there's something keeping them behind. Gordon hasn't accepted the circumstances of his death, the timing. The older gentleman I was talking to earlier—"

"Out when we first got here," Jeannie said, realization settling on her face. "You weren't talking to the owner of this place at all."

Melinda shook her head, a rueful little smile in place. "No. To her husband. He's waiting for her. He says she doesn't have much longer."

Jeannie covered her face. "I'm not sure I wanted to know that. I don't want to know *any* of this! I don't believe it, I don't believe it, I don't—" She stopped, and looked at Melinda. "But unless you're Steven Spielberg, you couldn't have rigged this place up. Even if you'd known about it before I brought you here."

"No," Melinda said. She shrugged, an apology of sorts. *I'm sorry you have to face this.*

"Okay, fine," Jeannie snapped. "Then just how is this about me? I'm sorry Gordon's dead. In fact, it really *sucks* that he's dead, after all he did to turn his life around. But I didn't do it."

Careful, careful . . . "The thing is," Melinda said, softly enough to bring Jeannie a step closer, "he thinks *Craig* did it."

Gordon rippled with anger—as much as he could muster after his previous display, and still it slapped Melinda with its underlying pain. *"I know Craig did it,"* he growled, and as diminished as he was, Jeannie, too, staggered a little beneath his emotional onslaught.

"Oh my God," she breathed. *"This* is what's wrong with Craig. This ghost!"

Melinda breathed a sigh of relief. Jeannie might not want the truth, and she might fight believing it, but if she'd figured it out so quickly, deep down, she did indeed believe. And she did understand the significance of how she responded. Melinda nodded. "Yes," she said. "That's exactly what's wrong with Craig."

"You've known all along," Jeannie said, blame infusing her words.

"Excuse me," Melinda told her, putting an incredulous laugh behind it, "but you barely wanted to listen to me even after a grand display of Gordon's temper. Do you really think I could have approached you any earlier? The truth is, I hadn't planned to say anything to you today, either."

"*I knew it,*" Gordon muttered, and in that moment he looked more human, more natural, than he had for some time. Woebegone rather than demanding . . . perhaps even on the edge of despair.

"Why not?" Jeannie said, and she was plenty demanding for both of them. "Why not help us?"

"Because it would have sounded like *this,*" Melinda said, adopting a more confrontational stance, and asked the questions Gordon had wanted voiced all along. "What else do you know about the night Gordon died? Craig was in that area—he was *there.* Gordon remembers seeing him as he died. Gordon died of blunt force trauma to the head and Craig had a tire iron. And Gordon is very, very sure that Craig killed him."

Jeannie made an inarticulate sound, then another; her hand landed at the base of her throat and she finally found words. "You can't be serious."

"You saw for yourself how Gordon feels about it," Melinda said. "I'd say that's pretty serious."

Gordon snorted. It wasn't a polite noise.

"You can't be—" Jeannie started again, and then shook her head. "No. I'm not even going to talk about this. Craig wouldn't hurt anyone. He barely knows how to raise his voice. Are you kidding me? I don't care what Gordon thinks. He's wrong."

"Waste of time," Gordon said, and glared at Melinda.

Her hands landed on her hips. "Really? And whose fault is that? Did you ever think I might know what I was doing before you came blasting in here to play bully?"

Gordon shot her a dark glower and disappeared. Ripples of anger lapped up against Melinda and faded.

swingbatterbatter . . . ?

"You have got to be kidding," Melinda muttered, but to her surprise, that was it. The faint chorus, the feel of a question mark behind it, the hint of something unspoken but badly wanting to be said . . .

The door slammed shut.

"Not again!" Jeannie cried. "I'm telling the truth, I swear. I'm telling the *truth*!"

But Gordon's presence had faded; Melinda felt nothing of him. "I don't think—"

swingbatterbatter?

It had that curious feeling to it, that faint hesitation. A polite knock. But Melinda, caught in the middle of things, one part of her mind tangled in *if not Gordon, then who?* and another part reluctant to shut out this struggling spirit . . . She left herself open. And although she vaguely heard Jeannie's startled cry of fear and thought she heard a man's voice, she—

swirling colors WHAM! reds and black and orange-to-green WHAM! and a voice cried "Careful-carefulcareful!" and the ants streamed from the swirl and—

"I'm calling for help!" Jeannie cried, and she was close to Melinda's ear, and Melinda's throat hurt, felt strained as though she'd been screaming.

"Whoa," she said, and her eyes opened reluctantly, fluttering with the effort. "Did I scream?"

"Loudly," Jeannie said. "Are you . . . are you okay? What happened? Who was that?"

"Who was who?" Melinda put a hand to her aching head. It wasn't meant to hold that many swirling colors. And it just really wasn't meant to hold ants at all.

"That man who closed the door." She stood, brushing off her pants, and held out a hand to Melinda.

Because of course Melinda was on the floor again, and this time it wasn't nearly as clean. She should have known better than to leave herself so open to this spirit. The poor soul was trying so hard to tell her something, and she hadn't the faintest idea what. In fact, if she'd ever suspected she might have an idea, she now knew that to be wishful thinking.

I don't have a clue. She took Jeannie's hand and climbed to her feet, heading for the door. "I have no idea. I barely heard him." She cast a rueful look over her shoulder to where Jeannie stood in the midst of jumbled furniture, a little forlorn . . . a little bewildered. As if her anger had deflated in the face of so many different assaults. "This gift of mine . . . They don't always get in line. That was something else altogether—something I'm handling, but I was distracted—"

"I can't imagine why," Jeannie said, wry asperity behind her words.

"Right," Melinda said. "Totally hard to fathom, under the circumstances." She gave the door a tug. It didn't open easily, but it did open, and once it started sliding, she threw her weight behind it, pushing it all the way back to reveal the gray daylight skies.

"Thank goodness!" Jeannie ran to the door, relief relaxing her features and lifting the corners of her mouth. "I was beginning to think we were trapped in the Twilight Zone."

"Not so far from the truth," Melinda admitted. "I wish I knew . . ." *Who had closed them in the second*

*time? What exactly had happened those moments her
swingbatterbatter spirit had been trying to get in touch?*
She sighed. No way to get those moments back. "Let
me make a few quick notes here, take some pictures.
I still want this washstand and a few other things,
but we'll definitely call it an afternoon."

"I think I'll just wait outside."

Melinda eyed the informal parking area, now
empty aside from the red Saturn. The dogs barked
hysterically from their outdoor kennel, quite sensibly offended by the turn of events on their turf;
dust lingered in the afternoon air. Jeannie followed
her gaze and said, "Oh, I heard a car engine—
down the driveway there, not up close. Whatever
that was about, the guy is gone. And seriously,
what *was* that about? Because that was very real, I
swear it was—I felt the pull on that door handle, I
heard that car engine."

"I really have no idea," Melinda said, and shook
her head. She almost opened her mouth to mention the rude message scrawled on the wood-
framed double doors of the store—and then
recalled her reluctant but lingering suspicions
about Craig Lusak. So no, maybe she wouldn't
mention that incident to Jeannie Lusak just yet. "It
sounds like whoever that was is gone, but . . . keep
an eye out?"

Jeannie snorted, albeit genteelly enough. "You'd
better believe it. You'll hurry, right?"

"You'd better believe it," Melinda echoed, with feeling.

But when she got out to the SUV some moments later, she found Jeannie staring at the slashing black words scrawled along the driver's side.

Leave it alone, bitch.

9

MELINDA PULLED INTO Jeannie Lusak's driveway and turned off the engine, but neither woman moved. Jeannie, Melinda was certain, felt as wrung-out as Melinda herself. Not long after they'd discovered the writing all over Melinda's Saturn—she had used windshield wiper fluid and tissue to wipe away that too-familiar dry-erase marker, though not before taking photos with the digital camera she'd tucked in her purse—their hostess had ambled out from the house again, apparently having missed all the action in spite of the dogs' nonstop barking.

And so Melinda had acquired the washstand and a few smaller pieces, and left with the smaller pieces and the woman's phone number and the intent to return with Jim's pickup, and a private wave from the woman's husband that no one else could see.

"When they sell," Melinda said, sitting there in

Jeannie's driveway in the SUV that had so recently had *bitch* written all over it, "I'll send you a check for spotter fees."

"Or apply them against that ring," Jeannie said, but there wasn't much spirit in her voice.

"I'm sorry things worked out as they did today." Melinda had wanted to talk to her, had wanted to pick her brain about Craig's activities the night Gordon had been killed, but she'd wanted to do it in a way that would have been far, far less traumatic. That might even have left some remnant of a budding friendship. "Gordon . . . he's so angry. And he's strong, and I thought if I could learn more about that night, he might leave Craig alone."

Jeannie's voice went bitter. "Only if Craig didn't do it, of course."

Melinda offered the slightest of apologetic shrugs. "Right."

"He came home late that night," Jeannie said tonelessly—a recitation. "He'd gotten held up at the office. And he got that flat at the edge of town, and he couldn't get the lug nuts to break. And Triple A would have been a forty-five-minute wait, so he went looking for help even though he's really not comfortable in that part of town at night. He couldn't find anyone at that gas station, and eventually the Triple A guy came and changed his flat, and he made it home. He talked to me on the phone while he waited, and he sounded perfectly normal—just tired and annoyed. And his good office clothes were ruined by grease and grime, but not by blood." She looked at Melinda. "Is that what you wanted earlier? His alibi?"

Melinda forbore to point out that it wasn't really an alibi at all. It was her version of what Craig told her, except for the part about the ruined clothes. And it was rehearsed, as though Jeannie had thought about it all the way home—which no doubt she had.

But her original reaction, her astonishment and spontaneous defense of Craig as a nonviolent man . . .

That spoke to Melinda.

It was too bad things had gotten all muddled up, and so quickly, too. If she was to learn more about Craig Lusak, she'd have to find another way to do it.

But she wasn't sure that was foremost on her mind, after Gordon's display of temper. Suddenly she was thinking about the bar, and what had happened there—about Howie's allusion to it. And she was especially thinking about the way the bar—and the site of Gordon's death—were both on the way home. Often she learned things at death sites, whether a spirit meant for her to or not: their reactions, their memories, things they unwittingly shared with her, or were moved to share with her.

"He knows I'm trying," Melinda said, injecting a positive note into her voice. "With any luck, what happened out there today will sober him up a little, make him take a second look at how he's been behaving and what he thinks he remembers. If that happens, maybe he'll back off for a while, and Craig will feel better."

"But you're not saying you believe me." Jeannie looked straight at her.

Melinda had to give her credit, and felt another moment's wistfulness at this potential friendship derailed. "The truth?" she asked, and waited for Jeannie's barely perceptible nod. "Gordon needs to cross over, and that's what matters to me. I want his killer caught, of course, but there are people seeing to that, people who know what they're doing. Unlike me. So I don't really know what I think about what Gordon's saying. But for the moment, I'm good with that. I'm pretty sure it'll be clear in time. So that part . . . it's not what matters right now."

"It matters to *me*," Jeannie said.

Melinda nodded, saddened all over again. "I know," she said, and watched as Jeannie got out of the car and walked up to her front door . . . and didn't look back.

So the Whetstone Bar wasn't *necessarily* on Melinda's way home.

But it wasn't necessarily out of the way, either.

The bar reminded Melinda of an old trailer

home—old enough to be tacky, not quite old enough to be cool again, not quite put together properly in the first place. Layers of fixes and a faux stone facade had done little for it; it looked as if it hadn't quite been done right in any of its incarnations. As a whole, it was the antithesis of the things chosen for Melinda's store—things well built the first time, well loved after that.

Resolutely, she put the Saturn into park and pulled the keys from the ignition. At nearly five o'clock, there were a couple of vehicles in the parking lot, but not so many that she felt uncomfortable going inside. Especially not when one of those vehicles was Howie's little truck.

The door opened stiffly, a heavy wooden thing that looked sturdier than many of the walls. Jukebox music already played in the background, something country and loud; stale alcohol infused the air, which stirred only sullenly in spite of the fans rotating overhead. Howie sat at the bar nursing a beer and didn't bother glancing her way as she moved into the open space of the bar. Classic bar configuration—booths along the outside walls, tables in the center around the pool table, and stools along the bar itself. Signs in the back corner pointed to the bathroom, past a bevy of tables that still had chairs racked on top. No little stage for live music in this place; no classy little touches. Just a halfhearted carryover of the faux stone motif, and a brief collection of outrageous knives that had been bolted into place on the wall.

Probably a wise idea at that.

Other than Howie, the bar held only the single bartender and one other customer, hunched over one of the tables and staring at his drink with fierce concentration. And, of course, the ghost leaning on the pool table. *"Don't even start with me,"* he said, and from the looks of him he'd been around about as long as the bar. Black leather jacket, ducktail hair, cocky slouch. Melinda lifted both hands in instant capitulation, a whoa, no-problem gesture. This wasn't a place she intended to get pushy.

The bartender looked her up and down, making it obvious. "You lost?"

"Looking for something to drink," she said. "If that's all right. And looking to help a friend."

Howie's head jerked up; his eyes narrowed when he saw her. He snorted softly. "A friend," he said. "Right."

"What'll you have?" The bartender wasn't interested and didn't pretend. Not a tall man, he was nonetheless broad and strong, with very little neck and a shaved-unto-shiny head.

"Whatever you've got on tap that's stout," she said. Not that she'd do anything other than sip— not on an empty stomach, with the drive to Grand-view ahead of her. She moved up to the bar, close enough to Howie so he gave her a glare—even if it seemed perfunctory.

"You're pushy," he said.

"I didn't know you'd be here." She dug into her pocket for a five and set it on the bar; it disappeared beneath the bartender's meaty hand as he slapped down a napkin and a careless mug of beer. "I was on my way home, and I'm still trying to help our mutual friend."

That caught the bartender's attention as he tucked her five away and hesitated on the verge of pocketing the change. "You know her?"

"No," Howie said, and the change immediately disappeared forever. "Met her once, that's all."

"Maybe you can help," Melinda told the bartender. After all, he now had a generous tip in his pocket. "I'm trying to pin down what happened to Gordon Reese on his last night here."

"What makes you think anything *happened*?" The bartender pulled a damp cloth from his shoulder, swiped down the beer he'd spilled from her glass, and slapped the cloth back into place as he gave her another once-over. "You're not a cop."

"I'm not," she agreed, readily enough. "Just trying to help a friend, like I said. And from what I've heard, it seems as though something did happen here the night Gordon was killed. Maybe not something big, but something important to Gordon."

"Drink up," said the bartender shortly. "I don't have anything to tell you, and you really don't want to be here when the regulars come in."

"My mistake." Melinda took a sip of the beer, found it stout indeed, not to mention flat and stale. And though the lack of welcome here was enough to make her want to turn around and leave, she put the glass back on its napkin and said, "I'd gotten the impression you were friends."

"Yeah?" The bartender snorted, gave Howie a look that said *will you get a load of this chick?* "Well, it's too late to help Gordon. And it's been more'n a year since he spent any time here, anyway."

"He came back to say good-bye," Melinda pointed out. "You must have been important to him."

The ghost by the pool table snorted. *"They're not going to tell you anything."*

She gave him a quick glance, just enough to let him know she'd heard him. And stalling just enough to think it through. *That implies there's something to tell.* "Look, I'm not trying to cause any trouble. I'm just trying to understand Gordon—to understand his last evening, and how it affected him."

The bartender scowled at her, a puzzled expression. "What's it to you?" But Howie looked away, unwilling to meet her eyes.

Howie knew.

"Howie," she said. "Please."

"Could be worse," the ghost said. *"Could be Greg. That kid didn't have a chance."*

"What about Greg?" Melinda asked warily. No one had even mentioned a Greg before now, but in desperation, she ignored the wily look on the man's face. He smirked as though he'd be just as pleased to mislead her—or worse yet, to send her right into trouble with the already uncooperative bartender.

"Greg?" the bartender said, as if the name was surprised right out of him. "Who said anything about Greg?"

"I heard his name recently." Melinda pushed the beer and napkin around as a unit, glancing over to the door as someone else entered—a man a decade older than Howie, with hard living worn into his face. His jeans were dirty, his T-shirt had a small ragged tear, and his arms bore scratches. He sat at the end of the bar and the bartender plopped a beer bottle in front of him, popping the cap without asking. A regular, then.

"Greg," Howie repeated, bemused. "That poor jerk. It was always a toss-up who'd go first, him or Gordon. Kind of thought Gordie had gotten past that, though."

"How long did it take them to find his body, anyway?" The bartender snorted. "That dumb bastard."

"You jerk," said the ghost, without any heat behind it. He held his hand over a pool ball, idly shifting it an inch. No one seemed to notice. *"Is that any way to speak of the dead? See if I let you win another game of pool any time soon."*

"A week," Howie said. "A whole week." He shook his head. "It really doesn't seem right. There wasn't any harm in Greg. In a lot of ways, he was the best of us. Him, and then Gordie. Neither of them should have gone first."

"You're right," Melinda said. "It's not fair. It's never fair. But you can help make it easier for everyone, if you'll just talk to me."

The door opened; another man entered, looking tired and not ready for conversation. The bartender lifted a hand at him and pulled out a glass and a bottle of whiskey. And the man at the end of the bar plunked his beer bottle on the wooden surface and snorted. "What are you, a reporter or some sort of do-gooder church lady?"

"Just someone trying to help a friend," Melinda responded, but she didn't look away from Howie as she spoke. The place was beginning to fill; she wouldn't linger much longer.

swingbatterbatter?

No, she thought, and shook her head ever so slightly, steeling herself in case he tried harder. "Not now."

"Busy in here," said the pool table ghost, ever so

dryly. He flicked a match with a thumbnail and lit himself a cigarette, more interested now.

No kidding, it was busy. She half expected Gordon to show up at any moment—and thought it interesting that he hadn't. If he was truly avoiding this place, then she could be right about the significance of what had happened here that night.

"'Not now' what?" Howie repeated, bewildered. His gaze flicked toward the pool table, furtively searched the air around him.

Oops. "I'm not giving up on my friend, not now," Melinda said. "Something happened here that night, I'm sure of it."

"Just plain nosy, then," the man at the end of the bar said. "You know, we come here to relax. We work hard and we come here to let go of it all. We don't come here to answer your questions. This is *our* place, lady. You don't belong here." He didn't shift in the chair; his hand remained relaxed, loosely curled around his beer. But he looked at her from beneath his brow, and he looked as though he meant it.

She took a deep breath and then a deliberate sip of her beer, which she pushed back slightly as she set it down. Another step and a half, taking most of her determination, and she stood right beside Howie, turning her low words into a private conversation. "I know you saw something," she said. "Just like I know you see things all the time. If you help me, I can help Gordon. And I just might be able to help you, too." She couldn't begin to do anything about his gift of perception, but she could explain it. Put it into context. Maybe change the way he looked at it. Maybe change the way he looked at his life.

For an instant, he met her gaze, his own eyes full of confusion . . . until they hardened, and he muttered, "I don't need your help." And then, louder—deliberately louder—"You need to go."

She nodded. "Okay," she said. "I'm going. But I'm not giving up." She turned, again quite deliberately, and left the bar. Not hurried, not rushed, but feeling their gazes on her back every step of the way. She reached the door much too slowly for the atavistic instincts urging her to flee, and still she forced herself to open it as though surrounded by an aura of calm.

And then, outside, she sighed deeply with relief, and said out loud, "Those were your *friends*?" just in case Gordon was there and listening. He made no response. Then again, she supposed she wouldn't respond in his place, either. What was there to say? And if he'd been watching, if he'd been expecting more of them . . .

"Well, there's a reason you left that life," she muttered, digging in her purse for her keys. She still had time to make it home for a late dinner, and this parking lot was filling up fast.

She stopped digging. Hand in purse, she froze. For there in the parking lot, not far from her own SUV, was a cream-colored old GMC. "Okay," she told herself. "No big deal. The new guy at the B&B stopped by for a drink here. Coincidences happen." But still it put a chill in her spine—a chill that only intensified when she unlocked the Saturn and slid behind the wheel, and her view through the window—gone unnoticed upon arrival, when she was so focused on the bar itself—turned out to be the road stretching toward town, the ratty little gas station, and just before that, the unofficial parking area beyond the small and empty former bait store.

The spot where Gordon had been killed.

He is out in the cold spring night, awkward on the ground, the stars fading into the night sky above. And there's Craig Lusak, wild around the eyes, tire jack in hand, looking over his shoulder, jogging away . . .

"Ah," she said softly. "So you *are* here." But he didn't show up, didn't say anything. Just that blink of memory, an interruption in her own thoughts.

Overhead, the gray sky was so full of imminent rain that she could just about taste it, but the gloom made it seem later than it was. She still had time. A moment or two. So she stuffed her purse down into the passenger foot well and got back out of the Saturn, glancing over her shoulder at the bar as she locked the door. Jukebox music swelled as someone else entered; two young couples traded smokes at the front edge of the parking lot. No one gave her a second glance. She headed off down the road, steps purposeful.

It took only a few moments to pass the old bait shop—little more than an old wooden shed with a prop-out window, something that had once taken advantage of the traffic to the little pond nearby. Beyond was the garage, still open; the bay door stood propped open and a small beater sucked up gas at the pump. And there, in between, crushed gravel washed out to hardscrabble dirt, a few desultory weeds flattened by the weekend overflow parking. Bits and pieces of yellow crime scene tape, escaped to the wild.

No one had washed away the blood.

He rotates his shoulders inside his leather jacket and strides confidently into the night. Away from the bar, past the phone booth that hasn't worked for nearly a year, past the bait shack and, just before the garage on the corner, he arrives at the wide gravel lot that serves as unofficial overflow parking for the Whetstone. None of it is lit, of course—not even the gas station after hours.

He catches the scent of beer and fresh cigarette smoke layered over old. Gravel crunches; movement flashes in the corner of his eye. He turns just fast enough to see a blur slashing toward him.

The world tips; it stops making sense. A blur of movement, a grunt of effort, a wet, sickening thud and then the stars overhead, blotted out on one side by the warmth trickling into his eye.

A long, long moment in which he is utterly alone, utterly baffled, utterly unable to understand what has just happened. A longer moment in which he begins to realize he is dying, and there is nothing he can do about it.

She couldn't feel her left side; she couldn't move it. The gravel bit into her shoulders, just as it had bitten into Gordon's.

Her shoulders.

Melinda sat up, brushed off her denim jacket, winced to find herself on top of bloody dirt and stone. "Right," she said. "It happened here. I knew that. But do you remember anything more about it? Did you *see* him?" She climbed to her feet, swiped clinging stone from the seat of her jeans. "Aside from afterward, I mean."

Silence. She wasn't even sure he remained. Lingering anger lapped against her, but it was tinged with frustration now, and she felt anxiety creep in—her own anxiety. "Gordon," she said. "Gordon, I'm *trying*. Please give me time—"

The voice from behind was droll, droll with an edge of nasty. "No wonder you don't take a hint. You're a fruitcake."

She whirled around, hand clenching over her

keys as she found the man from the end of the bar standing by the bait store, annoyed and scowling. "I'm not," she said, as evenly as only years of experience allowed. "I'm someone *trying to help*."

"Talking to Gordon?" he snorted.

"Talking out loud," she corrected. "Talking to myself." Which it seemed had only been the truth. No sign of Gordon now. It must have been very hard for him to come to this place at all. "Did you know him? Can you tell me anything about that night?"

He made a dismissive noise. "I'm new to the area. Never met the guy."

"Then why did you follow me?" She shifted the keys in her grip, easing them between her fingers—hoping they made as good a weapon as the self-defense gurus said they did. A drop of rain spatted on the ground beside her; another on her shoulder.

"Because you're messing with people around here," he said, and took a step closer. Rain hit his cheek, but he was intent on her; he didn't seem to notice.

swingbatterbatter!

The inner voice held an urgency Melinda hadn't heard before; she took it as concern—as warning. Realized suddenly that it had also been a warning in the barn, albeit one quickly gone out of hand. "Yes," she said to her unseen visitor, warily holding her ground if only because she sensed that moving would be a mistake, would trigger this man into action. "I know. But thank you."

"God, you *are* insane." And he *meant* it. She saw it on his face, then, the belief that she was less than a person, that she was *disposable*.

Fear shot down her spine. She drew on the confidence grown from years of dealing with cranky ghosts, from years of dealing with unhappy families and disbelieving friends and all those who had ever challenged and scorned her. "I'm *not*. I see things you don't," she said. Rain fell more swiftly, dampening the shoulders of her jacket. "Does that make me crazy, or you blind?"

He didn't hesitate. "It makes you trouble."

"Okay," she said, not about to argue with him. "Well, I'm leaving, so that takes care of that."

"Does it?" He asked as though he expected an answer.

"You're scaring me." She said it bluntly, trying to shock him out of his dangerous mind-set, the speculative look on his face. When he glanced over his shoulder to check that no one else was around, her hand clenched around the keys. She searched his face, trying to understand how things had suddenly gotten out of hand—and memorizing his features. Hair short on top, tight at the sides and back. Features a little too strong for that stark style, his nose dominating his face, his eyes a little too small and yet their intent far too clear, even in the gray light. Even in the rain. "I don't know you. Why would you even talk to me like this?"

He took a step closer. Rain ran down his temple, down the side of his nose. "I heard Carol crying," he said. "And still here you are, asking questions."

"All right, that's enough. I'm scared and I'm wet. You've done what you set out to do, okay?" She tried hard to keep the tremble from her voice, but now she was cold, too, and couldn't help it. "I'm leaving now." She put on her best matter-of-fact I'm-unstoppable face and struck out for the gravel shoulder, not far away and suddenly somehow representative of safety—even though she wouldn't truly be safe until she was behind the wheel of the Saturn, her foot pressed firmly to the accelerator, the heater blasting warmth at her, and the headlights aimed at Grandview.

She thought she was going to make it. She really thought she was going to make it. It was a last-minute thing, the way his hand shot out to grab her arm, and she startled and cried out, and her boots skidded on the wet gravel as she jerked against his hold. She turned on him with her eyes narrowed and mouth gone flat with pure determination. "Let me—"

Gordon rushed past. Gordon speed-jerked his way around the man, crossing through the juncture of the cruel grip on her arm; she felt the cold fury sink into her bones and so did the man. He snatched his hand away from her. "What did you—?"

"It's not me," she said, close to tears that things had come to this, that Gordon had taken up his anger again—and close to tears from the fear and relief battling it out in her chest. And now she couldn't even run, because she had no idea what Gordon would do to this man—what he *could* do to this man.

Because he came around again, nothing more than an acrid blur in the rain. Melinda hesitated, keys still at the ready but cold enough and scared enough to turn into a one-person huddle at the edge of the parking lot. She could see the reassuring red presence of the Saturn only a couple hundred feet away at the bar; the road ran beside her in a dark wet ribbon of asphalt, bordered by trees . . . and empty of traffic. No help there, not even so much as someone to dial a cell phone on the way past. She shivered as Gordon brushed past her and barreled straight through the man who would have . . . would have . . .

She didn't know what he'd had in mind. She didn't want to know.

The man doubled over at the impact of Gordon's energy—so full of anger, so hungry for revenge— and grunted as Gordon whipped through him again, and again, until finally the man dropped to his knees, stunned and bewildered, his aggression turned to pain.

"That's enough," Melinda said, hardly convincing through chattering teeth. Her jacket had soaked through; rain dampened the shoulders of her shirt and trickled down along her collarbones. "I mean it! That's enough, now! You're going to kill him!"

Gordon stopped—mere inches from her, as she'd grown to expect; she faced him as squarely as she could, with her arms crossed over her chest, hunched against the rain, tendrils of hair escaped from her ponytail and now plastered to the sides of her face.

"Would that be so bad?" he said. *"This one's never going to change. You can see it in his eyes. I think I should know . . . do I know?"* He shook his head sharply, dismissing that moment of question. *"He's cruel, and he likes it. At least I was never that."*

"So don't be it now," she snapped, knowing she shouldn't, but unable to stop herself.

"How did you . . ." the man whispered, looking at her with fear—blaming her for his pain.

"I *didn't*," she said, snapping at him, too. "But maybe you should keep it in mind next time." And before he could get up, she hurried down the road—quick steps at first, and then a jog, glancing over her shoulder to see that although he had climbed to his feet, he wasn't following her. He merely stared, still looking stunned, at the dark bloody gravel at his feet.

"Thank you," Melinda breathed, reaching her SUV, her key ready and fumbling but finally sliding into the lock.

A cold shiver washed over her, separate from the chill of the rain—bone deep and lasting. *It doesn't change anything,* Gordon said, nothing more than a voice in her ear. *I want Craig Lusak.*

"You want your *killer*," Melinda corrected him, yanking the driver's door open and diving inside, jabbing the key at the ignition and missing several times with her numbed fingers.

But she got no response, and she found that most chilling of all.

10

JIM DRAPED ANOTHER comforter around Melinda's shoulders as she curled up on the couch, looking smaller than he'd thought she could. "There you are," he said. "One warm shower, one mug of hot chocolate, the heat turned up, and every spare blanket in the house right here on this couch."

"And the fuzzy socks," she said, displaying one besocked foot, not to mention a lovely turn of ankle. "The fuzzy socks are crucial." And still, she pulled the comforter around her, layering it over the quilt, the knitted shawl, and the blanket he'd filched from the guest bedroom. Rain pounded steadily against the roof, pinging off the windows and splattering out of the gutters in a way that warned him he'd be up on a ladder soon enough, clearing blockages. She said, "I'm not sure I'll ever be warm again."

Looking at her face—pale and pinched, her

hair still damp from the shower—he believed it. Her lower lip still looked as though it could fall back into trembling—into that hurt look he'd do just about anything to prevent. To fix. "All right," he said. "I've had about as much of this as I can stand."

"What?" She looked at him with surprise, and maybe even a little alarm.

"I've reached my limit," he said. "You know, that point where the Guy Fix-It overdrive kicks in, and there's nothing I can do to stop it?"

"There's nothing you can do to fix it, either," she pointed out, far too sensibly. "Until Gordon knows who killed him—oh!"

For by then, his meaning had become clear—hard to avoid, in fact, as he scooped her up off the couch, blankets and all, and reversed himself to sit in the spot where she'd been, pulling her in on his lap. Suddenly the rain against the windows made things inside seem cozy.

"Ooh," she said, and settled in against him. "If this is your Guy Fix-It, I like your style."

"For now, it is. I won't guarantee that I won't go caveman if things keep up as they've been. What were you thinking, Mel, to go to that bar? Alone?"

"I was thinking it was on the way home, and I had questions to ask, and that this is theoretically a civilized country. And really, they weren't that bad. Not friendly, but hey, at least they were up front about that. It was afterwards . . ." She trailed off and shivered, and she suddenly felt fragile in his arms. Girly and fragile and vulnerable in ways he didn't even want to think—

"Hey," she said, mild complaint in her voice. "Gotta breathe, here."

He eased his hold on her. "Sorry," he said, resting his chin against the top of her head. "Involuntary caveman thing."

"And that's okay," she said, more agreeably than expected. "As long as it's just every once in a while." She snuggled closer to him, her face tucked into his neck, and breathed deeply. "Mm, you smell good."

He snorted. "I can't possibly. Only one of us has had a shower, and it wasn't me."

"That's okay. I've been wet enough for both of us." Her lashes, long as long came, tickled his neck—but oh yeah, in a *good* way.

In a *really* good . . .

Oh, but he wasn't that easy. "Hey, I may have some caveman peeking out, but I'm not entirely primordial. That changing-the-subject ploy is pretty transparent."

She released a sudden sigh. Damned if that, too, didn't feel good on his neck. "Darn. But good try, don't you think?"

"Excellent try. Effective, if not successful." He pulled the tangled blankets into some order, covering her fuzzy sock feet. "So who was this guy, anyway? What was his beef?"

She stilled against him, growing more thoughtful. "Someone who knows something, I think."

Instant alarm gripped him—he could see well enough where that line of thought would lead. "You're not going back to find out!" he said, the words blurted out even though he knew they were a mistake. Melinda Gordon was the boss of Melinda Gordon.

But when she pulled back to look up at him, she wore a wry little understanding smile. "No," she agreed. "Not alone, anyway." She found the damp ends of her hair, drew them together, twisted them slightly. "You know, it's the strangest thing. My other ghost warned me. You know, the one who's having such a hard time coming through? It's as much as he can do to repeat his *batterbatter* mantra in a different tone, but there he was, trying to warn me."

"His timing was a little off," Jim said, unable to keep the darkness from his voice as he recalled the moment when a sopping wet Melinda had tumbled into the house and into his arms, and shivered and choked around telling him what had happened at the bar and at the antiques barn before that.

"I'm not sure I would have understood, anyway," Melinda said. "Now I get it, though. Now I can see the compromise he's reached, for now, with trying to communicate. But you know, I've been thinking these spirits weren't related at all. Now I wonder. Unless it was just coincidence that he was there—both times—and he tried to warn me when he saw . . ." But she shook her head as her words trailed off. "That's hard to believe. He's just not that connected with us."

"Payne didn't have anything to say about what you've seen?" Not that Jim was entirely keen on Payne's growing involvement with Melinda's work. A brilliant man, a quirky man, a man crucial to some of her recent successes . . . but a dependable man? Jim wasn't so sure. And he got the distinct impression that all that quirky brilliance hid something brokenly dysfunctional, and damned if that didn't bring his own caveman right back out to play again.

Melinda, though, hadn't noticed his reaction. Small favors. "Not so far," she said. "I've been hoping some new element would come up—something he could work with. But really, it's just been more of the same. Gordon's mad and acting out, and my other guy still doesn't even have a name." She looked at him, sudden hope in her expression. "I don't suppose you've heard anything about the police getting any closer to an arrest?"

Reluctantly, he shook his head. "There's talk, but it's not promising. It was an impulse crime, probably took a matter of moments; the killer took the weapon with him. No witnesses, not a heck of a lot of evidence. I think they're hoping someone will come forward. That's why they're giving so much to the press on the human interest side of things."

"Hm," she said, thoughtful but with an edge of frustration. "And Jeannie said Craig couldn't possibly have done it, and anyway she'd seen his clothes—no blood. And still, you know—there he was, right at the scene. Gordon did see him. And there he was, too, right at the store when we got that hate graffiti—" She sat suddenly straighter. "But wait! He wasn't at the barn!"

Jim kept his silence, just met her gaze when it suddenly went stricken. He wasn't going to be the one to say it out loud. And so Melinda finally did. "But Jeannie was there. And she went out to the Saturn before I did. And she knew by then that I have concerns about Craig . . ." She stopped, pulled her hands from the blankets to cover her face. "Oh! I *hate* this! How can I even be thinking that?"

"You like her," he observed, finding the grief in her expression and guessing it came from *what could have been.*

"I think she could have been a good friend." Melinda didn't yet remove her hands. "She's got a great eye for antiques, and she's as nice as anyone I know, and she seems like a good person going through a hard time. I want to help, not *add* to her trouble!"

"You know," he said, struggling a little to balance his protective nature with the understanding of how Melinda felt about this whole complicated business—caught up by her earthbound spirits, as tangled as anyone in the living world, obligated to do her best by everyone—"maybe it's time to take what you know to the police."

She stiffened; her hands dropped to her lap. "I can't risk that yet." Her voice rose slightly at each word, grew more tense right along with her body. "I can't be known as the psychic weirdo ghost hunter. I just *can't*."

She wasn't any of those things. He knew it; she knew it.

But no one else would understand. They knew that, too.

11

WITH BRIGHT SUNSHINE returned, the square all full of green and bright color and good-morning smiles, a night in Jim's arms behind her—*what a difference it makes*. She'd figure out this mess with Gordon and Lusak somehow. Melinda hummed to herself as she approached the shop door, juggling the keys, her laptop bag, purse, and the still-warm croissants she'd brought in to share with Delia—the better to nibble with honey, of course.

"Here!" Delia ran up behind her, breathless and amused. "Let me get it."

Melinda dropped the keys into her hand, still jumbled. "Thanks—and good morning to you, too!"

"I guess there's still some spry left in these bones," Delia said, and made a face at herself. But she stopped suddenly short, and Melinda stopped just as short in response, puzzled until she followed Delia's gaze to the door.

Broken glass.

A gaping hole showed in place of the left-side door pane; glass littered the floor inside, scattered and crunched and quite obviously walked upon.

"Open it!" Melinda urged her.

"Shouldn't we wait, maybe call the police—"

"Yes," Melinda said. "But no! I need to see—"

The damage.

Delia finally managed the keys and pulled the door open. "You look, I'll call from out here."

Melinda walked carefully through the glass, crunching the smaller pieces anyway. Her arms tightened around the stack made of her laptop, purse, and croissant bag, and she hesitated in the center of the store, taking it all in. Shelves tipped over, clothes scattered, lamps tipped, and furniture askew . . .

She had to close her eyes against it. And realized, when pain shot up her arms, that she was clenching her armload too tightly. So she took a deep, determined breath and marched into the back room without even looking, depositing her things on the chair at the work desk. A quick glance around reassured her that the back room had gone untouched—she hoped the same for the downstairs storage—and she steeled herself to return to the sales floor.

It was just as bad the second time around. She had the fleeting thought that it looked like some-

thing Gordon would have done in a fit of anger—
and in that moment felt relief, for as problematical
as Gordon was, at least he was a known factor—
and then realized that of course Gordon wouldn't
have broken the front door to get inside.

So no. This was something new. Something unknown.

Melinda resisted the temptation to right a fallen
lamp. The scents of lavender, cloves, and vanilla
drew her attention to the lotions—broken jars,
there—and as if her earlier passage had released
it from stasis, one of the fragile glass ornaments
tipped out of the old clawed tub and smashed on
the floor. She winced.

Delia peered through the door. "They're coming. Hey, this doesn't look so bad . . ."

"You're kidding, right?" *Not so bad* wouldn't
have her stomach feeling this sick, or her hands
this cold.

"No, seriously. Look at it. Everything's topsy-
turvy, and yeah, some little things are broken, but
mostly it's just all stirred up." She shook her head.
"I have to say this much—working for you is never
boring."

Melinda didn't need a decoder to read between
those lines. "Oh, but this isn't part of that. At least,
this was done by very living, very human hands."
She gestured at the gaping hole in the front door.
"I have to admit, I did think of it, especially with

Gordon's recent behavior. But spirits don't need a doggy door."

Delia looked blankly at it for a moment and then laughed weakly. "Right. I guess not. So, just your random vandalism, then?"

"I'm not so sure." Melinda eased over to the counter, careful to avoid touching anything. The register was open, but Delia had no doubt left it that way—open and empty, with the tray carefully secured inside the safe in the back. The counter had been cleared of everything else—she could see the keepsake box on the floor just beyond—and she frowned at the marks on the otherwise gleaming marble surface, her steps unthinkingly growing quicker until there she was, looking down on a familiar message with that sick feeling in her stomach growing heavier by the moment.

Thick black marker, slashing letters, ugly words. The entire counter covered with it—not a single message this time, but words as jumbled as the store. *Bitch stay out of it nosy get out die!* Words so ugly she only let her gaze skip over them, blinking fast and hard.

Who?

Who had she threatened with her questions about Gordon? And *how*? At the time of the first message on the shop door glass, she'd spoken only to Lusak and Carol's family. And the Donovans lived a town away, while Lusak . . .

Worked here.

But *why?*

"What?" Delia said. "Melinda, what is it?"

Melinda spun wordlessly on her heel, scrambling into the back to grab up the hastily stowed cleaning supplies—always at the ready this past week, with the constant reappearance of hand and finger and nose prints—and returned seconds later to swipe the cloth broadly across the marble and *let it be that same dry-erase*—

"Melinda, what are you *doing?*" Delia's voice rose with incredulity. "That's evidence!"

Not anymore. She stared at the cleaned counter, and then just as swiftly stowed the rag and the spray she hadn't had to use. Why would anyone use dry-erase markers for vandalism, anyway? Vandalism was meant to make its mark—to damage. To hurt.

Convenience. They were something close to hand.

Impermanence. Because whoever this was wanted to make a point—but didn't want the evidence lingering around. *No more than Melinda did.*

She returned to the door, slipped outside to wait with Delia. "I know," she said. "I know it was evidence. But I don't want the police to know about it—not this, and not the writing on the door last week." She met Delia's disbelieving gaze head-on. "You have to understand, Delia—they're going to want to know what I'm supposed to *stay out of*. What I'm being nosy about. Sooner or later it'll get around that I'm asking about Gordon Reese. Sooner or later it'll get around *why*. And don't get me wrong—if this was something I had to face in order to help Gordon, I would. But I'm not sure it is. And it's a risk I can't take. Not yet."

Delia's expression softened slightly. "That sounds like the voice of experience."

Old hurts, still so fresh. Melinda blinked them back. "It is. Still, if it reaches the point that I really need to tell them, I will. Can you trust me on this?"

The nice thing about Delia—she wasn't a yes-man. She didn't just nod; she gave it an obvious moment's thought and *then* she nodded. "All right," she said. "If that's the way it needs to be."

"Besides, I have pictures of the first two—"

"Two?" Delia interrupted, her arched eyebrows climbing.

"Ah. Right. Yesterday, when I was antique hunting with Jeannie. *After* Gordon crashed the party. Before I bought the most gorgeous washstand you've ever seen. Busy day."

"Good," Delia said. "You'll be able to keep me entertained while we're cleaning this mess up." But her expression changed, and though Melinda correctly guessed someone was coming up behind her, when she turned, she was surprised to find it wasn't, after all, the officer they were expecting.

Craig Lusak approached; he had a carryout container of coffee—three cups—and an uneasy expression.

And Melinda thought, *Oh my God, it would be so much easier if you didn't show up right on the spot every time we discover we've had a visit from the dry-erase guy.*

Especially when he had the most to lose from the truth, if Gordon remembered correctly.

"Good morning," he said. "I'm not so sure about my timing here."

Exactly.

"We've definitely got a thing going on," Melinda said, nodding at the broken door glass. "Not that coffee isn't always welcome."

"Whatever your reason for stopping by, I think it's excellent timing," Delia proclaimed. "Who knows when we'll be able to break away for a coffee run, once the police get here?"

"The police?" Lusak said, looking at the broken glass but apparently not beyond. "Is it that bad?"

Melinda kept her voice matter-of-fact. "Pretty much trashed."

Lusak, already off balance, looked stunned. "Here in Grandview?"

"That about sums up my reaction," Melinda said. "At least it's mostly just a mess. We lost some stock, but I don't think any of the big pieces were damaged."

Lusak looked past her. "And here come the police. I guess I'd better come back later. If you don't mind? I'd like to talk."

Jeannie must have told him about her day. *All* about her day. "Sure." Melinda accepted the coffee with a grateful nod and put their conversation off with regret. Interesting that Jeannie had been open with him; she, at least, truly did believe in his innocence. Interesting that Lusak had come to her—not in anger, but with some anxiety. Bringing gifts of coffee, at that. His timing might be rotten, but if he'd meant to throw her off balance . . .

Well, good job.

And though Delia looked to be lost in nirvana with her first sip, she'd been paying a little more attention than that. "He sure wasn't interested in sticking around with the cops here."

"Noticed that, did you?" Melinda responded— but under her breath, because the cops were indeed here, familiar faces though she didn't know the men personally. She greeted them with a weary sort of smile. "Thanks for coming," she told them. "It looks as though we had visitors last night."

And they, too, were taken aback at the extent of the incursion—not just a simple snatch and grab, not even any apparent theft at all. Someone with a grudge, they swiftly concluded. And while Melinda admitted to having done a quick walk-through to get an idea of the damage, she said nothing of her even quicker cleaning activities; nor, though her lips pressed together as the opportunity passed, did Delia.

After a cursory investigation, note taking, and examination of the store, Melinda returned to assess it more carefully—things missing, things moved. Things out of place that seemed significant. And she could truthfully say that she saw nothing of the kind. A detective showed up and they went through it all again. Detective Johnson, efficient and polite and not terribly personable. Delia was already straightening things in their wake—pulling whole items away from broken ones, clearing the area around the smashed lotions; not putting things to right so much as clearing out the space to clean the worst of it. "Yeow," she said in the background. "Close call here at the honey table. What a mess *that* would have been."

Melinda winced at the thought. Maybe the honey-tasting and snack table hadn't been such a good idea after all. To the detective she said, "You're not taking fingerprints?"

He shrugged. While she knew some of the uniformed officers of this small town from both foot patrols and Jim's association with the precinct through the fire station, she hadn't seen this detective before. He was heading for retirement and worn, and she somehow didn't think there'd be a whole lot of action on her isolated little vandalism incident.

Which was fine, because she wasn't sure she wanted there to be.

Now he gestured at the door, at the register and counter. "It's a store; how many people touch that door on a daily basis? Now, if the money had been stolen, we'd dust the register, but from what you say, nothing was taken. It's doubtful the perp even touched anything in here. Probably bashed his way through with whatever he used to break that window."

"But we'll probably never know for sure," Melinda said, feeling him out.

"You want the truth? Unless we get a rash of these, we're not likely to find who did it. Doesn't mean we won't try; we'll do some footwork, see if anyone's talking. That's our best chance."

"Well, thank you," Melinda said. "I guess I'd better call my insurance, then."

"And get that door fixed. Put bars on it, maybe. You have someone you can call for the work?"

Bars? Wouldn't that just be welcoming! "I'm sure I can find someone," she told him—and then, seeing Delia at work with the chest of drawers that had ended up on its back, she added, "Delia, wait! I'm almost done here, I think."

Johnson nodded at that and gave her his card, and instructed her to call if she had any more trouble or if she thought of anything that might be of help.

"Wow," Delia said, after he'd gone. "I guess I expected more."

Melinda pulled the phone book up from behind the counter, flipping to the yellow pages and *glass*. "I'm not sure I did. He's right. If someone had been hurt or killed, they'd be combing this place for evidence, but . . ." She shrugged. "Someone broke in, smashed things around, and left. Didn't mess with the register, probably didn't stop long enough to leave prints anywhere."

"He stopped long enough to write a love letter all over the counter," Delia pointed out. Melinda just looked at her; Delia raised both hands in capitulation. "Okay, okay, leaving it alone."

"Those croissants are still in the back," Melinda said. "Why don't you take a break, and I'll get these calls made and be ready to help. And oh! I haven't checked downstairs yet. I just assumed, when the back was clear . . . It would be awful if he took out the furniture down there."

"I'll check it now," Delia said, and promptly went to do that very thing. A moment later, as Melinda scribbled down phone numbers, her voice floated back up the stairs. "It's all good! I'm going to clean up a little."

Melinda closed her eyes with relief. When she opened them again, ready to make that first phone call—to tell Jim about the break-in—she found herself no longer alone.

Craig Lusak. Looking uncertain.

As well he might.

But not angry. Not demanding. Not defiant. That was worthy of note, too. Even if a flicker of unease did travel down Melinda's spine at being here alone with him.

His gaze flickered toward the back room and the doorway to the lower storage.

"She'll be right out," Melinda said, working hard to keep any particular meaning from her voice.

"I figured. So I'll get right to the point. Jeannie told me what happened yesterday." Craig looked more than uneasy; he looked downright unwell. Weight lost, nervousness gained. His crisp, professional look was rumpled and worn around the edges, and although when Melinda had met him not so long ago, he had struck her as a perfectly competent lawyer, now . . .

Not so much. More like the public defender no one wanted to get.

Melinda nodded. "I thought she might." She put down her pen and paper and closed the phone book. "It must have been difficult for you to hear."

"Are you kidding?" His emphatic response made

her take a surprised and wary step back, but his next words made perfect sense. "It's an *answer*. A *reason*. The doctors can't find anything wrong with me. They're starting to get that look, the one that means the next diagnosis will be *It's all in your head*. This makes as much sense as anything."

"It's an answer," Melinda observed, searching his face for any signs of the sort of man who might kill. Or who might leave scrawly notes of nastiness. "It's not a solution. Gordon believes you killed him."

"And I can't blame him. I—" Lusak hesitated, closed his eyes, and took a deep breath. "I was in the area, after all. He could have seen me."

Those words, Melinda knew, weren't the ones he'd been about to say. But she let it pass—if only because she wanted more information before she truly confronted him.

"The thing is," Lusak added, and now the desperation crept in, "I can't . . . I *can't* go on like this. If you can talk to him . . . You *can* talk to him?"

There it was—that look. The one she was used to. Part skepticism, part hope, a whole lot of bafflement. She nodded; she kept her voice quiet. "I can talk to him," she said. "Call it a gift; I do. I help earthbound spirits cross over into the Light, when they've been caught up in things left undone. Although I have to admit, it's not generally this action-packed. Gordon is a challenge."

"I was only in the wrong place at the wrong time . . . can you convince him of that? Can you help me?"

"I've been trying to help all along." Melinda came around the counter, facing him more confidently. "Out in the square—I've been interrupting him. I've tried to talk him out of what he's doing, but he's very angry. He believes you killed him, and he's challenged me to prove that you didn't."

Lusak had a blank moment. "How?"

"By finding the man who did, if it wasn't you." Melinda gave him a wry smile. "Simple, isn't it? Unfortunately, that's not really what I do. My gifts lie elsewhere." She crossed her arms, raised an eyebrow at him. "Though it would help if you'd gone to the police, told them what you saw. What you know. If you'd even go to them now."

He shook his head; kept shaking it. The unthinking reaction of someone who couldn't, who wouldn't . . . "I didn't see anything," he pointed out, but his voice had gotten tight. "I can't tell them *anything*."

"You can tell them that much. Then they'll know when it *didn't* happen. That the area was clear right at that moment."

He shook his head again, much more decisive this time. "No. I can't get caught up in that. It could cost us everything." At her questioning look, he added, "The adoption. We've been waiting so long—we've been under a microscope. You have no idea. I won't risk that. There's nothing to gain, too much to lose."

She could understand his concerns. Those words, after all, were ones she might have said herself. But he might well feel differently after more attention from his own personal ghost. "I'll keep working on Gordon," she said. "But until then, I can tell you this much. Gordon is feeding off your reactions to him—your strong emotions. If you can control those, you can keep things from getting so bad."

Lusak laughed; it sounded hollow. "You mean, if I can keep from being terrified when he's turning me inside out or making the world do weird things around me?"

"I'm afraid that's exactly what I mean." She gave him an small and rueful smile. "I know it doesn't sound like much, but it'll make a difference."

He shook his head, an unconscious gesture; his expression had gone darkly bitter. "The way Jeannie talked, I thought you could really help."

"I'm doing my best." She fought to keep the edge from her voice—and from lashing out at him, gesturing at her wrecked store. Yesterday she'd faced a bully in the cold rain, one who would have done her harm; today her store looked like this? What was that a result of, if not her efforts to help?

Trying. Not yet actually helping.

So she took a breath and didn't lash out. "I can try to see if he'll talk to you. But frankly, his mind is made up. And you know what? I've seen what he saw, and I can understand why. I can also see pretty clearly that you're not telling me something—maybe something I could use to help Gordon understand what really happened. You're a personal lawyer—you tell me. What do you say to clients who can help themselves out of a situation but won't?"

He looked at her a long moment; his jaw clenched and his lips thinned, and the extended goatee hid none of it. He abruptly turned and left, jerking the door open and striding out.

That went well.

She stared after him for a moment, then sighed deeply, pulling her thoughts back to the store and to the list of phone numbers awaiting her.

"Wow," Delia said, appearing just inside the doorway to the back and stopping there with the croissant bag in hand, her lack of momentum making it pretty clear she'd done nothing more than bring herself into view from lurk mode. "That was intense." She made a vague gesture that encompassed herself and the doorway, setting her bracelets to jingling. "I thought it'd be better if I just waited."

"Good choice," Melinda agreed. "Take a break. I'll make these phone calls and then we can dive in together, decide if we need to call in professional cleaners to deal with this."

"With *this*?" Delia looked around the sales floor, waved away Melinda's concern. "Pshaw. You clearly haven't ever lived in the same house with a teen-aged boy."

"In fact, I haven't." An incredulous grin tugged at her mouth. "Did you say *pshaw*?"

"I certainly did. And I trust you aren't about to say anything that will make me feel any older than I already do."

"Old? You? Oh—" Melinda found herself at a loss for words, smiled big, and said, "Oh, *pshaw!*"

That got a laugh and Delia waved her off. "Go make your calls. I'm going to eat decadent amounts of honey and gear myself up for a nice salad for lunch as karma."

Melinda headed for the back. "Mm, I might just get my appetite back." As long as she didn't really look around the store . . . or think about those scrawled threats on the counter.

Or wonder just why they'd been there.

Or what she was going to do now, with Gordon still threatening Craig Lusak, still unwilling to cross over. Even if she did take what she knew to the police, what did she *know*, really? That Lusak wasn't telling her everything, that Howie wasn't telling her everything, that one of the Whetstone regulars was awfully protective of Carol Reese, that someone else had been trying to scare her off since she'd first started helping Gordon?

A whole lot of nothing, and the police weren't likely to hear any of it. Not once they realized she'd gathered all that information in the process of dealing with an earthbound spirit.

Of course, there were Gordon's memories. But they'd no doubt dismiss those out of hand.

"I don't hear dialing," Delia called back. "I hear worrying."

Melinda laughed, as much at herself as anything else. "Right you are. Dialing now." And she did, quickly connecting with the window replacement service, the insurance, and then—scribbling a few last notes to herself in the wake of the last—finally picking up the phone to hit the autodial for Jim's cell.

"Hey," he said, but she jumped, because his voice came from behind her, and when she whirled she found him right there in the doorway, spiff and handsome in his firehouse uniform.

"Hey," she said, and held out the phone. "I was just—"

"Too late. My girl gets her shop vandalized and I hear about it through town scuttlebutt? That's just wrong."

She wrinkled her nose. "You're right. But I've been—wait. You heard about this through *scuttlebutt*?"

"First things first," he said, and came in to envelop her in a size XL hug, long-lasting and just what she'd needed even if she hadn't realized it.

"Mm, perfect," she said, albeit somewhat muffled. "Slow day for you?"

"So far," he said. "I see a busy couple of hours in the near future, though."

She stepped back to hold him at arm's length. "How so?"

He gave a meaningful glance over his shoulder; she stepped around him to peer onto the sales floor and nearly squeaked her surprise. "What?"

The shop wasn't quite full of people, but it was close, and even now someone propped the broken front door open, the better to sweep up the scattered glass. A cashier from Village Java, one of the handy Virtual Eye Cyber Café techs, a waiter from Lentos, and a man Melinda had never seen, wearing the jaunty green apron from the village outdoor market.

"What?" she repeated, this time to Delia, who handed a broom to one person and directed two others to the tipped-over chest of drawers.

"Ask your husband—they came in on his heels!"

Jim came up behind her, resting a hand on her shoulder to gently squeeze. "I'd say you're getting a taste of small-town living."

"Things like this shouldn't happen here," agreed

the familiar old man in the middle of it all—a fussy librarian who'd passed years ago and was too content wandering the stacks of his beloved town library to cross over just yet. Wrinkled and bent, he wasn't above using his practiced translocation skills to flit from this person to that, invisibly supervising.

Melinda found herself speechless for those first few moments, and then she burst out, "Thank you! This is . . . this is amazing! I don't even know how I can—"

"Do you buy coffee a billion times a day?" the young woman from Village Java said wisely.

"And fruit from the market whenever we have it?"

"And when your laptop battery ran out the other day—" began the tech from the Virtual Eye Cyber Café, and then they all talked at once—only for a moment, after which there was a general burst of laughter and they got back to work. Delia moved quickly from place to place, supervising the straightening, offering cleaning supplies, shoving a trash can into the middle of the room. And Melinda found herself suddenly accosted by a woman with a gleam in her eye and a carousel horse doorstop in her hands. "How much is this?" she said. "It didn't take any damage. My grandaughter . . ."

"That's painted cast iron," Melinda said, easily falling into the enthusiastic discussion of her wares.

"It's from before 1920, and weighs a little over eight pounds, as you've probably figured out."

The woman made a wry face, hefting the thing. "She's more likely to use it to block her little brother *out* . . ."

"It's a ninety-dollar item," Melinda said. "But it seems to me we should have a clean-up sale today."

"Oh!" the woman said. And then to the room at large, "Did you hear that? Clean-up sale today!"

Melinda's eyes widened. "I haven't even opened the register yet—" But when she turned, she found the doorway still blocked by Jim's solid form, and she impulsively wrapped her arms around him. "I have a feeling I know who got this whole thing started."

"Give them credit," he said, quietly enough for his words to reach her ears only. "It didn't take much."

"That's nice," she said. "Really nice." Then she pulled back and gave his arm a poke. "Now, I need to get this place set up for business!"

But he didn't take her playful cue. Instead, one hand lingered on her arm, and his brows drew together ever so slightly. "Mel, about this. It's not coincidence, is it?"

She hesitated, glancing over her shoulder at the bustle of activity—at the amazing progress made in such short time—and then lowered her voice as she turned back to him. "No. There were threats written on the counter."

It didn't take him long to realize. "You didn't tell the police."

She shook her head. "It would have taken them places I'm not ready to go." And then, when he opened his mouth, concerned protest imminent, she put her fingers over it. Gently, just hovering, but enough to put his words on hold for the moment. "I *will*," she said, "if it comes to that. You know that, right?"

He tipped his head at her in that way that meant he wasn't altogether convinced.

"Look," she said, drawing him into the back with her. "I'm tackling this from as many angles as I can. Lusak knows what's going on, now—he's asked me for help. Maybe I can resolve this through him. There's something he's not telling me, and if I can get that information, maybe it'll be enough." She looked up at him, willing him to understand. To go with it just a little while longer.

To her surprise, he drew her in for a kiss. Not a laid-back Jim Clancy kiss, but a hard, possessive, lingering—

Oh, my.

"Caveman?" she asked, rather breathlessly, when he released her.

He looked at her for a long, searching moment, the battle within himself clear enough on his face.

Then he said, "Yeah. Definitely," and stepped away, leaving her room to fan herself expressively. But he wasn't about to let her lighten the mood. "Be careful," he said. "And call me if you need to."

"After that?" she said, and gave him a slow smile. "I'll find a reason to need to."

But he didn't smile back as he left.

12

MELINDA INSERTED THE register drawer with deft movements, and by then Delia had restored the counter with the phone, the keepsake box, and the pen holder—only half full at this point, but the pens would no doubt be scattered far and wide. "These people are amazing!" she said, rushing past with a new garbage bag to replace the one that had been filled already. Her cheeks were flushed, her eyes sparkled, and Melinda thought, darned if she wasn't loving it. Not the break-in, but the sudden whirl of social activity.

She scratched a note to herself—*open house at store?*—and stuck it into the keepsake box, then set about handling the sudden line of customers that formed when they saw she'd made ready. The carousel horse stop, an old sewing box, a collection of tatted table runners, and then Delia calling her away to discuss the provenance of a tidy little

steamer trunk lined with floral canvas. And then
to wince together over the jewelry display case—
self-contained wood frame, miraculously unbroken
glass cover, and velvet-lined pin board—which had
turned into such a jumble of chains and posts and
tangled pieces that Melinda reluctantly pulled it
aside for later attention.

"Oh," said an older lady, a receptionist Melinda had seen in the square, "you've got Honey Bs
honey here!"

"For the tasting," someone else added know-
ingly, and it prompted a small rush of interest in
that corner. Just as well, really, since it gave Melinda and Delia a chance to step back and look the
place over—and to exchange surprised glances at
how much had been done.

"Really," Delia said, "there's just the door to fix.
Everything else is a matter of fussing it back into
place. They even got the lotion mess up, can you
believe it?"

"I need to inventory what's left," Melinda said,
and grabbed a pad from the counter, jotting down
another in the series of notes-to-self that the day
had generated. "It's the only way I'll know what
we lost."

"Oh, I'll get that," Delia said, and Melinda
looked up to see the young Village Java clerk approaching with a desktop cast-iron mail sorter.
She nodded and returned to her notes, checking

her watch—the window guy had said he'd try to stop by in the late morning—and finding her ear caught by the conversation at the honey.

"That poor Donovan girl. She's had more than her share."

And as half the group nodded solemnly, Melinda asked the question on everyone else's mind. "How's that?"

"Oh," said the receptionist. "Of course you don't know . . . you haven't been here all that long, have you?"

"Just a couple of years," Melinda agreed.

"I guess it's been nearly ten years now," the woman said. "This happened in Bayview, of course, but I've got people there, so—"

"She had a friend," another woman said— younger, about Carol's age. "We were in the same senior class. Not that we hung out, but you know how it is around here; the classes are only so big. Everyone pretty much knows everyone's business, or at least you think you do."

"Oh, wait!" A fellow from the family-run convenience store just outside the square gave a squint of thought. "That guy who was mooning over her—"

"Wasn't good enough for her, you mean," the receptionist said. "Not that he deserved what happened, but she really only thought of him as a friend."

"Yes," said the younger woman. "But you know, a good friend. He was a sweet guy, really. Just didn't have a lot of direction. He was kind enough."

Melinda couldn't stand it any longer. "What *did* happen?"

"Drugs," said a handful of people at once, even several who had been savoring a mouthful of honey and biscuit and who quickly covered their mouths with their hands, abashed.

The old librarian sat primly in a Queen Anne chair, not even crushing the velvet seat upholstery. *"The young man died of an overdose. Or rather, he died from the fall he took while on those drugs, although public understanding was that he would have died from the drugs themselves if the accident hadn't taken him first."*

"Oh my God," Melinda said. "Acid trip." That's what Payne had said, in his sarcastically flippant way. *Acid trip.*

"Why, yes," the receptionist said, although not without casting a strange look in Melinda's direction. "I do believe he had LSD in his system."

"Carol really took it hard," the younger woman said. "It's just that there was no harm to him, you know? He made a good friend, even if they were sort of the odd couple. He just attached himself to her in eighth grade, and really, they never paid much attention to what the various cliques said." At Melinda's puzzled expression, she said, "You know—Carol was a cheerleader, and Greg was a slacker. Not much crossover there, generally."

"Lady and the Tramp," someone suggested, and that got a gentle round of laughter.

"This must be just terrible for her," Melinda realized. No wonder her family was so uptight, so protective.

"You know," the librarian said, rather pointedly, *"Your basement here is* full *of old books—all those boxes you got from the library archives. Perhaps you might feel inclined to dust off the yearbook collection you've got there. . . ."* And he disappeared, as if to say that taking the hint was now entirely up to her.

"Yes, exactly," the receptionist nodded, talking right over the librarian. "It's no wonder she moved back home, or that the family has closed in around her."

"They thought all that press would help flush out witnesses," the convenience store man said. "But I don't think it's done anything except keep Gordon's death right in the Donovans' faces."

"That boy pulled off a miracle with himself," the receptionist said. "I never would have believed it. He and his friends were notorious young men— *especially* Gordon and that young man who went upstate."

Melinda almost missed the reference. "Upstate . . . You mean, to prison?"

She nodded. "You see? That's the kind of boys

they were. That's what Gordon managed to turn around, once he connected with Carol."

"I had no idea," Melinda said. "I mean, obviously, I read the papers. But I didn't realize the extent of the changes Gordon made."

The younger woman sighed. "It really isn't fair."

They all chimed in at that, and then the receptionist looked up at the bookshelf with its nostalgic collection of children's books and the late nineteenth-century doll tucked in at the end and went, "Oh!" and the conversation shifted to the little finds they'd all made during the course of cleaning. Three shoppers came in the front, laughing and chatting and then stopping short at the sight that greeted them. "Duty calls!" Melinda said, breaking away from those who still hovered around the honey table and going to greet the new arrivals—to explain the circumstances and invite them to join in the impromptu gathering.

But she didn't linger on the sales floor, not any longer than she had to. She caught Delia's eye and tipped her head toward the lower level, her brows raised in question, and Delia didn't even break patter with the customer in hand as she lifted her chin in acknowledgment.

And so Melinda slipped away, all the way downstairs into storage. Because she didn't want to be interrupted, and she really, really didn't want to get caught—not by a customer.

"Greg?" she said, hovering at the bottom of the metal stairs and then sitting on the bottom step, just in case. "Greg, are you here? Is that you? Have you been drawn out because of what your friend Carol is going through? Because if it is, I under-stand a little better now. Maybe I can help you." And for Greg's sake, as well as Gordon's, she now knew where to look next. *Those yearbooks.* If she could find a picture of him, get his full name . . . get more details about what happened . . .

But the storage area was silent around her, aside from the creaking of the floorboards from the store above.

"Greg?" She fought to keep disappointment from her voice. It didn't mean she wasn't right—only that this struggling spirit wasn't currently in a place where he could hear her.

But then she heard it. Quiet . . . sad . . . ques-tioning. *Swing, batterbatter?*

"Yes!" Too early for celebration, but she couldn't stop the surge of excitement at this accomplish-ment for the spirit who'd tried so hard to com-municate. "I'll find out more, Greg. I know this much—it's been ten years since you died. A long time. It's not surprising that it's taking you a while to pull your energy together, but please, don't stop trying. I can help you; you can cross over, I know you can."

Not far away, near the old brick wall with the

thick timber supports, the air thickened. It swirled, rather like the swirl in her mind; Melinda wrapped her hand around the stair railing post, just in case. But reality didn't sweep out from beneath her; Day-Glo stench didn't wrap its tendrils through her thoughts. The air thickened and colors stirred within and the odd bitter stench came to her from her nose and not her mind. "That's good," she said. "That's great! Your name is Greg. You're here because your friend Carol is grieving, and she's thinking about you again. I'll find out more, but I know this much: ten years ago you died in an accident while overdosing on—"

SWINGBATTERBATTER!

The angry words smashed at her from inside and out; she cried out in dismay and clamped her hands against her ears, instantly knowing that she should never have released her hold on the railing post, for the dark ethereal mist sucked away with an almost audible sound and Greg, losing control, ended up back in her head—the smell of colors the taste of legs against her skin the *bite bite burning bite* to her bones—

"Stop it!" she cried. *"Stop it,* Greg!"

Gone.

Utterly gone.

Wow. *That* was sweet, gentle Greg? The spirit who'd tried to warn her about Gordon in the barn and about the man who accosted her in the parking lot? The spirit who, after his own shattering death, had been drawn to awareness by the distress of the young woman he'd once loved?

"Melinda?" Delia's voice floated down the stairs; from the sound of it, she was just inside the back room.

Which meant she'd heard something from the sales floor. And so had the others. "I'm fine!" she called, hasty words of reassurance. "I slipped on the stairs, that's all!"

"You're sure?"

"Totally. Completely. I'll be right up!"

But only after she sat for another moment. "I'm sorry," she said. "I didn't mean to upset you. I'll look into it, Greg. I'll figure it out."

And then she pried her clamped, whitened fingers from the rail post and stood, climbing the stairs to join the extemporaneous block party taking place in her store.

13

"Whoa." Melinda looked at the empty store, at everything subtly out of place, subtly *wrong* to her eye. But not bad . . . just something to get used to. Not to mention empty spots to fill. "I'll have to see what's ready to bring upstairs. What an amazing day!"

"It was," Delia said. "But hey, do you mind if I cut out a little early? I've got this thing tonight, and I'd planned to wear this"—she indicated her scoop-necked top, snug around her chest and shirred along the sides to emphasize her generous figure, then covered with an open sheer flowered blouse for a bit of modesty—"but as it turns out, I really need to shower and clean up before I go anywhere."

"Wow, date on a school night?" Melinda offered up an obvious double take.

"Oh, just a little thing—some friends of Tim's

are in town—and you know? It turns out that kid of mine is old enough to heat up his own dinner and do his homework without me looking over his shoulder." Delia reached for her purse, tucked away as it was behind the counter. She'd been prepared. "Bedtime—that's another story. I'll definitely be home before bedtime. So—?"

"Oh! So, go!" Melinda made shooing motions. "There's too much here to deal with before I leave, anyway. I have the feeling we'll be picking up after all this for the next week. Besides, Jim is meeting me here and we're walking over to Lentos for dinner, so I won't be much longer anyway."

"Ahh, young love."

"Don't you dare look wistful!" Melinda all but pushed her out the door. "Not with your own date planned! Go get beautiful. And have a good time!"

"Yes, ma'am!" Delia said over her shoulder, a snappy tone behind her salute. But as she reached the door, she said, "Now how—? We didn't even have any kids in here today, did we?"

"Not that I saw. More handprints on the window?" Someone had a powerfully fierce longing, to be leaving little ectoplasmic signs of his or her presence on the windows. But on the inside looking out? She still didn't get it. "Never mind. I'll get those tomorrow, too." Because, she didn't add, there was no point in cleaning them this evening. She'd probably only have to do it again in the morning.

"Okay, then . . . good night!"

Melinda waved one last time and pulled her laptop onto the counter, setting a box of yearbooks down beside it. She had a short wait for Jim; maybe she could learn something. "Greg?" she said, as the laptop booted up. "I'm sorry about earlier. It'll be okay. You'll see."

After a moment, his response—abashed and sorrowful—whispered through the room. *"Swing batterbatter . . ."*

"Apology accepted," she said, and smiled to herself. He'd lost his temper, but really, he *was* a sweet soul. It was no wonder Carol had mourned his loss.

Speaking of which . . . she looked at the phone, took a deep and bolstering breath. There was one quick way to get some of the information she needed. It just wasn't likely to be a pleasant way.

But Greg deserved the help, just as Gordon deserved the help. And so Melinda picked up the phone, and she dialed, and she breathed a sigh of relief when she recognized the voice of Carol's mother. "Mrs. Donovan? This is Melinda Gordon." Into the silence that followed, she said, "We spoke a few days ago . . ."

"I remember," the woman said grimly. "What's it going to take to get you to leave us alone?"

"Answering some of my questions would pretty much do the trick," Melinda said frankly. "But this isn't about Gordon."

Wary curiosity replaced the resentment. "What, then?"

"Greg."

"You must be kidding." The words came with more hostility than astonishment. "I'm going to hang up now. If you call again, we'll be in touch with the police."

Melinda spoke quickly, banking on the fact that most people didn't literally hang up if they bothered to threaten it. No, Mrs. Donovan wanted closure. She needed it.

After all, Melinda had heard that click of a dead line often enough over the years. Not everyone wanted to talk about the ghosts in their lives.

"If you talk to me," she said, "I'll go away." An empty promise, in truth; she couldn't go away until she'd seen Greg and Gordon into the Light—and kept Gordon from hurting Craig Lusak any more than he already had. "How much easier is that? And it means I won't have to ask Carol these same questions. I did think you'd prefer that I come to you first."

Fuming silence on the other end of the phone. And then, "*Why?* Why do you want to know these things? How can digging up our pain possibly be of any good to you?"

"I've told you why." Not the details, but this was one family who really didn't want to hear the details. Not yet. But . . . "Look at it this way. If you could help Gordon—or even Greg—find peace, wouldn't you want to do it?" Propping the phone on her shoulder, Melinda went to the Penthius search engine and typed in *greg overdose accident fatal.*

"That's a ridiculous question!"

"Wouldn't you, though?" Persistence with understanding—her best thing. "If you could?" And meanwhile Penthius came back with the polite query about changing search terms that meant *I got nothin'.*

Grandview, greg, overdose.

On the other end of the phone, silence. And then the sound of movement, and then finally the woman's voice came through lowered. Trying not to be overheard. Still angry, no doubt about that. "Of course I would. Just like I want peace for my daughter."

Penthius: *I got nothin'.* Melinda left it alone, tended to the conversation. "Exactly. And if it meant asking a few awkward questions, you'd do it anyway, I imagine."

"What do you think? I'm her *mother.*"

"And *I'm* trying to help people. I know you don't really understand that, but if you can put yourself in my shoes, and believe that I'm not trying to hurt anyone in your family . . . I'm only doing what I said all along. And if I can't get my answers from you, I'll dig them up in other ways. I'm sure it'll be harder, and it'll take me longer . . . and I can't guarantee that I won't draw attention."

More quietly yet, more angrily yet, with a little bit of quaver in her voice: "Was that a threat?"

"Absolutely not. More like full disclosure." She pulled a notepad out of the keepsake box, flipping a pen against it, biting her lip. Waiting and hoping.

"I still don't understand—"

Gah, this one was a bulldog. "And I don't think you're going to. But I need to know more about Greg—starting with a last name. And his relationship with Carol. Were they friends or more than friends?"

"Carol and Greg? Don't be—"

"Mrs. Donovan—please. I'm not judging anyone. I just need the information."

The sigh sounded like capitulation; Melinda held her own breath. But when Mrs. Donovan began to talk, she'd given up on her anger, if not the lingering threads of annoyance. "Greg Tuttle. Not a bad kid. He had a good heart. Doesn't mean I wanted to see my Carol with him. But there was never any chance of that happening."

Tuttle, Melinda scribed, hoping it spelled out as it sounded. "She didn't think of him that way?"

"She liked him a lot, she confided in him. I don't think she really saw what it was doing to him— that he'd fallen for her. He didn't bother to hide it from his friends. If you can call them that."

"Gordon was in that group, then?"

Her hesitation had a surprised quality about it, as if she'd never thought of it that way before. "I guess he was, in a way, though he never noticed Carol at that point; he always said as much, after they were together." She took a moment to think, then added, "Truth is, Greg never really fit in well with anyone. He ended up with the rough crew by default. They tolerated him, is the way I always saw it. And the way Carol saw it, I suspect, or she never would have developed a friendship with him in the first place."

"Do you know what happened? How Greg died?"

Mrs. Donovan sighed. "The drugs. It shocked us all; we knew he smoked pot and that he liked to experiment, but he wasn't an *addict*. At least, we never realized he was. Not like those other boys with their beer and their whiskey and that damned bar, never mind that they were still underage then. But Greg got into something—some horrible concoction of acid and pot and I don't know what all. And he ended up between here and there, off in the woods—the old gravel quarry. But they say he would have died anyway." This time her hesitation was sad. "I hope he didn't see it coming."

"I imagine he has no idea what really happened." Melinda couldn't keep the wry truth of it from her tone, but Mrs. Donovan didn't seem to notice.

In fact, she'd gone suddenly distracted, the phone making muffled noises as she moved it. In the distance she said, "No, that's fine, there's no need to stay over. You can start on that gutter tomorrow." When she came back to the phone, she said, musing, "It's really a little ironic, when you think about it—" and then she seemed to remember who she was talking to, and she interrupted herself, her voice growing brusque. "Is that enough? Do you have what you need to *go away*?"

"I might just," Melinda said. "And I appreciate it."

"Don't bother," the woman said, although her voice didn't grow quite as hard as it might have. "Just don't bother *us*." And she hung up.

Yup. No warning. No hesitation, no waiting for capitulation. Melinda would get nothing more from her, not for a while. She hung up the phone and pulled the laptop closer.

Greg Tuttle, she typed, glancing at one of the two watches she'd layered today; she had another hour before Jim would come off shift. *Quarry. Overdose.*

Oh, *much* better.

But the truth was, Mrs. Donovan had told her as much as she needed to know. How Carol had felt, how Greg had felt. An idea of where he'd fit into the social scheme of things. The articles she found—scant enough, with fewer newspapers on the Web ten years earlier—told her the impersonal details. The exact date, which didn't seem relevant since it had been fall and Greg had roused himself now in spring. The impressive combination of drugs in his system, when she already had a good idea what effect they'd had on him. The week it had taken to find his body, which made her wince. No one really seemed to know how he got out into that area in the first place; his beater mini truck had been found abandoned, but he couldn't have driven under the influence. The authorities concluded that he'd driven out to the area sober, found a private spot in the woods to partake, and run wild in exactly the wrong direction.

But Melinda tripped over the comment one of the interviewed high school kids had made—along with the usual bit about Greg's basic good nature, his lack of drive and goals and prospects—the puzzled side note that *no one went out there for a good time* because it was just too far from town.

"So why did you?" she murmured out loud. And then, clicking on the final search result link, she said more loudly into the empty store, "Jackpot!"

Class reunion Web page, including reunion details over the years . . . and an Absent Friends page. And there was Greg, as he looked the year before he died. "You were so young," Melinda murmured, looking at a marginally focused image of a young man caught grinning over his shoulder, throwing a hand of greeting up to the person behind the camera. "What were you even thinking? Acid and pot and PCP and Rohypnol and alcohol!" She book-marked the page; she'd print it when she got home. There might well be a tidbit or two buried in the classmate remembrances that would speak to him.

All in all, when she closed the laptop, satisfaction suffused her. And she still had half an hour before Jim would arrive; she'd pull on her work coat and get out the Prelude furniture cleaner and head downstairs to see how some of her recent acquisitions would clean up. And she still had to arrange for Jim's truck, so she could get the washstand, for which she'd already paid.

"I'm going downstairs to work for a little while," she said out loud. A golden dog hair drifted onto the counter from above; she picked it up and quite deliberately blew it off her fingers. "Anyone who needs to talk to me will find me down there."

But she had the place pretty much to herself as she pulled the work lights in close and pulled up her toolbox of old rags and cleaning gear. Vegetable oil soap for lighter jobs than the side table she planned to tackle, along with the Prelude and tools for getting at nooks and crannies and ancient caked-on polish—a plethora of old toothbrushes, quadruple-aught steel wool, a variety of plastic scrapers, sharpened dowels and toothpicks and heavy twine. She pulled out her vegetable brush, dipped it into the small cake pan of diluted cleaner, and carefully applied it to the wood, stroking with the grain.

"This is my favorite part," she said, just in case Greg was lingering. "You have to be gentle, and patient, but sometimes you uncover the most astonishing treasures. The grain of the wood starts to come through, and it's just the most gorgeous thing. I love how every piece is different." And she smiled to herself, because there, indeed, in the far corner, vaguely human-shaped swirls of color and darkness gathered and hovered and then, to all appearances, sat cross-legged on the floor. A little hard to tell, but if Melinda had to bet . . .

"I know this whole thing is upsetting," she told him, applying the cleaner to the inside of the details on a table leg and letting it sit while she worked an easier spot on the tabletop. "It's no wonder, really. It's been ten years, and I'm not sure you ever really knew what was happening."

A wash of sad wistfulness came from that corner—a careful sharing of confusion, of a wild stumbling run through the fall woods, golds and reds and browns and loud crunching noises.

"Ooh," she said, applying a toothbrush to a bit of carving on the edge. "That's better! That's so much better. I think, really, you just needed some pieces to focus on. We know you're here now because of Carol's grief, and we know what happened to you. There's really nothing keeping you here; it's all a matter of getting grounded enough so you can see the Light. I bet it won't take long."

But to her surprise, he withdrew—and though he solidified, he gave off an aura of stubborn resistance.

"I sure hope that's not about wanting to talk to Carol. Because I can give her a message when I think she'll hear it, but I really, really don't think she's in a place to—" No, that wasn't it. She felt again his sad wistfulness but nothing more. She picked up one of her thinner dowels to work on the corner that had been soaking, but stopped to look at him. "There's something else, isn't there?"

Batterbatterbatter, he said, words only inside her head. And then, with an effort she could feel and in a voice rusty and disused and possibly damaged by screaming, he said, *"Yes."*

She nearly dropped the dowel. "Greg! Go, you!" And then had to wince inwardly, because it meant she'd missed something; there was more to it than all that, and she caught a sudden glimpse of his urgency—felt it, and saw it in the abruptly increased whirl of colors in his nebulous form. But he'd done what he could for the moment, and with a blurp of surprised protest, he disappeared.

"Mel? You here?"

"Down here!" she called, and wiped the Prelude off with a rag, leaving distinct spots of glowing wood grain. She quickly covered the pan of diluted cleaner and tucked her tools away, and by the time Jim came halfway down the stairs and hesitated, she was pulling off the heavy lab coat she used to protect her clothes. "Told you having that key would come in handy." She grinned at him and hung the coat over the edge of a mirrored dresser. "And you thought I just wanted to be able to send you out to store-ish errands while I stayed all cozy at home."

"Don't tell me it hasn't crossed your mind," Jim said. "You about ready?"

"Totally ready," she said. "And starving! I'll be right up. Go check it out, why don't you? See the miracles we wrought in one day."

"You just want a last word with whoever it was you were talking to before I got here." He raised his brow in a knowing look.

"Caught," she said. "But not the least bit contrite. He's still . . . I'm not sure if he's shy, but he's struggling. So scoot."

"Cavemen do not scoot," he informed her. "But I'll see you upstairs."

And in only a few moments, she could hear him moving around up there, slow footsteps above her in the otherwise silent building. "Greg?" she asked. "Were you really through talking, or were you scared off? Because I have a few moments. He might be hungry, but he understands. So do I."

But whatever had spurred Greg's urgency, it didn't provide enough energy to bring him back.

Jim paced the store, avoiding the impulse to turn on the overheads. Even in the we're-closed lighting of a single vintage lamp in the back corner of the store, the place looked nothing like it had that morning. The chaos was gone, replaced by order; the damaged goods had been removed. The lingering and mingled scents of luxury lotions filled the air, along with the faint hint of Murphy's Oil Soap. Everything gleamed, giving off its usual tidy aura of someone cares for me. Except for the smudges on the front glass, visible only because the street light was placed just so, the sales floor bore no hint of its plundered state.

"Hey," Melinda said from behind him, her sidesaddle habit coat over her arm and her purse on her shoulder. "Looks pretty good, don't you think?"

"Looks amazing," he agreed. "You missed some window smudges. You want me to get those while you're closing up?"

"Nah. I'm just going to tuck my laptop away; no point in toting it over dinner, I'll just come back for it. Besides, those smudges aren't from this morning. Delia hasn't caught on yet—I don't *think*—but I've definitely got someone hanging around the inside of the store. Whether he wants out or thinks he can't get out or just likes to look through the window . . . haven't figured it out yet."

"He?"

"Oh, little boy ghost, definitely." She smiled at him as she pulled the laptop off the counter and found a spot for it in the whimsically disorganized shelving behind the register; she had that teasing twinkle that, well, made him smile, too. "Little girl ghosts tend to be tidier."

"You're just saying that."

She cocked her head, gave him a slantwise look. "Maybe," she said, in a tone that admitted nothing and managed to imply it knew everything.

He snorted and pretended to be immune to it. "Well, you'll figure out his problem sooner or later. It's not like you haven't had enough to fill your spirit-saving plate lately." He hesitated as she came back around the counter. "Look. About that. I don't know about you, but I've had a whole long day to think about it, and I couldn't think about anything *but*. I kept wondering what would have happened if you'd gotten here early this morning—if you'd been here when this guy trashed the place. And I'll tell you what—I keep wondering *why*, too."

She looked surprised. "Someone wants to make sure I get the message. I keep wavering between Craig Lusak and maybe that guy from the bar.

He was pretty protective." She casually linked her arm through his, as if this situation didn't have his hair standing on end, or hadn't brought her home to their doorstep shivering, soaked in tears the night before. "I think that's what he's wanted all along. And you know that old GMC that was at the Donovans'? It belongs to a man named Dave. He works there. And it was in the parking lot that night at the bar."

His eyes narrowed in spite of himself. "You think Dave is the one who came after you?"

Instead of nodding, she frowned in frustration. "The thing is, I don't know *why*. But if it's him, he's clearly invested."

"Fine," Jim said, his voice getting growly. "Then we need to make sure he understands that you've moved on."

She gave him a steady look. "Have I?"

"Mel, this guy's not playing games any longer!"

"No," she agreed, tucking herself up close. "I never thought he was. I just think what I'm doing is important. Not just to Gordon Reese, but to Craig Lusak. Regardless of whether he's guilty, about which I have serious doubts, even if the whole nasty note thing *does* look pretty bad."

"All the opportunity, none of the motive?"

"Something like that." She shrugged. "I know you just never know. But that's my feeling about it."

He slung an arm over her shoulder. "And I have

to say, you've got pretty good feelings when it comes to the people side of things."

"Hey, earthbound spirits *are* people. They've just left their bodies behind." She dug into her purse for her keys, and together they headed for the door. "Look, I hear you. I'm just not quite there yet. Because you know if I talk to the police, the investigation isn't going to stop at why this guy is messing with me, or with stopping *him*. It's going to go straight to why I've been in touch with Gordon's wife and her family."

He pushed the door open for her, then stood as she flipped the keys around, found the right one, and stuck it into the lock. "I don't get it. You've gone out on a limb before. You called the FAA last year—"

"And look what it got me! I was lucky that FAA inspector turned out to be understanding." She looked up at him. "Not that I wouldn't do it again, if I thought it would stop a plane crash. But you know what, it *didn't*. This is about putting an end to what's happening to Craig Lusak, and I'm already working on that. Besides, the police aren't likely to have much luck with it."

"No," he murmured. "I guess not. It just seems . . . you know, I don't like it. This thing with the store, it went too far."

"No argument there." She dropped her keys in her purse, lifted her head to consider the night air.

"I think I'll just brave the chill," she said, hugging her coat a little tighter. "It'll keep me moving and we'll get to the food even faster."

"I'm not sure I'm done with this conversation." He couldn't quite let it go, not at that; he led them out onto the quiet street.

She gave him a savvy look from beneath those long, sweeping lashes. "I think we can both agree that the sooner Gordon finds his peace and crosses over, the better."

A revving engine cut through the night, tinny and high-pitched; Jim stiffened, instantly glancing both ways to see where it came from. But he saw nothing, not at first. Not until a single tremendously bright halogen light burst on in the darkness, splashing directly into their faces and growing larger by the second.

"*Run,*" he said instantly, knowing that the motorcyclist had no intention of stopping. And he put words to action, springing forward—but Melinda didn't move. She stood as though mesmerized, staring at the fast-approaching headlight, her eloquent features etched in stark light and one hand slightly raised as though it could fend off the light. "*Mel!*" he shouted, and snatched her arm, jerking her after him.

"What?" she said, flabbergasted as she stumbled forward. "You mean you can—?" And her eyes widened, and she gave a little shriek, and then the tug between them lessened as she ran with him, leaping for the safety of the curb and the square beyond.

The trail bike roared past—close enough to snatch at them with its wind—and Jim released her arm to pull her in for a fierce hug. "You okay?" he asked, rubbing her arm where he'd grabbed her. "I didn't mean to—"

"No, no, I'm fine." But she sounded dazed, and she stared off into the night after the marauding trail bike, which had disappeared—although Jim could swear he heard the idle of an engine not all that far away. "I just . . . it was just so unreal, I thought it was . . . unreal!"

Understanding hit home. "A vision."

She nodded, shivered, and then looked up at him with one of those sudden bright smiles of hers that meant she'd put it behind her—or tried to. "I can't decide if I can put anything into my stomach after that. Let's go get closer to the food and see."

"What, you think that was coincidence?" He struggled to keep his voice level.

"Carelessness. Stupidity. Something like that." She had that determined sound to her voice, and when she moved out, her steps were brisk and quick, the heels of her short slouch boots hitting the pavement hard. Okay. He got the picture. She knew better, but—*not now.* She needed time to think.

He'd nearly caught up to her when that engine noise revved up again and he straightened, as alert as any man could be and yet seeing nothing, just the sidewalk leading to the central monument, flowers dulled by darkness, landscaping obscuring anything but the straightest view down the sidewalk in either direction. Melinda, too, stopped. "You don't think—"

"We need to get to Lentos," he said, not hiding the wary tone in his voice. Lentos—well lit, populated . . . and on the other side of the square. He took her hand, and if he held it a little too tightly, she didn't protest or pull away. The motorcycle revved—Jim had never considered it a taunting sound, but now he thought he always would—and the halogen headlamp abruptly painted them with blue-white light, this time bouncing eerily in the night.

Coming over the curb.

A sidewalk was plenty wide enough for a trail bike.

"The restaurant," Melinda breathed, and they took off running together, the sound of her boot heels—never meant for speed, never mind prolonged speed—quickly lost in the approaching engine noise, the bike itself still nothing more than a specter behind the blinding light. Shadows cast by that light bounced and stretched before them, growing shorter as the bike closed on them, the noise deafening but not quite obscuring the panicked sound Melinda made as she fell slightly behind, her steps uneven. He tugged her onward and then, with the engine noise filling the night and their shadows shrunk nearly to nothing, she stumbled.

Jim whirled; he snatched her up and held her close, standing against the light and waiting, waiting for that last moment when it might seem obvious in which direction he should throw them both—

And the light went out. An instant later, the bike went silent.

Melinda trembled in his arms; she gulped for air. His own breathing came none too steadily, as silence closed around them and the darkness again enfolded them. But then she pulled herself upright. She tucked hair behind her ear, and she said most definitely, "That is *not* what it means to go into the Light."

He snorted, searching over her head for any sign of the motorcyclist. "He's got to be walking it now—"

"Oh no you don't!" She followed that train of thought easily enough. "You stay right here with me! Besides, I don't think I can go another step in these heels. It's flats for me for the rest of the week, I swear." With a wary look over her shoulder, she turned her attention forward. "Look. We're almost there."

There, the other edge of the square—the street, and the familiar dark blue sign beyond, goldenrod letters welcoming, blue and white awning cheerful. Lentos, lit from within and looking busy and charming and emitting delicious aromas that just now registered on Jim's consciousness. "Okay," he said. "Dinner." And then, "But don't even try to tell me that was coincidence, or carelessness, or stupidity, or anything like it."

Somber, she met his gaze in the darkness. "I'll call Carol's mother tomorrow morning. I think she's come to terms with me. If she can make sure Dave knows I'm not a threat . . . well, if that's who it is, maybe he'll back off." Steadying herself with a hand on his arm, she stood on one foot and adjusted the boot on the other, making a face. "You know, I found some Bayview high school yearbooks in the basement today. I'd intended to look through them tonight, see what I could find about Greg—that's my *batterbatter* ghost. But I already learned so much from Mrs. Donovan, and after this day, I just want a good meal with a *really* good dessert, and to soak my feet and go to bed."

"They took a pounding, huh?"

"When's the last time *you* ran in heels?"

"Let's see." He pretended to ponder, then gave a decisive shake of his head. "That would be *never*. And that's exactly how I intend to keep it." He didn't give her any warning, then, just swooped her up, settled her in the cradle of his arms, and struck out across the street. She laughed—okay, it was a giggle, really, a young and delighted sound that tickled a grin from him.

But it wasn't a grin that lasted long. Because sooner or later, he'd have to put her down again. Even though whoever had chased them was still out there.

14

As if, after the previous day, Melinda could stop herself from getting to the store a good ninety minutes earlier than usual. She parked out front, telling herself she'd move the Saturn as soon as it came light, and ran to the store with her key out and ready, her steps cheerful in the ankle-high hiking sneakers she'd promised her feet today.

She locked the door behind her and looked the store over with a sigh of relief, and decided against turning up the heat; instead she snuggled into the thick sweater coat she'd pulled on against the early morning chill. Today, beneath the ginger-colored sweater, was a black day. Black jeans, black hiking sneakers, black sleeveless turtleneck. Hair sleek and parted in the middle, earrings high-contrast silver, more sensible and less dangle.

A deep breath brought her the pleasant scents of leftover hand lotion; she flipped on the lights and took a slow, careful walk around the sales floor, using her fresh morning eyes to inspect the details. All she found was a plethora of golden blond dog hair on her sweater, and she debated whether it was worth picking off, given that no one else could see it. "At least you've been keeping Homer busy," she muttered. And, "Give me a few days to get this stuff with Gordon and Greg sorted out. Then we'll see if we can't figure out what's up with you."

A glance at the windows showed her that her other lurking company had indeed been back during the night, so she grabbed the glass cleaner—it never seemed to be far away these days—and applied herself to the double front doors, especially the one with the blank new glass.

Satisfied with that, she headed for the back and sat down with the yearbooks, finding the year Carol and Gordon graduated and idly flipping through the pages of student photos and candids and "Senior Superlatives." She garnered little from it, other than images of Carol, Gordon, and Greg from ten years ago—Carol looking young and fresh and optimistic, Gordon with a dare-me smile and rough edges showing, and Greg distracted and a month past due for a haircut, but still exuding his own gentle charm.

"Look at you!" Melinda said, as though he might be there, lurking. "You were a cutie!" And she stopped herself from also saying out loud, "If

only you'd had a little more time to get your act together," because it wasn't something he needed to
hear even if she did suspect he would have turned
out as a perfectly nice guy. And she didn't sigh and
say, "You did it to yourself," in contrast to Gordon,
because, really, who wanted to hear that? Ever?
Never mind when whatever it was that you did
happened to have killed you.

So she put aside the yearbooks and checked
the time. Both watches informed her that it was
still too early to call the Honey Bs. No doubt the
household was up; no doubt they were busy handling their customers, breakfast, and morning
chores. She'd get a better reception if she waited.

Well, then. Time to do a little more work on
that clean-up job down below. And then she could
run over for first coffee and one of the big breakfast muffins that Village Java was savvy enough to
keep in a basket by the checkout. Later today she'd
handle the aftermath of the lunatic on the motorcycle who'd tried to run them down—or at least
happily chased them—and who'd likely trashed
her store, and never mind all the dry-erase threats
along the way.

Ironic, really. Those threats had been so easy to
wipe away, as ethereal as the spirits she was trying to
help. Maybe she'd taken them too lightly at that.

A tapping at the door pulled her away from the
stairs as she was about to take her first step down,

sending her heart into overdrive. One hand to her chest, she headed back out to the sales floor—and found, to her surprise, that Delia's son Ned waited there, looking not a little bit furtive. She quickly flipped the lock and let him in. "Ned! You're out early this morning."

"I was hoping you might be here." He looked no less furtive now that he was inside, a complicated backpack slung over still-narrow shoulders—although he did suddenly seem to stand taller than the last time she'd noticed. "I had to beat my mom here. Can I leave something for her?"

"Sure." She followed him to the counter, where he crouched down and *sooo* carefully eased his backpack to the floor, unzipping it with the care of a surgeon.

A teenaged surgeon with fumbling fingers, but nonetheless . . .

"You going to tell me what this is about?" Melinda leaned over the counter, sweater coat sleeves drawn up to the first knuckles of her hands and her weight on her forearms. She could see only the backpack, the careful fingers, the slow unzipping . . . Ned's tongue at the corner of his mouth, a childish gesture of concentration he'd no doubt be appalled about.

He didn't answer right away, not until he peeled open the backpack flap and pulled out a conical cellophane wrapper—and within that, a beautiful little rose, bright red and barely open from the bud. "I was kinda hoping you'd have a vase here."

Oh, my. "I have just the thing, in fact." She came around the counter and went straight to the shelving behind it—partly display, partly tucked odds and ends—and pulled out the delicate little milk glass bud vase she kept on hand for wildflower season. "How's this? You want me to put some water in it?"

He nodded, his concentration on the flower as he pulled away the cellophane, and when she came back, she found him ready and waiting. She pulled a little pair of scissors from the keepsake box, snipped the end of the stem away, and plunked it gently into the vase. "There you go," she said. "Do you have a card or anything?"

"No." He shook his head. "She'll know."

"Well, *I* don't know. Are you telling?"

He pondered the rosebud in its vase, moved it to a more obvious spot on the counter, and nodded in manly satisfaction. Then he returned to his oversized backpack, the zipper loud in the enclosed space behind the counter. "Well, you know how girls have friends?"

She laughed. "Well, *yeah*. Because I am one, in case you hadn't noticed. And I even have friends."

"No," he said, standing to slip the pack on so he looked like a bull in a china shop. "I mean, they *really* have friends. In that girl way. They dress the same and they like the same boys and they hold hands when they're scared, *that* kind of friend."

"Ah." She nodded. "Best friends. Best friends forever, except not the Hollywood kind where forever means five minutes just because it starts with the same letter."

"Right." He seemed relieved that she got it. "Like that. So, my mom had one of those, when she was my age. And I guess they talked about, you know, girl stuff, and things like whether they'd have families and how many kids and whatever."

"Oh?" Melinda raised her eyebrows. "And how many kids did your mom want to have?"

Ned made a disgusted noise. "She always just said she wanted one, a guy. You know, with dark hair and dark eyes and all that. You get it, right? Me. Well, she has to say that, she's my mom."

"Oh, I don't think she *has* to say anything," Melinda told him affectionately. "I think she *wants* to. World of difference there."

"Yeah, well, the point *is,* her friend went and died. Right when she and Mom were my age. So she's been all stuck in it, in case you haven't noticed."

"In fact, I have." The lightbulb went on, all right, big and bright. "*That's* what this has been about, all the business about you growing up and her getting old? Because she's not. You know that, right?"

A disgusted look this time, the sort that teenaged boys had the market on. "Puh-leeze," he said. "Do you have any idea how hard it was to beat her out of the house this morning?"

"I can guess." She nodded at the rose. "And this?"

"Today's her friend's birthday. Or it would have been." He stopped as he headed for the door, his features suddenly more animated. "Hey, I don't suppose . . . Maybe you've seen . . . ?"

"Around here?" Melinda gave a single, amused shake of her head. Ned had known about her gift nearly a year before Delia learned of it; he had readily accepted it. "Nuh-uh."

He shrugged. "Worth asking. Anyway, I thought maybe the rose would make her feel, I dunno, like not everyone had forgotten. Like it wasn't just her."

"Why, Ned Banks," Melinda said, a smile growing in spite of her awareness it would only discomfit him. "I think she's right. I think you *are* growing up."

And of course he looked away, and made a funny face, and said, "Yeah well." But when he glanced at the lightening sky out the window, he grimaced. "I'd better get out of here."

"If you don't want to be seen," she agreed. She waited at the door as he walked out and away, ready with a wave and a smile when he looked back. He gave a little up-nod of his head—again, so manly—and headed off in the direction of school.

She wandered back to the counter, positioned the vase *just so,* and then decided if Rick Payne wasn't in his office, he should be, and called.

Voice mail. Of course. Because really, who *was* at work this early except for her? "Hi, it's Melinda," she told the digital recording system. "I just wanted you to know, you were right. I mean, I know you weren't actually serious, but you were right. And if you want to know what that's all about, you can call me."

Not, perhaps, the kindest message she could have left. But anytime she could keep Professor Payne's wheels spinning, she considered it an accomplishment. He'd probably figure it out on his own at that. He had, after all, seen the vision with the ants.

Ned, it turned out, need not have worried about being caught out by his mother. Melinda had cleaned furniture, talked herself into that first cup of coffee and a muffin, and had just opened the store by the time Delia made an appearance. Not late, not by any means. And it was Melinda's own fault she'd gotten there so very, very early.

"Good morning!" Delia said, brightly cheerful. "Hey, isn't today the day you go grab that washstand with Jim? And oh, you've got a crumb thing going on right . . . *here.*" She brushed at her own chin with a hand already full of purse handles and a small gift bag and her keys; the other held what looked suspiciously like a yearbook.

Melinda swiped at her chin. "That's the plan. Jim's got some weird half-day thing going on. I'm not sure I'll ever understand the fire station shifts."

Delia gave her a wise look, depositing the yearbook on the counter. "Or he just swapped out some hours so he could do this with you and isn't making a big deal about it, because really, you two . . . Don't you know the honeymoon isn't supposed to last this long?"

"Goodness. You sure put some cheer in your Cheerios this morning. I take it last night's date went well?"

Delia didn't quite say *maaaaaybe* in an I'm-not-telling tone, but it was right there on her face—at least, before she changed the subject. "Nice to see we're free and clear of nasty messages this morning." She buffed an invisible spot on the counter with her sleeve.

"Yup, it's all good." Melinda let it hang there, waiting, and then, finally, Delia noticed the vase and the flower.

"There," she said. "You see? Jim's thinking of you."

Lips pressed together in a smile, Melinda shook her head once. "Nope."

"Well, who, then?" Delia trailed off as Melinda

waggled a finger in her direction. "No! This is . . . Someone left this for me?"

"Told him he should have used a card," Melinda said. "You can thank your son for that rose. He wanted you to feel loved today. And to know that someone else was thinking about your friend, too."

Delia gasped; her hand went to her throat and her eyes filled with tears, her cheerful morning mood abruptly hijacked by all the mom-Hallmark-moment signs. Not that Melinda couldn't relate; her own eyes stung with emotion. Delia said, "He told you about her?"

"In teenage boy language, he did. But I'd love to hear more about her, if you'd like."

When Delia spoke again, it was with obvious difficulty. "Maybe . . . not today." But when she ran her finger down the vase, she did it with a wistful smile. "But you know, later . . . that might be nice."

"Good. It's a date. Now, hold down the store for a few moments? I've got a phone call to make. Won't be long."

"Sure. I think we've got a few moments before—whoa, talk about speaking too soon!" Delia hastily stowed her things behind the counter as someone entered the store, and as Melinda escaped to the back, she overheard just enough to know the woman worked down the street and had heard about the vandalism, so had decided to stop by before work.

Take that, Mr. Dry-Erase Marker.

Not a particularly daunting name for a villain, at that. Especially not one whose vandalism had resulted in their best sales day in weeks and now looked to have some great follow-up potential.

What had happened the night before, now . . .

Totally different matter. And enough to drive her to make this phone call she dreaded. And indeed, when she had Mrs. Donovan on the phone, the woman's exasperated anger drew a big wince from her. "I know, I know," Melinda said. "But I'm not calling for the reason you think I am." And then, quickly, before the woman could reject her, she added, "Maybe you heard something about my store being vandalized yesterday."

Not likely, but it was an opening. "What does that have to do with us? If you need replacement honey, come and buy it."

"You have a man working there—Dave, you said his name was. He seems pretty . . . well, I guess I'd call him dedicated."

"And what does that have to do with *you?*"

She'd definitely used up her patience points on the previous phone call. "Just tell me this. After yesterday, after we talked—and I'm *not* calling to ask you more about Gordon or Carol or Greg, I swear I'm not—are you good with me? Do you get

I'm not out to hurt any of you or cause trouble for your daughter?"

"I might, if you hadn't called again," Mrs. Donovan said meaningfully. Then she hesitated. "Truth is, none of what we talked about showed up on any of those Web sites or in the local rag. So no, I don't get you and I don't like you and I don't want you to keep calling, but I don't have a *problem* with you. Is that what you wanted to know?" Her voice went wry and dark. "You've had a sudden attack of conscience and need us to make it okay?"

"No, not at all," Melinda said, as evenly as possible. "I need you to make that clear to the dedicated man you have working for you. And by any chance is that a dry-erase board off the side of the honey shack? With the hours posted?"

"Yes, of course it—" she started, and then stopped herself. "What is it you're not saying?"

"I'm saying," Melinda said, her words getting a little too distinct, a little too pointed, as she thought of the shop, of the motorcycle, "that it would be best if your dedicated employee understood that your family doesn't perceive me as a problem."

"That . . . that almost sounds like a threat of your own."

"I'm sorry, but it's really quite the opposite— more like a desperate request." She hated speaking around it; for someone who had grown up greeting strangers with the very direct words that their dead loved one was right *there,* it was much easier to come right out and say, *Your dedicated employee has probably been wreaking havoc here.* But as soon as she voiced her conviction out loud, the tenor of the exchange would deteriorate into denial and defensiveness. Let it stay at thoughtful and mildly confused for a while. "Anyway, I don't want to take up more of your time. Just, if you have a chance to make that clear—"

"I'll keep it in mind." And from the baffled if not friendly response, Melinda thought she probably would, if only because this confusing conversation would stay on her mind.

15

IN THE LATE morning the store activity slowed to a crawl—standard operating procedure right before lunch.

"And normal is good," Melinda said to no one in particular, at the counter making her wish list of items she'd like to see in the store. No customers, no phone calls, not even any ghosts. In particular, no sign of Gordon. In fact, she hadn't seen him since the incident in the antique-filled barn two days earlier, and she hoped he was off pondering the situation with some thoughtfulness—hoped that she might actually be making some progress there, even if she was no closer to understanding what had really happened that night. Neither, it seemed from Jim's recent phone conversation, were the police.

"It's kind of nice to have a few moments." Delia slowly turned a page in her yearbook. "Oh, look—

there I am. Six months before I learned to pluck my eyebrows and six months *after* I should have started doing it."

Melinda laughed, leaning into Delia's space to see. "You are so mean to *you*," she said, but then stopped, giving the image a double take. "Whoa. You aren't kidding, either."

"Ha. You probably have the kind of brows that grew naturally into shape."

"Something like that," Melinda admitted. "But you don't want to know about the various leg hair adventures."

"You are so wrong! I want to know every embarrassing detail!" But Delia's gaze drifted back to the yearbook, and her finger hovered over the image of the girl standing beside her in the underclassman candid. "There we are," she said. "Not long before . . ."

"She died," Melinda finished for her, softly.

"And this thing with Gordon Reese—it feels the same somehow, y'know? All that potential, just . . . cut off. I guess that drove it home."

Melinda could see how it would. "I'm so sorry. If life was fair, she'd still be right here with you."

"And now Ned is her age. It just makes me feel . . ." Delia wiped invisible dust from the page. "Guilty. And old."

"Okay, now you *are* kidding. You practically danced through that door this morning."

Delia gave her a look. "Maybe I'm compensating."

"*I* think you're learning how to live again. And I also think that's not a bad legacy for your friend."

Delia laughed outright. "Party enough for both of us?"

Melinda couldn't help but grin. "Maybe not exactly . . ."

"I swear, sometimes I think Ned's been enough of a challenge for two kids. At least two kids." She touched the vase again. "But still, he's a good one."

"Of course he is." The conversation died off as Delia flipped over to the next page, and Melinda thought, *Time to give her some space.* "Listen, it's quiet. If you can hold down the fort, I'll head downstairs and get back to the cleaning. With that washstand coming in this afternoon, we'll need the space down there. Besides, that little table will fit perfectly into that new space over by the clothes rack."

"Sure," Delia murmured, already distracted. Melinda slipped away and had her foot on the first step when Delia's voice, gone from distracted to alarmed in an instant, called her back. "Melinda, I think you'd better—" and then she ran out of words.

Melinda spun and ran back to the sales floor, just in time to see Jeannie Lusak staggering for the door with her arm around her husband's waist; even as she reached for the door, he stumbled and almost went down—his face pasty and sweating, his eyes unfocused, his hand groping for and missing the door.

And no wonder. Gordon speed-jerked around him in a manic blur of anger; before Melinda even reached the front of the store, the waves of anger and frustration slammed into her, and she, too, almost went down, taken by surprise at the strength of it. But she recovered herself quickly enough, and by then Delia was beside her, pulling the door open as Melinda ducked through to put Lusak's other arm around her shoulders. They staggered in as a trio, and Delia yanked the Queen Anne chair away from the bathtub glass ornament pile and put it behind Lusak before he fell.

Gordon took advantage of that, too, jerking through Lusak three times in quick succession, while Lusak hunched in response, groaning with each intrusion—while Gordon emerged looking stronger and more determined and a little more manic. *As if that's even possible.* In these few moments he stood still enough for a good look, Melinda found his features distorted, his eyes fiery, and his entire tone gone to burnt sepia—crisp with his emotion, edges etched into her sight. Only his wounds were in color—bright, startling red, more crimson than any true blood had ever been, permanently oozing down the side of his face. Runnels of blood dripped off his brow, trailed down to fall from his chin. The drops never landed, and the blood never slowed.

"Gordon," she said. "What are you doing? What's gotten into you?"

"Ask that question of him!*"* Gordon said, and made his point by going through Lusak one more time. The man turned such an odd shade of gray that Melinda took a quick step forward, bracing for him to faint.

Jeannie tightened her hand on Lusak's shoulders. "This has been going on almost since we went out to the barn," she said. "Since that night. Since . . . what happened in the barn that day." And she looked utterly miserable. Her tidy appearance had started to unravel—her camp blouse partially untucked, her narrow belt not quite lined up at the front of her neatly pleated pants, and that same corduroy jacket she'd worn to the barn, only this time it matched nothing.

"This isn't your fault," Melinda said, sharply enough to reach the woman.

"You said you'd help . . ." Lusak's voice came weak and wheezy.

"God, he needs to be in a hospital," Delia said. "I'm calling the fire station."

"No!" Jeannie cried, and Lusak wheezed, and

Melinda blurted in alarm, all in unison. Jeannie added, "You don't get it. Doctors *can't help*."

"Surely there's something—"

"You said *you'd* help," Lusak repeated, looking at Melinda.

She didn't give an inch, much as she felt for him. "This isn't *my* fault, either. You know as well as I do that you've been keeping something from me, something very important. If I knew what that was, maybe I could stop this. Maybe I could have stopped it a week ago."

"You told him that Gordon couldn't hurt him!" Jeannie said, another accusation, albeit a more desperate one.

Gordon appeared directly before her, and the strength of his emotions was enough to rock her back a step; she put an arm up as though to blindly ward him off. Gordon leaned in to shout in her face, his voice taking on the hollow, grinding quality of his initial days after death. *"He hurt me! Now I'm going to hurt him plenty before I take him down."* And Jeannie flinched, although she couldn't hear him any better than she could see him.

"You said you were going to wait!" Melinda said to him. She wanted to stamp her foot, she really did. "You said you'd give me some time!"

"You!" Gordon said, and speed-whirled on her. *"You're the one who told him to stay calm, stay cool,*

*to not let me get to him. That it would weaken me.
That I couldn't affect him if he didn't let me."*

Lusak lifted his head. "He did seem to wait. To
back off. And when I felt him, I did as you said.
And you were right, it worked—but only for a
while. Then . . . I don't know, I just couldn't seem
to—"

Melinda looked at Gordon's satisfied smirk, at
Lusak's defeat. "He realized what you were doing,"
she said. "He stepped things up and you weren't
prepared. You thought the strategy had stopped
working, instead of understanding that he'd turned
the volume all the way up at once. So you gave up
on it."

Dazed at the revelation, Lusak murmured,
"Maybe I did." But then he shook his head. "It
doesn't matter now; it's too late. I can't fight him
any longer."

"HA!" Gordon said, though he cast a sly, quick
look at Melinda as he did so. *"I win! See you on the
other side!"* And out he went.

Lusak slumped in the chair as though he'd truly
given up, his pulse pounding visibly at his throat,
his breathing ragged. Delia drew Melinda aside, if
only a token step. "I really think he needs to be in
the hospital. Maybe they can't stop the cause, but
they can support him while you . . ." She trailed
off, suddenly uncertain.

"While I what?" Melinda said, not bothering

with the charade of lowering her voice. "Take care of Gordon? I don't think that's going to happen."

"You said—" Lusak started.

"Oh, stop it!" She turned on him in frustration, the sweater coat flaring wide; her fisted hands landed on her hips. "You know what, you're right. I said I'd *help*. I didn't say I'd do it all. I didn't say I'd carry you. Look, Gordon's not here right now. *Tell* me what you've been holding back!"

"It's not relevant!" Lusak shouted, straightening just long enough to do it, to glare at her, and then to sag back again.

Jeannie stepped back so she could look him in the face, her hand trailing off his arm. "Craig?"

Grimly, Melinda crossed her arms—a nonverbal challenge. "If it wasn't relevant, you wouldn't have thought of it just now. And the last time we had this conversation. And probably every single time we've talked about Gordon Reese."

Lusak stared mutely at her, his jaw hard.

"*Craig,*" Jeannie said. She crouched beside him, taking his lax hand from his lap. "If there's something—*anything*—that can make a difference . . . !"

He looked away from them all, muttered something.

"You know I couldn't hear that," Melinda said.

Jeannie sent her an imploring look. "Please," she said. "He's had such a hard time. I know this is frustrating . . . I know you've been trying. I couldn't have been in the barn that day and *not* know what this takes out of you. He's just—"

Lusak's other hand closed over hers. "Don't make excuses for me, Jeannie. That's just the problem." He took a deep breath, wobbly though it was, and looked back at them—from Jeannie to Delia and finally to Melinda, where his gaze rested. "I *was* there that night." Jeannie gasped; he shook his head. "Not like that. It was like I said; I was going to the gas station. But I was spooked. That's not a great section of road for a flat, and going past that bar . . ."

Melinda gave him a moment after he trailed off, and another, and then would have prodded him, but Jeannie squeezed his hand and he sighed and said, "I wasn't walking. I was frightened. I ran. Well, jogged. And yes, I had the tire iron, but I was shaking so hard, I don't know if I even could have used it. And I heard a noise. Just past the old bait shop. Someone in pain, or someone falling . . . I thought maybe it could have been a raccoon—" He stopped, his jaw working, and started again. "No. I knew it was human. And you know what? I ran faster. I saw the station was closed and I got out of there. And then when I read about Gordon's death . . ."

Jeannie reached up to place her hand along his pale cheek. "Oh, Craig. You couldn't have saved him. He was so badly hurt—"

"I could have *tried*," Lusak said, with the certainty of utter truth.

Melinda closed her eyes, let the implications of it all wash through her.

No wonder.

No wonder he'd been so reluctant. No wonder he felt the guilt she'd perceived in him. But she softened her challenging stance, let her arms drop, let her mouth relax—her relief coming through. For the first time, she truly believed Lusak hadn't done it, that all he'd been hiding was what he *hadn't* done. "Yes," she said, not without understanding. "You could have. And you'll have to live with that—even though Jeannie is right. Gordon was dying by the time you went past."

He shot her a sharp look. "You *know* that?"

With the gravel sharp at her back, her hand twitching and spasming while the rest of her body utterly failed to do her bidding, the world going all *starry starry night* on her and yet . . . all an imposed memory—boy, did she know it. "I do."

He closed his eyes in utter relief; his jaw, only moments ago so hard, suddenly trembled. When he looked at her again, it was with unshed tears; his voice was quiet and steady. "But I didn't know that at the time. For all I knew, I could have made a difference. And I was too afraid."

"Craig . . ." Jeannie said, hesitating on words.

"Not exactly the kind of example a child needs,"

he said, putting an edge to the words. "Not the kind of thing that will impress the adoption agency."

Of course he'd been thinking of the adoption . . . their long wait, their climbing hopes it would be over soon. "Well, right," Melinda said. "Because any adoption agency prefers that their children go to a family where the father runs headlong into situations he's not actually prepared to deal with."

Lusak blinked, trying to process that.

"Don't you get it?" Jeannie asked. "You are who you are. You're not a physically confrontational guy. You think I don't know that? You're not a rescuer the way Melinda's Jim is a rescuer; your fight is in the courtroom, when you have to fight at all, but even then, you try to mediate things out. It's who you *are*, Craig. Am I supposed to be surprised to find out you reacted this way?"

"Don't tell me you're not disappointed," Lusak said, bitterness edging his words. "I didn't even call for help. I was afraid to get involved—afraid even that would interfere with the adoption. But look at me now: if the social worker saw me, she'd take us off the waiting list as soon as she could whip the red marker from her pocket."

"I think she uses a PDA," Jeannie said, in a tone that was meant to prod him with a little humor.

"If you'd called for help," Melinda said, "then

Gordon might have seen that. It might have clarified what was probably his last living observation. It might have prevented this entire vendetta."

"Wow," Delia murmured, as Jeannie turned to give Melinda a horrified look. "You don't mince words, do you?"

Melinda spared her a quick smile. "The thing about helping earthbound spirits . . . In the end, it's all about the truth. Sometimes it's factual truth—like where those safe deposit box keys are hidden, or where the heirloom necklace ended up. But usually it's about emotional truth. So in situations like this, I tend to cut to the chase. Because the point is, maybe we can use this information to stop Gordon *now*."

Lusak snorted. "Why would he even believe me? I'm only trying to save my own neck. Again."

"Maybe he won't," Melinda agreed. "But you've gotten to know him, in a way, just as I have, and surely you see that he's probably going to understand exactly why you kept this to yourself. And I'm not saying he'll take it *well*, but I think he's going to believe you're not the killer. Because you see—he's had time to get to know you, too."

"Fine," Lusak said, without enthusiasm, without any real belief it would work.

"Hey," Jeannie said sharply, standing up beside the chair. "*Now* is when you need to be a fighter." She took his face between both hands, turned it so he had to look at her. "You hear me? Everything we have together depends on it, and don't you dare tell me that's not worth fighting for."

His eyes filled; he put his hands over hers and nodded.

Melinda glanced at Delia. "You know, you might . . ." *Flee. Run away. Get thee hence.*

Delia picked up on Melinda's intent right away. "And wonder what's going on? No, thank you." She settled in behind the counter.

"Gordon?" Melinda said, alert for any flicker of movement, any ripple of anger. "Gordon, are you here? We'd really like to talk to you."

Nothing. Jeannie's shoulders slightly hunched as if expecting a blow and Lusak clearly steeled himself for the misery Gordon could so easily inflict, but Melinda shook her head, letting them know . . . *nothing.*

"Gordon Reese!" Lusak shouted—a pale imitation of a shout, really, hoarse and thready. "I need to talk to you! I need you to hear me!"

Warily, Melinda looked around the shop; she even went to the doors and looked outside the shop—at the square, up and down the street. She half expected to see Gordon across the street in the square, angry and taunting.

But he wasn't.

"I don't think he's coming," she said slowly. "I think, in his heart, he knows he's wrong. He knows he's reached the point where he has to face that fact—or make the biggest mistake of his existence. I don't think he's ready to do it."

"He's waiting until you're not with us," Craig said bitterly. "When he can attack me and not have to answer for it."

"But . . ." Jeannie, so strong a moment ago, suddenly looked near tears. "We can't go on like this. *Craig* can't go on like this."

"You know," Melinda said, looking at Lusak, "I think you're right. He's so angry, he's hurting so badly, he's striking out. He needs a reminder of who he *is*, not who he was." She bit her lip, thought of Carol and her family, and shook her head.

"What?" Jeannie asked, leaving Lusak to approach Melinda, to take her arm, her grip just a little too desperate for comfort. "Please!"

"Gordon's wife, her family—they're so emotional about his death, so defensive. If we go there, looking to show him who he *is*, and he sees that we're upsetting her . . ."

Jeannie closed her eyes, taking in a deep breath; she looked as though she'd been punched. "It could be a last straw for him."

"Go to where he died," Delia said, still behind the counter.

Lusak looked agape at her. "Are you kidding? If he's going to be angry about something—!"

Delia shrugged. "Hey, first you have to get his attention. Right now you can't even do that. But from what I understand, that whole area is about what he *left*. What he *isn't*. So, turn it on him, why don't you?"

Surprised and gratified, Melinda nodded. "She's right. It's a place to start."

But Lusak made a funny noise; what color he'd regained in the past moments now fled, and he lurched to the side. Jeannie ran back to him, her hands on his cheek, his forehead, smoothing back his hair—frantic gestures, trying to understand and fix things with just a touch. "What is it?" she asked, looking at Melinda.

Melinda crouched by the arm of Lusak's chair, and as soon as she got that close, she felt it; she gasped. "I didn't even know he could do that," she said. "He *shouldn't*—" but she didn't finish, because the list of what an earthbound spirit should and shouldn't be able to do had undergone complete revisions of late.

"*What?*" Jeannie demanded, stroking Lusak's back.

"He's still got me," Lusak said, the words barely audible. "Doesn't he? Somehow, he's still got me."

"There's some sort of connection," Melinda admitted. A thin echo of anger, a reverberation of dark satisfaction. She held her hands out, feeling it emanate from Lusak in radiant waves, a warmth and a sharp edge of pain; she shuddered. "We've got to get to Gordon. *Now.*"

"Are you sure the hospital isn't—" Delia cut herself off, her attention on the door, and Melinda followed her gaze as she finished, "Thank goodness!"

Jim swung the door open and came in free-striding and oblivious—only to stop short as he took in the scene before him.

"The thing is," Melinda said, looking right at him, knowing he was putting the pieces together, "a hospital can treat his symptoms. But they can't stop the cause, and unless we do that—"

"No!" Jeannie said, her voice catching. "No, don't even say it. Don't even *think* it. This is all a horrible mistake!"

"Maybe it's what I deserve," Lusak said, and his shoulders had gone tense, his hands trembling.

"Of course it isn't." Melinda made her voice brisk. She stood, giving Jim the slightest of nods. "Was what you did heroic? Not in anyone's book. But it was human. It was *understandable*. And you didn't know someone was dying."

He shook his head. "I thought . . . I didn't really think. I just ran. It wasn't until I heard the news . . ."

"There you are." She leaned into Jim slightly as his hand slid around her waist, resting on her hip. "This is my husband, Jim. He's a paramedic, and he can take care of Craig on the way to Bayview.

Because I think Delia's exactly right—we've got to get his attention. We don't have time to waste."

Jim took one look at Lusak; his arm tightened around her. "And he's not going to the hospital because . . . ?"

She loved that he assumed there was a reason. "Because Gordon has a connection to him, some sort of drain on him, and no one at the hospital can stop that. And Jim, we *have* to stop it."

He met her gaze, held it a moment . . . and nodded. Got it, just like that. But Jeannie gave a little shriek of dismay and Lusak slumped over, and Melinda broke away to reach him. "My keys are in my purse," she said over her shoulder to Jim. "We've got to go *now*."

He moved, and fast; she heard the flurry of motion between him and Delia, the quick exchange of words even as Jim headed out the back. But her attention was on Craig Lusak, on Jeannie's whitened knuckles where she gripped the back of the chair.

Melinda took his shoulders, shook him gently. "Craig," she said sharply. "You need to hear me. This is just like when he's here, do you understand that? *Don't fear him*. Don't give him anything of yourself!" For she knew just what had happened, kicked herself for not anticipating that it would. He'd learned of the connection and his fear had kicked back in—kicked right up to high as he sat there awaiting his fate—and instead of doing everything she could to stop it, she'd let her urgency show.

And so Gordon had taken yet more from him.

"Come *on*, Craig," she said. "Hold on to yourself!"

16

By the time Jim pulled around front with the SUV, Melinda and Jeannie had roused Craig and hoisted him through the door, with Delia holding it open and wishing them luck and looking after them in a way that spoke of her bemused wariness of the whole thing. Craig staggered to the rear of the Saturn and crawled inside, and Jeannie fumbled for the seat belt around his waist, then flung herself into place while Melinda slammed the door and ran to the passenger side. "Go," she told Jim, reaching for her own belt. "Just *go!*"

And he did, pulling away from the curb and succinctly navigating their way out of Grandview, and then pushing the speed up and over the limit as they hit the state road outside town, slowing down only when a motorcyclist recklessly ripped past them. Jeannie murmured to Craig the whole while, and Melinda twisted around to keep an eye on him. He seemed to be recovering slightly, and she caught his gaze as he straightened, realizing for the first time that they were on the road and out of town. He asked, "Where?"

"On the way to Bayview," she told him. "And until we get there, you just need to remember what I said: he can't hurt you. It doesn't matter what you did or didn't do; it doesn't matter how angry he is. He can only touch you if you give him that power."

He mustered a dark little half grin, more a twist of the lips than a real smile. "That would be easier to believe if he hadn't already done so much."

"You know she's right, Craig," Jeannie pleaded. "You *know* it got better when you believed it, these past couple days. That's why he pushed it to this point in the first place—he knows it, too!"

"All right, all right. He can't touch me. He can't—"

SWINGBATTERBATTER!

Jim snapped a sudden curse, slamming on the brakes; Melinda cried out in surprise as the motion flung her forward and then back, the Saturn slewing sideways, the driver's side growing light on the wheels until the vehicle hung in the air, ready to roll. Melinda had the blurred impression of bulk across the road, bulk and brown and green quickly spinning out of view again. The back end of the

Saturn slammed to a stop with a crunch of metal and glass.

There was, for the moment, silence. Melinda's throat hurt; she realized she'd been screaming. In the back seat, Jeannie gasped, as though she'd only just started breathing again. Craig groaned. "What . . . ?"

"Tree," Jim said, sounding dazed. "There's a tree across the road. How—?"

"Are you okay?" Melinda did a quick self-check, arms and legs, and ran a hand across her chest where the seat belt had bruised, pressing it against her aching collarbone.

"I'm good," Jim said, sounding more certain, looking over at her to put a hand on her arm, then to the side of her face, catching and holding her gaze while she nodded, answering that unasked question. *I'm okay.* Without looking back, he asked, "Jeannie? Craig?"

"Just shook up, I think," Jeannie said, as Melinda fumbled with her seat belt.

Jim forced the driver's door open. "We might be able to pull this out of the way. It's not that big. It must have just come dow—" But he never finished the sentence, and Melinda finally freed herself and joined him. "Melinda," he said, his voice odd beyond the mere effects of the wild ride. "This tree's been cut."

She saw it then, two feet in diameter of sturdy

ash, strong gray trunk with tight branches, fresh green leaves with serrated edges—and a cleanly cut base.

Swingbatterbatter, just a whisper now, startled and suddenly wary, suddenly understanding. Melinda took it in, pushed it aside.

"Why would anyone—?" she started, and, "But if someone did this, they must still be here," and then, "Could it even *be* an accident?"

Jeannie stepped out of the Saturn, eyes fixed on the fresh stump, and blurted, "This can't be right!"

Jim touched a hand to his temple, glanced at it and away, but not before Melinda had seen the gleam of blood. "Jim, your head!" She grabbed his arm, turning him just enough to see the generous runnels of blood streaming from inside his hairline.

"Scalp wound, Mel. You know how those are."

"That doesn't mean you should just ignore it! You know better than that—or you should!"

"Looks pretty nasty," Jeannie agreed. "Look, we've all got phones. Let's just call for help."

Jim glanced back at the SUV, where Craig leaned heavily on the open passenger door, eyeing the tree. "And then what?" Jim asked Melinda quietly. "Isn't that exactly what you wanted to avoid? *Help?*"

She bit her lip, quite suddenly aware of all the aches and pains from being whipped around. "See what you think about moving the tree," she said. "I'll get the first aid kit. We'll decide then."

The next few moments were so full of bustle that Melinda didn't have time to think, just to do. She scrambled over the back seat into the cargo area because the tailgate was crunched closed, and tossed through the jumbled contents there to pull out a blanket and then the heavy and complete backcountry first aid kit augmented with the supplies only a paramedic could get his hands on. The blanket she gave to Lusak, and then as she stood outside the Saturn and opened the kit, using the seat as a table, she asked him, "Are you doing all right? Any sign of Gordon?"

"No," Lusak said, surprised, as though he just realized it. "In fact, I feel better. As though maybe the accident shook him up? Does that make sense?"

"Depends." She quickly sorted through the kit, hunting alcohol wipes and butterfly bandages and hoping they'd both be adequate but thinking, *So much blood from one spot* . . . "He might have gotten more than he bargained for. Or it might have been . . ." She hesitated, searching for words along with the supplies.

"What?" Lusak's anxiety broke her momentary fugue.

"An eye-opener," she finished, spotting the butterfly bandages with a small cry of triumph. "You know, in a way he got what he wanted; you were afraid for your life. And maybe he realized that's not what he really wants."

"Do you think so?" Lusak frowned in doubt. He stood straighter, less pale. He looked less vulnerable—and again like the man Melinda had found herself doubting, wondering if he was capable of killing, wondering what he was hiding.

Now she knew he hid only his fears and his failings, but the knowledge inspired no more confidence than before. And she couldn't lie. She could only say, "I *hope* so."

"Melinda!" Jeannie called, and Melinda glanced over to find Jim bent over, hands on his knees. She grabbed the bandages and wipes, dropping pieces behind her, and stuffed the items into the big cargo pockets of her sweater coat as she ran—hating that sudden spike of fear, the tight band around the base of her throat. All her experience with helping people, all her common sense, the extreme worldliness brought on by dealing with death from such a young age—it all vanished in the face of Jim doubled over, hands on knees and blood dripping from his head.

"Jim," she said breathlessly, skidding to a stop before him and slipping on the crushed green leaves as easily as slipping on ice. She steadied herself, took a breath, and then took both his upper arms in her hands. "Maybe you'd better sit down. On this convenient tree trunk, even."

"I'm okay," he said, so matter-of-factly it couldn't help but reassure her. "It happens. Hit my head, lost some blood. Lucky I didn't fai—whoo—"

She would have bet that last word was supposed to be *whoops* but didn't dwell on it. Not with Jim going down in slow motion right in front of her. And he didn't truly faint, not completely, just ended up on his hands and knees looking momentarily, utterly stupid. From there she had a most excellent view of the gash in his high forehead—how deep it was, how fast the blood still welled up. *More than alcohol wipes and gauze pads, for sure.*

"Here," Jeannie said, and she'd come from the car with a roll of gauze in her hand. Melinda ripped it open, wadded it up, and pressed it to Jim's head.

"Hey! Ow!" But when his hand wandered up to protest what she'd done, she took it and firmly pushed it down on the gauze.

"There," she said. "Do some good for yourself. Especially since tape isn't going to work right there, and we need pressure." Amazing, to sound so casual and feel so sick at the same time.

"Mel, I'm all right. Seriously. Just give me a moment. We'll pull this tree out of here and we can go on. I'll get this looked at in Bayview. We're halfway there, anyway."

"Right," she said, not even pretending to be convinced, and pulled out one of those wipes to clean off his face, or at least part of it. Strong face, strong bones and lines, straight and classical under her hand. Paler than he probably thought, too.

"Feel better?" he asked when she was done, hand still pressing the gauze in place as he sat back on his heels.

"Not enough," she said, with some asperity. "Maybe someone else will come along, be able to help with this thing."

"This time of day? It's not a busy road even at rush hour."

"He's right," Lusak said, coming up from the SUV with the blanket still draped over his shoulders. "No one takes this road for commuting; there are too many icy patches in the winter, too many blind curves in the summer. And it takes us straight to that wrong end of town."

A new voice startled them all. "You're already in the wrong end of town."

As one, they startled, drawing a little closer together. Jim straightened too fast and wove a little on his feet; Melinda edged up beside him and tried to make it look as though he hadn't—as though he stood there completely on his own, as though he and Craig and Jeannie and she were untouched and ready for anything.

Even for a cocky intruder standing at the edge of the road, motorcycle helmet propped on his hip, twisted and predatory grin on his face. A familiar face; a familiar grin. *Dave.* Melinda gasped to see him, and Jim tightened his arm around her. "He's the one?"

"Yes," she said. "At the bar parking lot. He would have—"

"Yes," Dave agreed. "I would have. You deserved it then, and you deserve it now. And still, you didn't learn your lesson. Still calling Carol's family, still haunting her."

"Interesting you should use that word," Melinda murmured.

Jim's grip tightened another fraction, this time a warning. He straightened—almost imperceptible, that, but Melinda felt it and she knew it to be what it was, his unconscious attempt to gather up against whatever lay ahead. She assessed the man with a more calculating eye. And then her husband asked what they all wanted to know. "What do you want?"

"I *wanted* your wife to leave Carol's family alone. She's too good for the likes of you—and still you kept coming back, kept calling." He dropped the helmet aside, a deliberate movement that somehow seemed ominous. "Even this morning, you called. Stupid bitch. Last mistake you'll make."

"I called her *mother,*" Melinda said. "Because *I*

didn't want Carol upset, either." In the corner of her eye, she saw Jim's warning, the slightest shake of his head. And though she felt an instant of resistance, it didn't last any longer than that. This was his world—dealing with the living. The *sick*.

Because she had no doubt this man was, in his own way, very sick indeed. So she went for distraction. "Who *are* you?" she said. "You must care for Carol and her family very much. Have you known them long?"

"Don't even bother," he said, and snorted with disapproval—but he wasn't the only one there, and he wasn't the only one answering. Gordon's emotions shot through the scene, an arrow of anger and surprise, and a name echoing in her head—*Davedavedavedave*—followed by his confusion, the flickering images of a much younger Dave, of Greg, and of young Howie—one from the yearbook, which she'd seen without truly absorbing it until this moment; one of them sharing a tough laugh outside the Whetstone, flicking careless cigarette ashes to the gravel with the exchange of some crude remark. And then Gordon was gone, withdrawing his bafflement, not ready to face either his past or his present.

"It's too late," Dave was saying. "You should have left her alone. Now you'll join the others." He glanced down the road, and for an instant Melinda hoped he'd heard an approaching car—but there was nothing, and Dave relaxed, and then gestured toward the other side of the road. The woods grew thick there, thick and young at the edge, more scattered toward the interior.

"No," Jim said, matter-of-fact and full of the calm authority he used in the highly charged, highly emotional emergencies to which he responded. "We're not going anywhere." And then, to their small, huddled group, "Let's go. Back in the car."

"I don't think so!" Dave's voice had risen to an edge that quite suddenly reminded Melinda of the wild chase through the square, the motorcycle engine revving, the light pinning them in the darkness. Full of threat, not quite in control.

She didn't have to look to know he was armed.

Jeannie hadn't expected it though; she gasped. "He's got a gun! Oh my God, why are you even doing this? Haven't we been through enough?"

Dave frowned at her. "I don't even know who you are, except that you're stupid enough to end up with *her* again. I saw you at the antique barn—I guess you didn't get the point, either."

"You did all of that," Melinda said, and couldn't help but shake her head. "The barn, the threats . . . my shop. The motorcycle."

No guilt there. He looked pleased with himself, if anything. "I followed you to the barn. You weren't watching for a motorcycle then, were you?

And the marker—clever as hell, don't you think? Not much in the way of evidence there."

"I've got pictures," she said tightly. "They'll be found."

"And they'll lead nowhere. So get your asses into the woods," he said, and gestured with the gun. "There's a path there—you'll see it. You'll understand soon enough."

"Listen, let's talk about this—" Jim said.

"Melinda?" Jeannie cut him off, looking at Melinda for guidance, eyes wide and frightened, her arm tucked around Lusak's waist.

"I think we'd better," Melinda said. "For the moment. I can't help but wonder . . ."

Gordon had helped her once. Hadn't wanted anyone else interfering in his own scenario. Had given her just enough of an edge to get away. Maybe . . . ?

To Jeannie, she said, "Just remember we're not alone." *She hoped.*

Startled, Jeannie responded, "And you think that's *good*?"

"*Now,*" Dave said, and his voice came as a sudden hiss of malice, a frightening glimpse into the violence lurking just beneath the surface. Melinda flinched; she saw again, quite suddenly, the wild gleam of his eye in the wet dusk as he came for her in the very spot Gordon had died. He saw her reaction; he latched on to it with cruel satisfaction. "That's right," he said. "You tell them. Get them moving. Let them know I mean it. Whatever happened before—that little storm burst—it's not going to happen again."

"Jim," she said, and there came the tremble in her voice, the one she'd been trying to avoid, but now this man had struck through to the fear of what he'd wrought that afternoon. "We'd really better . . ."

He kept his own voice to a fervent murmur in her ear. "Mel, that's crazy—we can't go into the woods with him at *gunpoint*. We may never—"

Swingbatterbatter!

Those quick warning words disappeared into an explosive blast of sound; wood chips flew around them and Melinda ducked against Jim, covering her face, feeling him flinch and feeling the sudden startle of stinging impacts up and down her arm. "Jim!"

"I'm fine," he said quickly, although that's what he'd said about his head and all she could see in her mind's eye was the suddenly huge sight of the gaping gun barrel that had been pointed his way, so she stepped back to check him out and found yes, he was horribly pale, the gauze lost in the fuss, the blood streaming—and then suddenly Jeannie shrieked a wordless warning, and the tree limbs trembled beside them, and their strange and oddly driven assailant had run out along the trunk and jumped down beside them. As he landed, he casually backhanded Jim with the gun and sent him staggering back and then sprawling, tangled, in the tree limbs.

"No!" Melinda cried, leaping for Jim—only to wrench up short, very short, her arm twisted and shoulder burning with pain, and she couldn't help a sob of frustration, sensing Jeannie and Lusak frozen in fear and knowing Lusak would do nothing, the man who had run from noises in the dark as Gordon Reese died.

Swingbatterbatter . . . Greg's presence came quietly, a sad apology of some sort, and suddenly Melinda understood . . . because Greg hadn't responded when she'd spoken of his return for Carol—he'd merely gotten distant—but when she thought back on it, she saw he'd tried to warn her every time Dave was about to show his hand.

For Greg, it wasn't about Carol at all—not anymore.

She had the feeling she was also about to understand just what had drawn him back—drawn him to come to her for help.

A noisy old diesel pickup approached from the other side of the road, the engine rumbling to a stop; a door slammed shortly afterward, but Melinda couldn't see anyone over the expanse of the tree. She could hear the muttered curse, though, and then the shout of a question, the voice of an older man. "Anyone over there call this in yet?"

Dave didn't miss a beat. With one work-booted foot planted on Jim's stomach, the gun jammed into Melinda's side so hard she suddenly couldn't breathe—or maybe that was just the sudden anticipation of that same explosion, this time ripping through her body—he called back, "Not yet. No cell phones here. Maybe you'd better do it."

A loud grunt. "No use for a cell phone. I'll drive back the other way."

No! Melinda willed the man to pay closer attention, to realize the tree had been cut, to see that they'd all frozen in fear, that Jim was down on the tree limbs looking dazed and hurt and trying so hard to pull himself together. *No, don't go! Don't leave us!*

The truck door slammed; the engine cranked painfully to life. The gears whined in reverse, shifted noisily, and faded away. Melinda met Jeannie's terrified gaze as she clung desperately to Lusak. And Melinda remembered, then, what she herself had said only a few moments ago. *We're not alone.* "Greg," she said—and he was here, flashing in and out, distressed, connected to all this in some way she was only beginning to understand— yet not focused enough, not strong enough, to do so much as distract Dave. "Gordon! You must be here somewhere; you must be able to hear me! Please!"

"Into the woods," Dave growled. "Now. All of you." And he shoved the gun into her ribs for good measure.

She jerked away from him, defiant in spite of the tremble of her chin and lip, furious in spite of the fear, and reached down for Jim, bracing to help him up. "It's okay," she told him. "We just have to trust. We're not alone."

Dave just laughed. "Being nosy got you into this. Being crazy isn't going to get you out."

Leaf litter still wet from the heavy rain softened Melinda's steps; twigs and branches snagged at her sweater coat. She slipped free of yet another, turning back to look at Jim, at Jeannie and Craig struggling behind him. But behind them all came Dave, the gun ready and attitude loaded. "Just keep walking," he said. "The path is clear enough. Almost as clear as it was ten years ago." And he grinned at that, although Melinda couldn't fathom why.

She caught Jim's glance before she straightened back around—brief, but it was enough. She saw that he, too, frowned at the comment, and she knew from the very way he held his shoulders that he was still looking for opportunity. "*Trust,*" she mouthed at him, eyeing the blood soaking into the shoulder of his dark jacket. Because he wasn't strong enough, wasn't steady enough—and no more was Lusak behind him, although she'd felt nothing of Gordon, and thought that if he wasn't helping, he at least had left them alone.

"Frankly, *alone* doesn't really work for me right now," she muttered to the thin air ahead, following the path every bit as easily as Dave said. Narrow but clear, winding between the trees . . . It should have been beautiful, this spring day, with kinglets darting around in a small flock to scold them from alongside the path, other birds rooting around in the ground cover, and chipmunks crying alarm to each other, strong sharp chirps echoing through the trees. Beautiful, and not closed and dark and desperate.

We shouldn't have come with him. He'd had a gun in her ribs. *I should have done something, anything, should have stopped him . . . run from him . . .*

Right. Because she was *so* about to leave Jim and Jeannie and Craig Lusak there to deal with the consequences. Especially when this man was after *her*. After her for being . . . nosy?

But even Mrs. Donovan had relaxed, had accepted, however grudgingly, that Melinda did not mean their family harm. She hadn't been friendly, she'd by no means welcomed their contact, but she hadn't sounded like the kind of woman who would instigate *this*. Merely a mother protecting her own.

No, this was all about Dave. A self-assigned protector. A man who'd only worked at the B&B for a short while, and yet who seemed to know the family and to know the Whetstone . . .

And who'd known Gordon. Who'd known Greg. Who'd been there, in Gordon's memories, that startled flash of contact by the fallen tree before Gordon had fled again.

"Gordon," she said, between her teeth, barely avoiding a fall over a protruding root covered by leaves, "you're strong. You've been taking energy from Craig for days. You know you can help us here. You know that somehow, this is still about you—still about Carol." He was listening. He *had* to be listening. "Even before you changed your life, were you really the kind of man who could watch four people die and not care?"

Ahead, light bloomed—an open area of some sort. The path, up until now largely clean, widened; it turned spotted with beer cans and broken bottles, and tiny little fire pits off to the side.

"Teen hangout," Jim said, and he didn't sound good—winded, his voice ragged. How hard had he hit his head on that window, anyway? How hard had Dave hit him afterward?

"Won't do you any good," Dave said, too cheerfully. "No one comes here during the day. Well, no one but me."

The woods abruptly ended, the ground turning rocky and hard, the growth over it little more than

stubby grasses and scraggly remnants of wildflow-
ers from the previous year. Melinda squinted in the
sunshine and stumbled over a jutting rock, stopping to let her vision adjust as Jim came up close
behind her and Jeannie and Craig moved up to the
side.

"Melinda," Jeannie said, talking fast and grabbing this first opportunity, "what is this about?
Who *is* this man?"

"I hardly know where to start," Melinda said,
turning to Jim—the back of her hand on his
cheek, a quick smile as she met his gaze, letting
him know she was there, was doing her best. "His
name is Dave. He works for the Donovans, Carol's
family. Gordon knows him. And he's the one who
closed us in the barn and who trashed my store.
All apparently because Carol was upset at my first
visit. Or maybe there's more?" She raised her voice,
aimed it Dave's way.

"What," Dave snorted, "like I *owe* you the
truth because I'm gonna shove you down into that
quarry?"

Shove us down into—

"Oh my God," she said. "The *quarry*." And,
now that her eyes had adjusted, there it was, or the
lip of it anyway, not truly recognizable for what it
was from this shallow depression in the landscape.
She looked around more carefully now—found
signs of the old truck road going into the woods

from the opposite direction, found scattered blocks of discarded limestone. "Greg . . . *Greg* was found in a quarry."

Dave grinned, unpleasant and cruel. "Greg was doped up, didn't you hear? There's no telling what he was doing out here."

"Oh, I think there probably is," Melinda said tightly. "But I don't understand *why*."

Swirlingcolors tumblingsmells the bounce of air against skin . . .

"You're falling," she said, suddenly understanding that much of it, struggling to maintain her balance between Greg's *then* and her *now*. She felt his wash of relief at that understanding—felt him strengthen, as he began to complete his own understanding. "You fell here," she told him. "You were experimenting, and you didn't know where you were walking, and—"

But he suddenly stood there, right at the lip of the quarry, looking over—very much himself, just as she'd seen him waving in the memorial of the class Web site: hair a little too long, flannel shirt unbuttoned over a T-shirt, jeans comfortably worn. But unlike in those photos, now he frowned—a thoughtful scowl—arms crossed, so close to the edge that Melinda couldn't help but fear for his safety, even knowing he couldn't possibly fall.

And he frowned at Dave. He frowned, and he said quite distinctly, *"You drove out with me. In my beater truck. God, I was the only one who could keep that thing running. And your motorcycle—we had it in the back. Do you still ride a motorcycle, Dave?"*

Jim moved up close behind her, his warmth along her back. "Greg's here?"

"What the hell is *wrong* with you people?" Dave said.

"Yes," Melinda said clearly. "He's here." She looked at Dave. "You don't need to tell us what this is all about, actually. Greg is going to do that." Or enough of it, she thought, so she could put it together from there.

"You're not only crazy, you *believe* it." He made a face that was half sneer, half disdain. "Damned good thing I'm getting you out of Carol's life."

"You do a lot of that?" Jim asked, weaving slightly against Melinda. "Getting people out of Carol's life?"

She pushed up against him, trying to steady him, struggled to keep worry from distracting her. "He says you came out here in his truck, with your motorcycle in the back."

"Parked it right where that tree went down. And the drugs . . . the drugs were his." Greg seemed to realize it for the first time. *"They were his, but he . . . he only smoked a little pot. A different joint than mine. So we'd each have our own, he said."*

"You gave him those drugs," Melinda said, eyes narrowing, watching Dave's startlement grow through defensiveness to anger. "You brought him to the path, you brought him out here. Which of those little fire rings did you sit at, Dave? Did you even try to stop him from running over the edge of the quarry?"

"Good God," Lusak exclaimed, abruptly sitting down behind her. "It's not just Gordon, now. What the hell is going on here, Melinda? Besides this guy waiting to kill us?"

Melinda didn't take her eyes from Dave—from the gun. "The truth is, I'm not exactly sure. These two men died ten years apart, and I've been thinking they were completely separate situations—except that at first I thought Greg was drawn out by Carol's grief, and now I think maybe it was something else."

Dave made a show of bashing himself upside the head with the body of the gun. "I get it, I get it. Unique stalling technique. Make me demand an explanation from *you*. That's a good one, really it is."

"You brought me here," Greg said to Dave, bemusment coloring his voice, *"and I died. I took your drugs and I ran over the edge of this—"* He stopped, frowning, hesitating on that memory. *"Didn't I? Run over the edge?"*

"Oh my God," Melinda breathed, her gaze jerking from Greg back to Dave. "You pushed him. You took him to that edge and you pushed him."

Dave shook his head—shook it emphatically, with abrupt fury. His neck reddened, his face reddened, and his eyes went narrow and deep. "No!" And then, louder, "*No!* I didn't! He didn't need pushing! I just took him to the edge! I just—he thought he was good enough for her!" He snorted, shook his head. "You should have seen how easy it was, how fast he took the bait. Free drugs, that's all it took. He came right out with me, took it all— as trusting as a baby. But I had to be sure. And no one ever figured it out." He pulled himself together, approached Melinda in a few swift strides, grabbing her by the arm, twisting it as he yanked her in close. "How did you? Huh? Who told you? Who have you told?"

"Hey!" Jim surged forward, shoving between them. "That's enough!"

"Back off!" Dave snarled, flinging Melinda aside with such force that she stumbled and fell and didn't really see what happened next, just heard the impact and the surprised sound of pain, and then Jim landed heavily beside her, twisted around himself, his limbs slack and his eyes, barely visible though cracked lids, rolled back. Melinda cried something incomprehensible and threw herself at him, touching his face, his shoulders, the side of his head, finding the split and purpling lump; she turned to Dave in fury. "You hit him *again*? Why don't you just shoot us all and get it over with?"

Jeannie cried out in fear. *"Melinda!"*

"You killed me?" Greg said over it all, full of disbelief and hurt.

But Melinda barely heard either of them. She climbed to her feet, ignoring the awkwardness of her long sweater, and stalked over to Dave. "That's what you want, isn't it? To get rid of us? Because I'm *nosy*? Well, go ahead—but just so you know, it's not going to end there. Because you're not alone anymore, and I'm pretty much the only person who can change that."

"You killed *me?"* Greg said, a little more loudly this time, a little closer.

"You," Dave said, grabbing the front of Melinda's sweater. "Whatever you're talking about, just shut up! This'll all be over soon, and *that* will be the end of it, just like—"

"Just like Greg?" Melinda said, lowering her voice. It still trembled; her mind's eye still froze on the sight of Jim, fallen behind her. "Because he didn't deserve to be near Carol? And me, because I'm a problem for Carol? What else have you done, Dave? Who else have you done it to?"

Greg stepped between them, stepped right up to Dave. He couldn't have looked more lost-puppy-dog if he'd tried, with his hair mussed and brown eyes hurt and soulful—except for the building anger. Melinda felt it as much as she saw it. *"You* killed *me?"* he said. *"Dave?"* And tried to put a hand on Dave's arm, only to watch it pass through flesh.

Dave jumped; he turned on her, his hand fisting more tightly into her sweater coat. "What are you doing?"

"Nothing," she said sharply. "What am I supposed to be doing, with you shaking me up like this, and when all I can think of is how badly you've hurt my husband?"

He glanced around—into the bright sunshine, though there was nothing of it on his face, and his cruelty had gone furtive. For an instant she thought he might latch on to Jeannie and Lusak, on the ground together not far from Jim; Lusak, it seemed, had gone about as far as he was able. But Dave looked back to her, scowl growing. "I felt it," he said. "I felt—"

"*Me,*" said Greg, and this time gave Dave a punch—what would have been a solid blow to the shoulder—and though his fist went right through, Dave flinched and shied away. Greg only did it again. "*You son of a bitch! You couldn't have her, so no one can?*"

"That's Greg you feel," Melinda said, surprised at her own calm—but now they were on *her* turf. "He's here with us. He's been confused, but recent events have drawn him out. And he never realized what you'd done, not until now."

The rustling noise behind her should have

warned her; Dave's sudden scowl definitely widened her eyes, and she flinched wildly as he drew the gun up, her calm shattering as it exploded into noise, the sound so loud it slapped against her face. But she didn't feel any pain, and she didn't see any blood, and she whirled to realize that Dave had fired the shot into the ground near Jeannie and Craig and that, to judge by their frozen, terrified midcrawl postures, they'd been heading for the trail.

Dave pointed the gun more directly at them. *"No,"* he said. But his attention shifted back to Melinda, and just as fast he stalked up to her, pushing her back a step, then another, flat-handing her shoulder while she flailed to catch her balance, the long and heavy sweater catching up on the backs of her thighs. *"You,"* he said, "are trying my patience. What the hell is this all about? What're you talking about? *Greg?* That softheaded idiot never knew a thing!"

"He does now," she said, nearly choking on the words—from fear, from her stumbling, from the way he slammed her backward another step even as she answered him. "Haven't you figured it out? I'm in touch with Greg. I've been in touch with Gordon. That's what this has been all about from the start. I've been trying to bring them some peace, that's all. Greg's been so confused, so resistant, I couldn't understand what was going on.

Not until now. But they're both tied to Carol, and that's why I called on her and her mother . . ." Her eyes widened slightly; Dave had stopped pushing her, had stepped back as she spoke, giving her that look, the one she was so used to. The you-must-be-kidding look, the one full of mixed fear and denial and scorn, and something else—not guilt, but . . . an extra edge of fear. Of wary alarm, as he looked around—as if he would suddenly see signs of either Gordon or Greg himself. She shook her head, an unconscious gesture, and stepped back from him of her own volition. "They *were* both tied to Carol," she realized. "I don't understand it—I don't have all the pieces yet—but you did it, didn't you? It wasn't just Greg. It was *Gordon*. You killed them both."

And suddenly, as much as she'd been hoping for help from Gordon, she now dreaded his arrival. His anger-fed power, his temper—his ability to manipulate the energies around them.

"Gordon," Dave said tightly, "didn't deserve her, either."

"But *why*?" Melinda cried. "He did everything for her; he changed his *life*. She's devastated to lose him, can't you see that?"

"She'll get over it." He said it so assertively, so dismissively, Melinda found herself without words.

Greg had been staring at his ineffective hand,

staring at Dave in horror as his understanding grew, his sudden comprehension of just *why* he had died. *"You can't do that!"* he said. *"You can't decide other people's lives for them! You just get it* wrong. *Do you really think Carol would have seen me as anything more than a friend? I'm not stupid, Dave—even I knew I didn't have a chance with her. It didn't stop me from wanting, but hell! Look at me!"* He gestured at himself—his lanky, not quite mature body, his features not yet hardened into their final cast. *"I was a kid! When you're eighteen, who* doesn't *want what you can't have?"*

"Greg says," Melinda told Dave, keeping her voice steady, "that you killed him for nothing. That Carol always knew better. And that when you make other people's decisions for them, you get it wrong. You've been controlling Carol's life all along, haven't you? In one way or another."

"Greg's an idiot. Lived an idiot, died that way."

"You bastard!" Greg lifted the hand he'd been staring at, slamming it home through Dave— his eyes widening as he felt the impact this time. *Learning.*

He wasn't the only one. Dave shouted "Hey!" and jerked around toward Greg, glare at full bore and gun ready.

"That's Greg again," Melinda said. "You can't treat people the way you have and think they won't react—somehow, some way. Greg's new to this, but he's learning. I think . . . I think you should just let us go. Maybe I can help you."

But Dave's expression only hardened with resolve, his eyes narrowing down and his jaw jutting slightly. "Get up," he said to Jeannie and Craig. "Get *him* up. Drag him, I don't care. And get over to the quarry."

17

FINALLY, GORDON APPEARED, sitting on a large chunk of limestone, his posture far too casual, and his voice—when he spoke—far too soft. *"Gone squeamish, Dave? Whoever killed me wasn't squeamish. No, not at all."* But his wounds had disappeared, and instead of his crisp-edged anger, he looked resigned. Accepting.

Just when we could use a good hissy fit.

"What was it you used?" Gordon said, far too thoughtful for a man pondering his own violent death. Melinda didn't know whether to trust this new side of Gordon or run from it. *"I'm remembering, now, I think. A baseball bat, wasn't it?"*

Oh my God. Greg had been trying to warn her all along . . .

"Swing, batter batter," Greg said softly in the background, as if only now understanding himself.

"Gordon's here, now," Melinda told the others, and then quickly glanced at Lusak, who had been climbing to his feet as ordered but now hesitated, fear in his eye, at her words. "I don't think you'll have any problem."

"No," Gordon said. *"He's a coward and he left me to die, but he didn't kill me. I'm not even sure I'm sorry for what I did, but I'm done with him."* But when he looked at Dave, the burnt sienna anger washed over his form, building slowly, as if someone had a volume knob and had begun to turn it up.

"Well, my *God,*" Dave said, sarcasm lacing his voice. "Let's just have a *party.*"

"Right," Melinda said, her words just as edged. "The people you've killed and the ones you're about to." But just behind her, Jim groaned, and she instantly turned and dropped down beside him. "Hey," she said. "Don't try to move just yet." A pause, with a glare at Dave. "We're still sorting things out." But when his eyes fluttered open, there was little recognition there, just dazed confusion, and she bit her lip and looked away and took a deep breath—and then, through blurred vision, saw that they were no longer alone, no longer just the four hostages, the killer, and the two already dead.

There, hesitating in horror at the end of the path, stood Carol. And her mother, and—not quite fitting in at all—Howie. "Be careful!" Melinda blurted. "He's got a gun!"

"We heard it," Howie said, and he no longer looked confused or frightened; he stared straight at Gordon and Greg, and if he squinted—if he obviously saw very little of what she did, he still gave his head a grim shake, and he still stepped forward.

Not so far forward that he put Carol behind him, though. "Dave," Carol said. "What have you *done?*"

For the first time, Dave faltered. The gun wobbled down to a lower position. "Carol," he said, and just that. But only for a moment, and then he gathered himself. "You shouldn't have come. I'm taking care of things for you. I've always taken care of things for you."

She shook her head, golden brown hair awry from what must have been a hurried run down the path, her cheeks flushed . . . her eyes horrified. "I don't even want to know," she told him. "I don't think I can even bear to know!"

Melinda bit her lip; said nothing. She leaned down and kissed Jim's forehead and she watched Greg and Gordon's growing interest and resentment, and she let the moments play out between Carol and Dave—because Carol was the one with the power here, at least when it came to Dave. He'd done this for her, in his own sick way. Over the years, he'd done for her. And now maybe she could stop him.

And then two needlessly murdered men could find their peace, and this would be over for all of them. "Be okay," Melinda murmured, so close to Jim's ear no one else could possibly hear. "Oh, please be okay."

Dave took a step toward Carol; a note of pleading entered his voice. "Go home. I'm taking care of this."

She ignored him; she looked at Melinda. "Did I hear you right? He killed Greg, all those years ago?"

Dave didn't give her a chance to respond. "He didn't deserve you!" he shouted, that pleading note still in place. "You have to understand—he just didn't deserve you! I took care of it for you. You didn't have to worry about him; you didn't have any chance of being tied down by him."

Carol recoiled. "Greg was my *friend*! He was sweet and kind and he was my *friend*!"

Dave frowned; he'd had a moment to think. "How did you even get here?"

"What do you think?" Carol's mother snapped. Either she hadn't noticed the gun or she felt no fear of it. "After what Melinda said on the phone— asking me to make sure you knew there were no hard feelings between us—I got to thinking. I thought about the strange little things that have happened since you came back from upstate. I thought about why she'd have reason to ask about that whiteboard when you keep losing the markers, and you better believe I heard about the vandalism at her store. I thought about the things that happened around Carol before you got sent upstate." She crossed her arms, her expression wavering between righteous anger and hurt. "We took you in, Dave. We gave you a job. We gave you a second chance!"

Upstate. He'd been in prison. Had Gordon mentioned something about one of his guys going to prison? Or had she seen it in the paper—something about beating a man to within an inch of his life? Didn't matter. She understood better now. She'd be willing to bet, too, that that man had looked wrong at Carol—and no one had put those pieces together. Just like they hadn't ever realized that Greg's death had been more than a sad, early end to a young man's lackadaisical life.

But Carol didn't quite wait for her mother to finish. "We weren't sure," she said, looking at Melinda. "Just . . . worried. We were on our way to see you. We came the back way; we always used that road, just like Greg used to use it, just like Gordon liked to use it. All of you did, didn't you? And when we reached that tree—"

"The helmet," Howie interrupted. "We found it. And the bike, off the road. And you're not the only one who remembers this path." He shifted uncomfortably, looked away from them all, but not without one last glance at Melinda. "And . . . I don't think it's what you see, but I can see enough, if I don't drink it away."

"Is it true?" Carol said, talking over him, all of them talking over each other, layers of sound that beat against Melinda and fanned Dave's impatience, that unnerving gleam in his eye. "Howie says . . . he says Gordon is here. That you can see him, and that's why you came to me." Her challenge turned into something forlorn, her fair complexion gone splotchy red with emotion on top of the flush of exertion. "Why didn't you tell me?"

Careful, here. With Dave ready to explode and Gordon glowering himself back into a fit of fury and Jim just now stirring, thinking about rolling over to his side—or more likely, not thinking at all—it was not the time for deep philosophy. "You didn't seem ready to hear it," she said, simply enough. "I would have, if the time had come. If Gordon had needed that in order to go into the Light, or if I'd felt it would comfort you. But I was just upsetting you."

"What?" Jim said, and batted irritably at nothing in the vague vicinity of his head, then made an aborted effort to sit up. Melinda quickly slid in closer, slipping her crooked leg beneath his shoulders as he moved and wrapping her arms around him. *Oh, God, you're supposed to be the strong one.*

"But if I'd known!" Carol cried, anguish in her voice, her features crumpling.

"It's not that simple," Melinda told her, cradling Jim, shushing him with a glance at Dave. He appeared wild-eyed, unpredictable. If he thought Jim was too much trouble . . .

Just keep talking. Keep it low-key. Work it through. It was what she always did—persisted when it came to helping earthbound spirits, even when those left behind were all tangled up in themselves. "Gordon's been struggling with what happened; he's been angry. And he's been blaming Craig, because Craig . . ." She suddenly wasn't sure just what to say, not with Craig Lusak watching with horror on his face and Jeannie's arms entwined through his. He was still on the ground, still hoping not to die, but not yet doing anything about it.

Not yet.

"Because I was *there*," Lusak said for her, although he hesitated at the shock on Carol's face, the anger blooming in Howie's expression. But he swallowed visibly and, with a nervous glance at Dave, who seemed to have decided to be amused by the entire thing, added, "I was there, and even though nothing could have been done by that time, I didn't try."

Dave snorted. "That makes no sense, man. You *are* a loser. No wonder you got caught up in this."

"It makes perfect sense to me," Melinda said, daring that much. "He didn't know at the time that he couldn't have made a difference. It matters. It's not fair to either Gordon or Craig to pretend it doesn't."

And Gordon said quietly, *"But now I do know who to blame."*

Dave, blissfully ignorant of that burnt ire, only snorted again. "Howie, man, get Carol out of here. Get her damned *mother* out of here. And you. You turned your back often enough. It's time to do it again."

Howie shook his head, his words coming slow. "I don't think so. Not for this."

"Mel?" Jim put a hand to his head—it must have ached fiercely—and this time it was a more directed movement, a more purposeful one, even if his aim wasn't quite steady.

"I'm here," she said quickly, leaning over his ear. "I'm taking care of it. And I need you to rest, because we've got a washstand to pick up, and it's too heavy for me to handle on my own."

"What about . . . ?" He struggled up, made it to a hunched sort of sitting position, and squinted around, still obviously determined to act.

"Jim, I'm serious. I need you to stay down so I can deal with this. There's too much happening." And, still feeling his resistance, still knowing he was barely pulling off the upright position, she leaned in close and gave him an out. "At least for now?"

And he subsided just in time, his nod almost imperceptible, his catch of pained breath even less so. Just in time, because Gordon had left his rock and stalked among them.

Stalking Dave, now.

"Yeah," he said. *"I know who to blame."*

"Gordon, please," she said, looking at him only in her peripheral vision—looking, in fact, off to the rock where he'd been. Because if Dave realized how close his old friend had gotten, he might well just put an end to all of this—the discussion, the witnesses, the emotional, guilt-ravaged encounter in the woods. "Think about this. It's not the last mark you want to make on this world. It's not the last thing you want Carol to see of you. You're better than this, and you know it."

Gordon laughed, and the bitter sound reverberated slightly, distorting as it had when she'd first seen him. His egregious head wound had returned, streams of red threading along the natural contours of his face, exaggerated gashes of clotted blood and gore along his temple. *"You don't get it,"* he said. *"You'll never get it, because you think you can see the best in everyone. You think you can make it all right."* He said the words with a sneer of exaggerated niceness, and slid right back into hard-edged anger. *"Well, you* can't. *Because I'm not who everyone thought I was—who they thought I'd become."*

He'd let go of the old life, but the old life hadn't let go of him. The guys calling, stopping by to see if they could lure him out to get Whet. So here he is. Official good-byes. A beer for the road.

"The way I see it," Mikey Gomez says, smacking his beer down on the scarred bar hard enough to draw the slanting, warning gaze of Lou the bartender-owner-bouncer, a man big enough to fill all three jobs, "you're saying we're not good enough for you anymore."

Gordon swallows his own beer. "You asshole, always gotta make it about you, don't you?"

Howie grins down at the bar, snorting through his nose. He's had one too many, although it's not yet late; Gordon thinks Howie arrived a couple of beers ahead of the game—paying too much attention, as usual, to the unoccupied pool tables, at least until he put away a few. Always the cheap stuff for Howie, always in quantity. He used to claim that the pool balls moved on their own, but enough razzing from the guys put an end to that.

Dave Schmidt, down at the far end of the bar, just looks away. Gordon catches a glimpse of a frown. Dave wasn't like that before he went upstate—always hard, always tough, and hell,

he'd beaten that kid nearly to death, hadn't he?—
but who knew what prison did to a guy. Gordon's
probably lucky he'll never find out—lucky he
turned himself around.

But Mikey takes it all in good stride, because
Mikey always does. "Buy me a beer, then, you—"
and he spews a string of expletives that makes
Howie duck his head and Lou roll his eyes and
everyone in earshot—not so many, on a weekday
evening, a gentler crowd with some young couples
and even a few tired white-collar guys—break out
into laughter.

Except one.

"You think that's funny?" The guy's got a black
biker do-rag and lots of black leather, but he's
skinny beneath that jacket—bad teeth, bad skin,
too much meth. A little antsy, a little cocky. Just
passing through. "You even think about what he's
saying? What's going on here? Or are you all such
little asswipes that you really buy this whole thing,
this good-luck-with-your-new-life crap? Your
buddy there has it right, you know—you're not
good enough anymore."

Lou flips a damp towel over his shoulder, leaving his hands free. He gives the fellow the eye. Any
local would have known to pay attention, but not
this guy. He sneers at them all, at their silence.
"Yeah," he says. "Asswipes."

"Hey," Howie protests, not as mean as it's probably meant to sound, not with all that beer behind it. "Guy's gonna put family first, now. Nothing wrong with that, you got a family to do it with."

"Pussy-whipped, you mean," says skinny biker guy. In the corner, Dave scowls. Always an odd one, with a weird sense of chivalry for a guy who didn't hesitate to get rough—sometimes too rough—if the moment struck him. He'd come right back to Bayview after his release from prison, and Gordon had gotten him a part-time caretaker job at the B&B, freeing himself up to do more of the management and financials. Carol, he knew, was still doubtful about it, but Dave would prove himself.

Still, kind of surprising he didn't speak up now—didn't stand up for the man who'd helped him out upon his return here, only a couple of bucks left in his pocket and most folks looking the other way when they saw him. Gordon, looking at the biker, feels his temper begin to simmer. As if this jerkwad knew anything about him. As if he knew what it had taken—the work, the willpower—to turn things around into a life he could actually look forward to instead of just live through?

Howie glances at him and, even through the beer blear, sees Gordon's edge. He's always been the one to read Gordon the best, the sidekick who knew when to say the right thing. The one friend who's stayed in touch without expecting raucous bar nights and midnight flings. "You don't even know us," he says, simple enough. "You just oughta go get some air."

Lou nods, but it's Gordon he watches.

For Lou knows, too—knows that Gordon has only covered up that temper of his, not replaced it. Pretends it doesn't exist, but hasn't eradicated it. And realizing that makes Gordon angrier, makes him feel like a failure. Puts an instant flare of fear in his belly—fear that Carol will see the truth and walk away. *Imposter.*

And meanwhile skinny biker guy sneers. "God," he says. "He's pissing on the lot of you, and you still defend him. Pussy-whipped by proxy."

Mikey stands up from his corner; Lou looks over with a sharp, scowling shake of his head, and Mikey subsides, but Gordon does not. The temper tightens his spine; it balls his fists. Lou says to the biker, "You've had enough, mister. Your drinks are on me. Now go get some of that night air."

Skinny biker jerk makes a rude noise. The jukebox song ends; no one moves to kick up a new one. Two pool balls click together, or what sounds like it, because there's no one over by the tables. Skinny biker jerk looks around, shrugs. "Done here anyway," he says, pushing his drink toward the center of the table that he alone occupies. And Howie relaxes, as though he thinks that's the end of it, and Lou's wary eye gets less mean, and Mikey pretends like nothing ever happened, taking another big gulp of his beer.

And skinny biker jerk gets up to leave, and on the way out, he gives Gordon a little shove.

And Gordon's temper explodes.

Skinny biker guy flies across the room, slung and flung, slams into the fake rock lining the inside front wall. Gordon dives after him and half a dozen hands land on him—his arms, his shoulders—and he fights them all, lost in the burnt red roar of temper released . . .

Glorying in it.

"You see?" Gordon asked, impatient as Melinda pressed her hands to her head, overwhelmed by the images and the emotion, rocked by the violence within him. *"That's the real me. What I couldn't fix."*

Dazed, she lifted her head, looking directly at Dave. "That's why?" she asked, groping for understanding. "He wasn't good enough for Carol because . . . what, because he lost his temper in the bar that night?"

"Because he pretended to be something he wasn't," Dave spat. "He *pretended* to be changed, and she believed him. Lying sonofabitch!"

Gordon pulsated with his building fury; his words howled around Melinda in a shattering reverberation. *"It was all I could do!"* And then, chest heaving with emotion, eyes glowing with it, voice thick and hoarse, he said, *"But you're right. It wasn't good enough. None of it was good enough. That's who I am. Maybe I had to die for it—but now, so do you."*

"Gordon!"

Jim tensed under her hand. "That can't be good."

"It's not," she told him, voice low, watching as Gordon flipped into speed-jerk mode, as the dead winter's leaves and dried grasses began to stir.

"Oh, God," said Howie.

Carol's voice, pitched high and frightened: "What's happening? What's going on? Is he still here? Is Gordon here?"

"Gordon," Melinda said, rising to her feet to stand at Jim's shoulder, her leg still touching him, still clinging to that warmth and to the strength she drew from him even when he was too wobbly to stand himself. "Gordon, *please*." Never mind that he could well save them all—Craig and Jeannie getting to their feet now as Dave grew wild-eyed and distracted, Melinda terrified for Jim and now for Carol and her mother and even Howie, too. If Gordon did this thing, she would lose him. He'd never cross into the Light; he'd never accept it. And there was so much darkness here these days, just waiting for someone to falter, to give up on themselves . . .

"Stop it!" Dave shouted, staggering back against the wind, his fear edging toward an out-of-control retaliation, the gun wavering wildly in his hand in spite of his efforts to aim it—at Melinda, at Jeannie, at Carol. It discharged, a wasted bullet kicking up rock and dirt from the ground; Melinda jumped in spite of herself, her heart hammering into overtime as Dave shouted, "If that's really you, Gordon, you'd better just stop it, dammit, or I'm going to shoot them all right now!"

"Gordon . . ." She couldn't even see him, now, just a blur, with the wind rising to bluster in her face; she squinted, raising a hand against the little twigs and tiny gravel that pelted her. "Gordon, it was a flawed moment, from a man who was doing his best! Ask Carol—" In desperation, she whirled around to face Carol. "He lost his temper at the Whetstone, that's what this is all about! He hurt a man there, and he thinks it takes away from everything he did—all he accomplished. From the life he made with you."

Gordon jerked to a bruising stop, so close to her face that Melinda stiffened, stifling a shriek. Jim struggled to his feet, gathered her up from behind, stood for her, as steady as anyone in the wind, holding her as she flinched from Gordon's shout, his bitter words. *I died for it! Is there any greater betrayal?*

"Oh—" Melinda couldn't immediately separate

herself from his emotion—from the heartbreak she felt lurking beneath his anger. Jim's arms tightened around her waist, pulling her in close; she forced her mouth to stop the tremble, her closed throat to allow the words. "*You* didn't do that, Gordon. You made a mistake, that's all. *You weren't perfect.* None of us is." To Carol, she said, "He thinks he betrayed you, because he lost his temper in that bar and it ultimately led to his death."

Carol gaped in clear astonishment. "You must be kidding! Gordon Reese, do you think I didn't know you still had a temper? Do you think I didn't know it when I married you? What kind of idiot do you think I am?"

Gordon stopped short, starkly astonished. The wind raged around them; Craig drew Jeannie to her feet, then stepped away from her—stepped between her and Dave and the wavering gun, and barely reacted when Dave pulled the trigger again, cursing as the gun jerked in his grip, his aim gone completely awry. "*You knew?*" Gordon cried.

"He's surprised that you knew," Melinda said, a dry understatement, the wind whipping strands of hair into her face to catch on her lashes and lips.

"Oh, Gordon," Carol said, closing her eyes there on the edge of his raging wind, covering her mouth. Her mother stepped up behind her, put hands on her shoulders; Howie, too, stepped in close. "Gordon, of course I knew. I knew you missed those nights out with your friends, and I knew you cursed up a storm when you thought I couldn't hear, and I knew you kept a six-pack stashed in the garage, and that sometimes you drank it all in one night. But I knew you were *trying* and that, for the most part, you were succeeding. You were—you *are*—the man I love. How can you ever doubt that? How can you even think I would have been with you, if you weren't exactly who and what I wanted?"

For an instant, the wind died. Only an instant. Long enough for Dave to stagger into balance, for Melinda to relax against Jim, feeling the ragged nature of his breathing and the effort it cost him just to stand there.

Just long enough for Carol to look at Melinda in grateful surprise. "He heard me." And then, "You heard me! Thank God. Gordon, I don't want to lose you. But you can't go on like this. You have to find your peace. I need to be able to tell your baby girl that you're at rest . . . that you're waiting for me."

But the wind stirred. Gordon circled them so fast that Melinda almost missed it, *might* have missed it had Dave not made a gargling noise, paling as Gordon punched right through him. Staggering, Dave clutched the gun with both hands, bringing it to bear on Melinda. "Make it stop!" he shouted, and Melinda squeaked on a gasp, drawing in that breath and sticking there, unable to quite let it out at the sight of that gaping barrel pointed her way.

"I'll *make it stop!*" Gordon raged. "*Just as you stopped my life—stopped me. For nothing! Did you hear her? She loves me! She needed me—our family needed me! And you took it all away!*"

"*From me, too,*" Greg said, standing by the edge of the quarry, his quiet demeanor gone hard. "*He took everything from me.*"

And he watched as Gordon punched through Dave yet again, as Dave stumbled back to find his faltering balance, the gun dipping away. Lusak set Jeannie aside, took a more confident step forward, and Carol cried denial as she and her mother huddled together against the wind and Howie shouted, "No, man! Gordon, no! This isn't you! You were never like *this,* not ever!"

"Gordon!" Melinda held tightly to Jim's hands where they clasped over her waist, drawing strength from their contact. Jim ducked his head against hers, hiding from the wind, but she squinted into it, hunting Gordon—needing to see him, to read his burnt-edged fury and the pulsating glow that marked his path. "Gordon, you made something of yourself! You changed your life! You made good decisions, and you should stand by them, not throw them away because of *what someone else has done.*"

Abruptly, the wind died.

Leaf dust and twigs settled gently in the still air.

Carol emerged from her huddle, finding Melinda's glance with hope in her eyes; she took a step forward—and caught sight of Dave, still there at the head of the trail.

And Gordon appeared. His scruffy jeans and boots and leather jacket were clean and neat; his features, lacking the burnt sienna effect of his anger, had softened into handsomeness. He looked at himself; he looked around. *"Oh,"* he said, surprise coloring his voice, opening his posture. *"I guess . . . I guess that's true."* He stepped closer to Carol. *"You . . . you were the best decision I ever made. What would it say about us if I can't stand by that?"*

"It's okay," Melinda said, talking to Carol but squeezing Jim's hand. "He's chosen to honor what he had with you."

Carol's face crumpled with relief and grief and sheer reaction; her mother hugged her, pressing a kiss to her cheek and murmuring comforting words too low to be heard.

"Yeah, yeah, that's enough of that." Dave, too, had recovered himself. "You know, I've had enough of *all* this. Gordon's here, Greg's here, it's all real sentimental. But they're *dead*. I killed them for a *reason.*"

Melinda flinched at the expression that passed

over Greg's face then, the flicker of hardness. Dave, aggressively oblivious, ignored her reaction and its implication. "Carol, you'll get over it. We'll do fine on your place, you and me and your folks. It's time for you to show some appreciation for what I've done. And the rest of you just shoulda minded your own damned business. Especially you, Howie. You shoulda known not to mess with me."

And just like that, he raised the gun and pulled the trigger. Melinda flinched from the explosive noise, ducking into Jim; his arms tightened around her. She opened her eyes in time to see Howie crumple slowly to the ground, utter astonishment on his face.

Lusak made a gargling noise, a desperate noise. It rose to a shout and he suddenly dropped his shoulder and charged, startling a cry from Jeannie. Dave reacted an instant too late; Lusak slammed into him and the gun went flying, skittering across the ground to slide right over the quarry edge, clattering all the way down.

Dave swore so explosively the words came out garbled, and he went down beneath Lusak—but only for a moment. Instantly he battered his way back up to land hard, swift blows to Lusak's ribs, his neck, his face, until Lusak ducked and grappled close, flailing with his fists, both men far too close to the edge.

Jim pushed away from Melinda, a stumbling

lunge to reach the men, falling short and then scrabbling forward again as Jeannie rushed up to Melinda's side and grabbed her arm, both of them hesitating for fear of making it worse—for fear of adding that final extra piece that would push all three men over the edge.

"Wow," Howie said incongruously in the background. "Gordon, man, I really see you."

"No!" Carol said fiercely. "You will *not*. It's not that bad, Howie, I swear it's not!"

"Over," Dave grunted, clawing at Lusak, twisting him toward the edge. "You. *Go!*"

"No!" Jeannie cried, leaping forward.

Melinda snatched her back. "They're too close!"

Another desperate, staggering lunge, and Jim planted his hands on Lusak's jacket, yanked him back and away—and then he faltered, falling to his hands and knees, fingers digging against rock and grit, his expression so very determined and yet not quite focused. As Dave snatched him up, hands fisting up Jim's jacket, Jim's defensive swing went wild, nearly bringing them both down. And now it was Jeannie holding Melinda back, rocks bouncing over the quarry edge and Dave's boots slipping over the ground. Jim dug in, resisting, the air full of harsh breathing and grunting effort and gasps, as Lusak regained his feet and hesitated, no more able than Melinda or Jeannie to intervene without bringing them all down.

And then Jim's foot skidded over the edge, and Melinda shook Jeannie off, rushing forward to duck in low as she reached the men. She kicked at Dave with all her might, hanging on to Jim's jacket and hammering at Dave's knee with sheer ferocity while Dave yanked back so hard that even Melinda staggered a short step forward. Dave shouted unintelligible words that she almost instantly realized had included, *"—take you with me—!"*

And Greg, oh-so-quiet, oh-so-gentle, the laid-back boy who had trusted, who had lacked drive and action, said, *"I don't think so,"* and gently placed his hands on either side of Dave's head and—

swirling color and darkness, Day-Glo stench and the taste of ants, spinning groundless vertigo splash—

A man's hoarse scream filled what remained of Melinda's senses and suddenly she was tumbling back, Jim falling on top of her, tangling limbs, solid substantial blessed familiarity, and she regained her vision just in time to see Dave—

Dave, arms windmilling, mouth agape . . . expression nothing but terror as he fell away into open space and down.

Melinda, clutching tightly at Jim, pulled him even closer as Dave's scream ended with the solid crunching thump of impact.

"Whoa," Jim said, a groaning sigh. "I really need to sit down."

"You *are* sitting," Melinda informed him. "In fact, you're doing it on *me*." He shifted, his hand patting the ground.

"Technically, I'm lying on you. And boy, do I wish it was under different circumstances." But as he said it he rolled aside, giving her room to scramble out from beneath.

"You must be feeling better." She ended up on her knees beside him—and got her first good look at his face. Bloodied and gritty on one side, horribly bruised on the other. "Oh, your poor head!"

He winced. "Yeah. Later. Howie—?"

And so she helped him over to Howie, where Mrs. Donovan had already pulled out a cell phone from the prodigious fanny pack she wore, the only one among them who hadn't left her purse behind at the growing collection of vehicles beside the fallen tree.

There, he took a quick look—the bullet hole into the left lower rib cage, the blood at Howie's mouth—and had them roll Howie onto his wounded side. Mrs. Donovan then quickly flung the granola contents of a sandwich baggie to the woods so he could plaster the limp baggie to the sucking wound with Howie's own blood.

Melinda eased back, nearly bumping into a hushed Jeannie—and nearly passing through Gordon.

"I'm sorry," Lusak said. "I got you into this—"

all of it. And . . . well, you saw. I'm not very good with my fists."

"You were wonderful," Jeannie said fiercely, and she hugged him. "You've been sick and exhausted and do you think I don't know how hard that was for you? You were *stupendous.*"

Melinda smiled, looking over at Jim—unsteady even on his knees, but reassuring Howie anyway, reassuring Carol and Mrs. Donovan. She knew well enough how hard he'd go down when the local crew finally made it out here and Howie didn't need him anymore. "I think we always know our men just a little better than they think."

Gordon just shook his head. *"I had no idea . . ."*

Melinda must have responded to him—some flicker of expression, some fleeting smile—for Lusak came to attention. "Is he here?" he asked, going wary. "Is he—?"

Still mad at me? She heard that well enough, unspoken or not.

"He's right here." Melinda nodded at Gordon, who grinned at Lusak's discomfiture.

"Hey, tell him we're good now." He gave it a moment's thought, nodded. *"Tell him I understand. And hey, with a soft swing like that, he probably made the right decision to run past that bait shack."*

Melinda took a breath, smiled, and told Lusak, "He understands why you didn't stop to help that night," and then glanced back to Gordon with a clear message in her expression: *That's as close as I'm going to get.*

Gordon just grinned. He disappeared, showing up almost immediately at Carol's side—at Howie's side, where he exchanged a few words with Howie, during which Carol looked up and over to Melinda. Carol knew Gordon was there, that was clear enough; she knew, and she wanted . . .

She wanted what she couldn't have. Melinda knew that sad and wistful expression. But she also knew it was the front edge of acceptance.

"I always thought Howie was different," Greg said, appearing at her side more faintly than he'd been earlier. After a moment he solidified. *"I kinda feel like maybe I'm just getting to know him, after seeing him here today. Coming out for Carol like that . . . Who would have figured?"*

"She has a lot of people who love her." Melinda nodded at Carol, confirming Gordon's presence, but her gaze quickly slid back to Jim, watching him for any sign of faltering as he directed Mrs. Donovan in gathering up branches to use against Howie's back, propping him up. Craig and Jeannie Lusak hastened over to help, leaving Melinda near the edge of the quarry—not looking over, and strangely not worried about encountering Dave's spirit. She thought that like Greg, it would take Dave a while to pull himself together, and she could only hope that a spirit as damaged as his could find the way to cross over without her help. She looked over at Greg. "Is there anything else I can do for you? Would you like to talk to Carol, or anyone else?"

Greg gave it some thought; he was solid, now, standing at the very lip of the quarry without concern for the drop behind him, no sign of confusion in his expression or manner. *"You know,"* he said, *"I'm sorry it took me so long to get my act together. So many times I tried to warn you, but I know I just wasn't making sense. That whole batter thing . . . I guess Dave swinging that bat was the first thing I really saw. The only anchor I had for a while."*

"You did your best," she told him. "And now?"

"You know?" He gave it another moment's thought; nodded. *"I'm good. It's going to get out— what Dave did—and that's enough."*

She gave him a long look, seeing in his expression a quiet solidity that hadn't been apparent in any of his photos. "It's more than that, isn't it?"

"Do you think?" The notion seemed to surprise him; he took his attention from Carol to look more directly at Melinda, and then, when she didn't respond immediately, that surprise turned into a nod. *"You know, you're right. You've heard what they all said about me: Nice kid. Didn't have direction, took the easy way. Went with the flow. I heard it enough—along with the ever-popular* never amount to anything.*"*

"I can believe it." And she did, and she had no doubt he'd felt all the unspoken judgments behind even the kinder words.

He nodded again. *"Dave thought he could have his way with me . . . and you know, he was right. But he thought, after all this time, that I hadn't changed. Hadn't learned anything from taking his drugs, from feeling that final shove . . . from lingering long enough to feel the ants and flies at my dying body."*

"Greg," she said, "I am so sorry—"

"No, don't you get it? Here we are, and he was wrong. I did what I had to do. I didn't save myself, but I was finally a friend to Carol when she really needed me, in the way she needed me. I did something that needed *to be done."*

"You saved my life," Melinda said. "And my husband's, and I can't tell you what that means to me. I have to admit, I was a little worried about how this was going to affect you. What happened just now." She took a breath, said it out loud—because with Greg's fate at stake, flinching at the hard words wasn't fair to either of them. "Killing Dave."

But it took only a moment before Greg shrugged. *"I didn't push him. I didn't put him on the edge of that quarry. I didn't even bring him out here in the first place, with or without that gun in his hand. I only gave him a taste of what it was like, here on the edge, when he turned me loose with his killer cocktail in my system. It's a justice of sorts."*

"A very hard justice."

He shrugged again. *"Sometimes we really do get what's coming to us. And sometimes I guess it even comes from someone like me."*

"You know," Melinda said, pulling her sweater coat more tightly around herself as the cool air bit through the fading adrenaline to raise goose bumps, "I think they were wrong. All those people who said you didn't have direction, that you wouldn't amount to anything. I think you were just a late bloomer."

He grinned at her, quite suddenly—boyish and charming, as sweet as everyone ever said. *"A little too late. But thanks."* And almost immediately, he blinked and squinted and said, *"Hey, I shook those drugs—"*

Melinda laughed. "I think that's the Light. I think you're ready."

"Hey," Greg said, *"I think you're right."*

18

"HEY, WOW—GREAT DAY for a picnic in the square," Rick Payne said, descending on Melinda and Jim's quiet park bench in a whirlwind of obliviousness. He took a second look at Jim and winced. "That's a heck of a ding you've got there. Must hurt, huh?"

Jim unconsciously reached up to touch a bruise of spreading and dramatic coloration, stopping himself just in time. "Now that you mention it."

Melinda had less restraint; she sent Payne a purely cross look. "Your timing is rotten."

Not that it affected him. "Been trying to reach you, by the way," Payne said, leaning over the back of the bench to pluck a cherry tomato from the shared salad sitting on the bench between them. Melinda thought she saw Jim's fork hovering into attack position, but he showed heroic restraint and waited for the hand to retreat before forking salad onto his plate beside the turkey, cheese, and apple slice sandwich she'd made up that morning—very much an offering of appreciation, after he'd missed a day of work while the world stopped spinning around him and they'd spent countless hours giving statements regarding Dave's death and what they'd learned from him of Gordon's death, and of Greg's death so long ago.

Got too close to the quarry edge during the struggle—that had been their unanimous story, and Carol's suggestion. "That Gordon and Greg were here," she'd said, "that's private."

Melinda couldn't argue with that. But Payne was still hovering, and that, she could argue with. "Trying to reach me, why? No, wait. Don't tell me. You want to gloat about being right."

"You wound me!" he exclaimed, straightening so as to better gesture with his hand over his heart. But with a lopsided grin, he added, "And how well you know me. Yes, indeed, gloating was part of my plan. But mainly I wanted to know . . . what was I right about? You know, so I can properly calibrate my gloating."

Melinda teased a baby carrot from the salad and bit into it. "Haven't you read the paper? It was the acid trip. I know it was just an offhand comment, but you *were* right. Those images Greg was throwing at me came from the time of his death, and the drugs he was on when he fell. The ants . . . I'm not entirely sure if that happened before or after he died. I don't think he was, either. But you were right about that, too. They eat dead things. They went for Greg."

Payne frowned. "And that whole *batterbatter* chant?"

"Just trying to warn me, the best he could. Dave used a baseball bat on Gordon."

"Oh," Payne said. And then, most expressively, "That's almost too much information."

"You *haven't* been reading the paper," Melinda decided.

"A failing," he said. "It's more fun to read the supermarket rags and deconstruct the alien abduction stories. So Greg, he's . . ." and he made a whirly gesture.

Melinda crossed her arms and just looked at him.

"Really good sandwich, babe," Jim said, apparently having decided that the only way to have this picnic lunch together was to go ahead and have it. She thought he might have something there.

"Thank you," she said. "Your mom wants credit for giving up the recipe, by the way." And then, over her shoulder to Payne, "Yes. Greg crossed over."

"What about the other fellow? The one who started it all? And is it true, it was all over a girl?"

"A woman." Melinda raised her gaze to a flicker of movement, found Gordon standing behind Payne—still neat and tidy, his expression tinged with regret and acceptance. "And Gordon . . . he hasn't crossed over yet. In fact, he's right behind you."

Payne stiffened with alarm, scooting over to the side. "What? Here? Now?"

Jim offered her a juicy cherry tomato from the salad and wiped dressing from the corner of her mouth afterward; Melinda nodded as she chewed. "Here," she said, after she swallowed. "Now." And to Gordon, "Is there something I can do for you? Are you ready to talk to them?"

For he'd left, those several days earlier at the cliff, leaving behind a wistful Carol—although during Melinda's brief visit with Howie at the hospital, it seemed as though both Carol and her mother had quickly taken Howie into the fold and had already cleared space for him to recuperate at the Honey Bs.

"If you don't mind," Gordon said, *"I think it's time."*

"Let me check with Delia," she said. And to Jim, "Okay?"

"Hey," he said. "It's what you do. And that was a *great* sandwich. I hope you saved Mom's recipe. C'mere."

For a moment, she could almost forget that Rick

Payne was there, that Gordon waited, that they were, indeed, in the middle of a very public square where more than one person chose to lunch in the gorgeous warmth of the spring day.

For a moment.

And then she broke away from Jim's very thorough kiss, rescued a smear of shared mayonnaise from his lip, and stuck her finger in her mouth without much thinking about it.

"Whoa," said Payne. "That was pretty hot, kids."

Melinda slanted him a look and left it at that. To Gordon, she said, "All right then. Let's see what we can do," and got up from her picnic lunch and her recovering and heroic husband, and went to see about helping Gordon find his closure and his crossing point.

"Well?" Delia asked as Melinda breezed into the store, purse hitched over one shoulder so she could carry in the hot caffeine thank-you treat for Delia—not to mention the herbal tea that had called to Melinda herself, soothing and thoughtful. "How was it and ooh, thank you."

"It was . . ." Melinda stopped, considered the afternoon, and nodded. "It was fine. Did I see more window smudges on the way in?"

"I was just about to get those. But hey, you can't leave it at that! Details, woman, I want details!"

Melinda tucked her purse away behind the counter and sipped at the tea, which had cooled to the perfect temperature during the walk across the square. "Well," she said, "I can't say they were surprised to see me."

In fact, they'd been a lot more welcoming than the last time Melinda had stopped by the B&B, and they'd shown her, with some excitement, the room they'd prepared for Howie.

"He only saw Gordon that one time, really," Carol had confided in her, the baby sleeping in a sling around her shoulder, almost too big for it now. "Otherwise it's just as it's always been—the glimpses. But you know, now that he understands what he's seeing, I don't think it bothers him as much. I don't think he'll fight it like he always has. You know—the drinking."

Melinda thought of her mother—in denial for most of Melinda's life, and suffering migraines for it—and couldn't help a wistful smile. "That's good," she said. "And I'm glad you've got a place for him here while he recovers."

"As if we could do anything else, after the way he was hurt," Mrs. Donovan said, as brusque as she could be, that fanny pack sitting over her hip as it always did, stuffed just as full as ever. "Why, if he hadn't come to us . . ." And she stopped, her eyes suddenly filling, her cheeks flushed high with emotion. "I just can't believe it was Dave all along—first Greg, then Carol's beau after high school, and then—" She struggled with the words, finally bursting out, "I can't believe we took him in when he was released from prison! We thought that he deserved a second chance—Gordon thought it!—and we took that man right into our house!"

"You had no way of knowing," Melinda told her. "You did a compassionate thing. Just as you're doing a compassionate thing for Howie."

"You see," Gordon said, suddenly standing there behind her, *"you see why I changed for her. Why she brought it out in me."*

"Yes," Melinda said. "I do see."

"He's here." Carol looked at Melinda, looked around her. "I know he is."

Melinda nodded. "He asked me to come to see you, actually."

"Bring them outside," Gordon said. *"To the porch swing. I always loved the porch swing."*

"He wants to go out to the porch," Melinda told them. "To the—"

"Swing," Carol finished, and nodded. "He loved that swing." And when they got there, only Carol sat; Melinda stood aside, leaving room for Gordon; Mrs. Donovan stood in the B&B doorway, while Mr. Donovan—heretofore an invisible presence spending his retirement hours in the kitchen with baking experiments—came out to stand behind her, his flannel shirtsleeves rolled up around his forearms and a stained apron around his waist. Carol sat and sighed and, without even realizing it, leaned slightly into the arm Gordon had put around her shoulders, his fingers curling around to tickle the baby's head. The baby, in the way of children, happily grasped at what no one else but Melinda could see.

Carol smiled, smoothing back the baby's hair—dark, like Gordon's—and said, "I just wish it could stay like this, now. Even though he's not here, I know he's *here*."

"I know," Melinda said, leaning back against the porch rail to look out over the yard, fresh spring green grass, lush blooming flowers. Gordon, she knew—looking at him, looking at his pride in his home and family—had felt welcome here. As would Howie, whatever role he would ultimately play in this family. Uncle, she thought, looking at the baby. "But you know that it can't stay this way. Not if he's truly at peace. And I think he's reached that point."

Gordon nodded. *"I need you to tell her . . . it's because of her that I can find this place at all. I don't regret a thing. Not the changes, not what I left behind, not the way it turned out. It was worth it, and it made me into who I am."*

"He's so glad for his time with you," Melinda told Carol. "He doesn't regret the choices he made."

"But if he hadn't—" Carol burst out almost immediately . . . and stopped, just as quickly, when Gordon pressed his fingers against her lips. Her own hand rose to her mouth, a wondering expression on her face; Melinda nodded ever so slightly.

"He doesn't want you to go there," she suggested.

"If I hadn't," Gordon said, echoing Carol's words, *"I might be alive right now, I might not. Instead I had the most wonderful years a man could have, and I learned who I could really be. I saw my daughter born. I saw my wife turn into the most wonderful mother. You tell her . . ."* He looked down at the baby, who gurgled at him, and for the first time he seemed at a loss for words. *"You tell her I love her."*

"He says that being with you is what made him alive," Melinda told her. "And he wants you to be sure to tell the baby how much he loves her, every day."

"Yes," Carol said, suddenly fierce. "I can do that."

Gordon stood; Carol looked puzzled at the loss of a presence she couldn't quite feel in the first place. He turned to the Donovans. *"Tell them thank you for taking me in. And tell Howie to do right by them."*

Melinda nodded. That she could gladly do.

And then he got that look on his face, the wonder she'd come to know so well.

"He's ready to cross into the Light," she told Carol, gently, knowing the woman wasn't quite ready for it yet, knowing her eyes would fill and redden, that her face would crumple. "This is what you've done for him, what you've given him." She glanced at Gordon, saw his hesitation. "He needs to know you'll be all right. He needs that one last gift—not belief in him, but belief in yourself."

"Oh!" Carol said, startled. She exchanged a quick look with her parents, found their support, and turned back to Melinda—and then to the open space on the porch she'd figured out to be Gordon, from the attention Melinda had paid it. "Yes. I can do that. Believe in me as I believed in him. That's only fair, isn't it? I can definitely do that."

"I love you," Gordon said, and was gone.

"Hey," Delia said, a voice from the here and now, a tiny bit sharp and a tiny bit worried. "Are you crying?"

"No," Melinda said automatically, suddenly pulled out of recent memory to focus on the store around her. "I mean . . . maybe. But it's okay. It's *good* crying. Gordon crossed over into the Light, Carol has accepted his death and can work through her grief, Howie has more of a family waiting for him than he ever expected . . ."

But Delia didn't look entirely convinced at the happy ending. "What about Dave?"

Melinda had to admit, "I don't know about Dave. He might have crossed over as soon as he died; he might have gone to the Dark. It depends on who he *was* deep down—whether he was just confused and sick, or whether he was truly . . ."

"Evil," Delia finished, and quite firmly, too.

"Evil," Melinda whispered, echoing her. She took a deep breath, pushing her tea aside. "Okay, then, what do I need to get done here? There must be catching up to do after I played hooky for half the afternoon, and I definitely want to be home on time this evening. That man of mine deserves more than a special turkey sandwich after what he's been through. Creamy chicken lasagna, that's what I'm thinking."

"I bet that's not *all* you're thinking," Delia said, but her expression quickly turned all *what?* and *who, me?* as Melinda shot a look her way.

"That," she said, "would be too much sharing. I'm going back to get the window cleaning stuff. Now that this whole thing with Gordon is settled, maybe I can get to the bottom of our window smears."

She took her purse in the back, and the tea as well, and spent a few moments perusing messages and sifting through the day's mail. A nice thank-you card from the woman who'd sold them the washstand—and an invitation to return. *A definite yes.* And soon, to judge by her husband's solicitous vigil. She put that in her to-do pile as the store phone rang; Delia called out a claim to it and quickly picked up, and Melinda paid it little attention as she finally scooped up the spray bottle of cleaner and the latest of the rags appropriated from her downstairs supply of refinishing stores.

She hit the store front just as Delia hung up the phone, her expression a little stunned, but a grin spreading on her face. "That was Jeannie Lusak," she said. "She didn't have time to talk, but she wanted you to know that they've gotten the call from the adoption agency. There's the baby they've been looking for and an older sister, and it looks like they're going to take them both."

"That's wonder—" But if Melinda's exclamation started off with sincerity, it cut short with a startled and inarticulate sound. For there, pressed up against the front window and looking out, was a young boy—and then an old man, and then a young boy again. Right up against the glass, yearning and listening and waiting. "Can I help you?" she said, or started to say, but that, too, was lost—for not only did a scattering of golden-blond hair settle onto her clothes, but from outside, she heard a bark. Nothing like Homer's sharp bark, this was deep-throated and joyful and came from outside, and the spirit—an old man again—straightened in quivering expectation.

"I knew it!" he said, and again, "I knew it!"

On impulse, Melinda quietly went to those front doors and pushed one of them open, letting it stand that way as she stepped back.

"Should I even ask?" Delia wondered, and let the question fall into silence when Melinda could not bring herself to intrude on the moment by answering.

For the moment meant a huge golden dog—a retriever like Delia's Bob, if bigger and coarser and exuberantly out-of-control—came bounding across the street, through the single car that got in his way and straight through the open doors, straight into the arms of the old man-now-turned-boy as they came together with a thump of overjoyed impact, the boy pounding the dog's sides with thin arms and the dog's tail wagging so hard it stirred a breeze across the floor of the shop. "I knew it!" the boy said, his voice muffled by fur and by the happy panting of his faithful friend. Finally he stood, one hand still buried in the fur over the dog's shoulders, and said, with quite some dignity for the nine-year-old he appeared to be, "Thank you for giving us a place to meet." And then to the dog he said, "Let's go, boy! You've been waiting long enough, I think!" and like that, with a brief fresh breeze of light, they were gone.

"What—?" Delia asked.

"I'll tell you later." Melinda glanced at the cleaning supplies in hand and found herself putting them aside. "For now . . . you know, I think I'll just leave those smears for a while."